For _____

Witches of Cahokia

Hope you enjoy

Raymond Scott Edge

Raymond Scott Edge

Redoubt Books

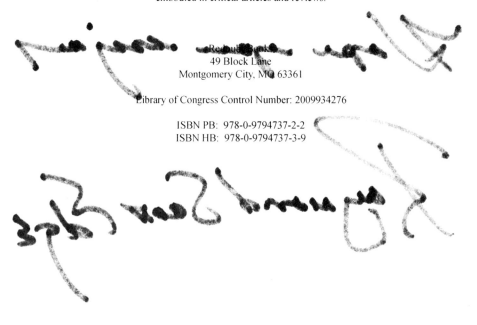

Redoubt Books
49 Block Lane
Montgomery City, MO 63361

Library of Congress Control Number: 2009934276

ISBN PB: 978-0-9794737-2-2
ISBN HB: 978-0-9794737-3-9

Printed in the United States of America

This book is dedicated to my children—Scott, Christopher, Erin, Jason, and Micah. Such an amazing adventure you have shared with me. You are the gifts that keep on giving.

Chapter 1 - She Who Remembers

The strain of placing the limestone slabs into the wall pulled at Snow Pine's muscles. She rubbed her back, relaxed in the half darkness, and surveyed her work with satisfaction. Cooled by the perspiration of her efforts, she watched the boy as he happily moved back and forth between the light and darkness marking the cave entrance. She picked up another broken slab of limestone, heavy and cold to the touch. With each placement, the opening into the shallow alcove became smaller. *Soon my love, you will be safe,* she thought, and placed the next stone in the wall erected to protect the body of Sun Kai from discovery by anyone or anything that might seek shelter in the cave. "My love, what shall I do without you?" she asked aloud, knowing only stillness would answer. At first she planned to block the outer entrance to the cave to protect the body. Her mind rebelled at the thought, since she herself would be blocked from visiting.

The opening had shrunken to the size of a single stone, which she picked from the pile, then hesitated in the placement. *Two worlds, two lives,* she thought. The first began long ago in an ancient land and belonged to the man who now lay hidden behind the stone barrier. How far they had come, so far from home, and now his body lay in this cave beyond any map. She smiled as bittersweet thoughts of him filled her mind: his smell, the sound of his voice, his dreams, the way his body felt. Even as she entered this second life beyond the cave entrance, she knew that her love for Sun Kai would never change. "Not while I breathe," she said. His last words again came to mind, a final request that she watch, wait, and remember. He was right. One day his people would come, and she must be ready so his body could be taken and buried in his homeland. *He deserves that,* she thought, *to be buried with his ancestors, not here, not lost and alone.* Steeling her resolve for the task, she placed the last stone.

The alcove sealed, she stretched and pushed her fingers into the muscles of her back, massaging away the strain. Her attention was brought to the cave entrance as the playing boy bounced a rock off the wall and yelled in pleasure.

She called to him, "Be careful out there, Little Sun." The boy was a miniature copy of his father, tall and thin, dark of eye and hair. She moved toward the light, scooped up the child, and stepped into the day. The boy wriggled in her arms, and she tossed him into the air. The next life had begun. "I will watch, wait and remember," she sang to the boy. "I am she who remembers."

The light of the day lit her hair and warmed her body as she walked toward the valley entrance. The path was little more than an animal trail, and she noted with approval the trees, bushes, vines, flowers, and grasses that filled this wild and verdant place. Looking back to the cave's entrance located high on the hillside overlooking the trail, she was satisfied that the opening was hidden among the bushes and vines. *It will do,* she thought. *It will do.*

Her stride was strong and sure; her eyes warmed in delight at the gurgling of the little boy balanced on her shoulders. Although she'd been the wife of Sun Kai and made the trip with him from far away Chin'in, Snow Pine's full body, face with strong nose and chin, spoke more of Mediterranean people than Asian, a gift from her nomadic ancestry that moved into northern Chin'in a thousand years before. On this day, however, as she moved along the path away from the hidden grave, her mind was focused not on the past, but the immediate future, and how she was to make a place for herself and son among her adopted people in this new land. Along her way, Snow Pine scanned the flora and began to select those having medicinal value. Spotting a green plant, she moved from the trail to dig several ginseng roots. The plant was very similar to those used in Chin'in, except perhaps a bit hotter, which when overused, caused nosebleeds. Such a strange land, she thought. Even things familiar are so different.

Leaving the valley, Snow Pine turned her attention to the horizon and the small notch that indicated the pass leading to the Trading People village. She remembered the day when she'd been traded. Her heart ached at the memory. What a terrible time. If it were not for the boy growing in her body, she wouldn't have had the will to live. Her painful memories of the loss of Sun Kai and the others was like a dark blanket shutting out all feelings and desire for the future. Yet the one thing that kept her moving forward was the child swelling her belly, Sun Kai's child. "You saved my life, little man" she said, kissing and bouncing him until he laughed and grabbed her hair.

Chapter 2 ~ A New Home

As Snow Pine neared the village, she remembered when she first arrived. She'd not seen the village as they approached because she was tied like an animal in the bottom of the canoe. Snow Pine was pulled from the craft and paraded back and forth, like trade goods. After a deal was struck, the Village of the Trading People became her new home. At first she'd slept in the lodge for strangers. As a foreign woman, swelling with child, she was essentially ignored, a thing of low value.

Seven lunar cycles had passed when the sickness came. The disease fell especially hard on the village children and nothing the Council of Elders or village Shaman recommended lowered the temperatures or eased their pain. Her first thoughts were to gather herbs to protect herself and the baby within, but seeing the suffering of the families, she dug extra roots and offered them to the afflicted. The villagers at first were reluctant to place their sick ones in the care of a foreign woman, but one by one, the desperate families took her offerings. Snow Pine remembered how being needed slowly built a bond between them. *Often it is crisis that provides the way forward.*

Beaver Lodge, Village Chief for harvest and trade, quickly saw the advantage of having a healing woman in his lodge and sought to purchase her. His request to the Council of Elders was approved, as a woman alone with a child needed the support of a man, and her reputation as a healer gave her value. After a time, following the birth of the boy, Beaver Lodge called upon her to become a sister wife. Snow Pine closed her eyes in remembrance. With Sun Kai dead anyplace was as good as another. The needs of the boy sealed the decision.

Beaver Lodge was darker and taller than Sun Kai. His color was more like the soil of this new land, less yellow, and his eyes were not almond shaped in the manner of the people of Chin'in. When they lay together, his body weight, hair texture, and smell at first startled her—not unpleasant, just terribly different. Afterwards, when he turned his back and lay sleeping, she stared into the darkness, thinking of the past. It was during these times of aloneness, she became overwhelmed by her loss and cried for Sun Kai. Yet, for all the differences between the two men, there were similarities. Both were loyal to friends and family, both sought to live in harmony with the land, and both had an insatiable curiosity in regard to understanding the patterns of life that surrounded them. She remembered how excited Sun Kai had been with his plans for bringing water to their regional capital in Chin'in. No, she thought to herself. Do not spend your time remembering the past. Remember the now. Her thoughts refocused on Beaver Lodge and his appreciation and interest in the healing practices of her people and the many nights they'd been spent at the fire discussing herbs she used for medicine. On several occasions he allowed her to go on trading trips with him to broaden her acquaintance with the plants of this new place.

Her feeling for Beaver Lodge were not like those she shared with Sun Kai. She knew Beaver Lodge would never be the man of her heart, but Sun Kai was dead, and Beaver Lodge was her future. He was a good man, and if she did not exactly love him, she at least respected him. Perhaps, that would be enough for this new life. Beaver Lodge was the Civil Chief among the trading people who plied the great river. *He is a good man,* she thought. Her mind drifted back to her homeland. The Chin'in were a cultured people with many skills and technologies unknown to these people.

Beaver Lodge and his family were kind, and Snow Pine quickly resigned herself to living among them alongside the great river. She set up a small booth in the marketplace to trade herbs with travelers, which added to her new family's wealth.

She was at her booth when life again turned. Fawn Heart, first wife to Beaver Lodge, came running, her face flushed with excitement.

"You should see it," she cried. It is a monster!"

Snow Pine taking hold of Fawn Heart's hands, said, "A monster, Dear One, where?"

"On the cliff above the village, a great creature has been painted on the cliff." At first as Fawn Heart described the painting, it only seemed mildly interesting to Snow Pine, but as the villagers began to talk about the creature and how it ate children and threatened the village, she decided to view the thing for herself. Arriving at the foot of the cliff, she saw the painting and was overwhelmed with emotion. *Someone lives,* she thought. One of her party survived. It was too much to hope that it was Sun Kai, but someone survived. She looked at the small hole high on the cliff wall from which the warriors said the thing came and went during the night, and knew that there must be a second opening. *My people are advanced,* she thought, *but we do not fly.*

As Snow Pine made her way back to the village, a thousand questions filled her mind, but only one mattered: "Who?" She barely closed her eyes that night, and in the early morning she gathered the boy, found the pouch for collecting herbs, and went again to the cliff painting overlooking the village. The cliff wall was too steep and the painting too high to be reached from where she stood. *There must be a second entrance,* she thought. Perhaps in the valley on the other side of the cliff. She placed the boy on her shoulders and moved toward the trail leading from the village. By the end of the first day of searching, Snow Pine sank into despair. Feeling defeat, she decided to return to the village. *Perhaps, it is not them,* she thought. No, I cannot loose them again. Who else would paint a Chin'in Dragon?

Chapter 3 ~ Sun Kai Restored and Lost

The next morning at daylight she was up and feeding the child. "Today is the day, Little Sun. Today is the day!" Gathering the boy, she made her way back to the valley beyond the cliff-side painting. *A second entrance to the cliff opening must be there,* she thought. *It must be.*

And then he was there, standing in the trail before them. Snow Pine's heart cried out as she looked at him. "Ancestors be blessed. It is you." It was not the Sun Kai of her past, the man who stood tall and strong, whose very presence provided security. Rather, it was a hurt thing, bent and dirty, who shuffled as he walked. But he was alive! Snow Pine's mind raced as she ran forward; although bent, dirty, or hurt, it was Sun Kai. He practically collapsed as Snow Pine embraced him strongly. He fell back, then struggled to stand. She could see fresh blood staining his side. "Where is your shelter?" she cried. "You must lay down." He pointed upward toward a clump of bushes. Putting her arms under his and trying to avoid the injured area, she provided support and partially carried him to the cave. How light he now seemed, almost like a child.

Sun Kai slipped into unconsciousness, and she laid him on her cape. Her senses rebelled at the smell of contagion that filled the space, bile filling her mouth. *This will not do,* she thought, as she undressed him and threw his belongings beyond the cave entrance. "Little Sun, Momma needs you to wait outside; I will be with you soon." As the boy moved away, she could see his fear of the hairy, dirty man. She looked down on Sun Kai who lay unconscious. Tears filled her eyes, and pain took her breath. *I cannot lose you again,* she thought, taking ointments and herbs from her bag.

During the night Snow Pine brought cedar boughs and sage to burn, which refreshed the cave air. Tears wet her chin and chest as she rubbed healing ointments into his wounds. She surveyed the cuts, bruises, and breaks that hadn't healed properly. These were things she could in time repair, yet what caused her most concern was a dark swelling, hot to the touch, on his left abdomen. When she pushed on the place, he grunted in pain. "Ancestors, please, help," she said, knowing not even they could reach such a deep wound.

It was late in the morning when Sun Kai awoke. Snow Pine placed the boy next to his father so that the first thing he saw upon awakening was Little Sun. "Your father is a great man," she said, "a mighty warrior." When his eyes opened and came into focus, she smiled, and held up the boy. "Welcome back, my love. Our paths have ever been one. I shall never doubt." She placed the boy in his arms and lay beside him, careful not to push against his injuries.

There was joy in being together, but each day he grew weaker. It was as she feared. While she could heal the cuts and bruises, her medicines could not reach his internal wounds. On the last morning, she placed the boy in Sun Kai's arms and lay down beside them. "Wait, watch, remember," he said. "They will come." His eyes then closed as if asleep, and he was gone.

Snow Pine relived the weeks she spent tending Sun Kai in the cave as she and Little Sun returned to the village. Sun Kai's last words echoed in her mind, "They will come. They will come,"

"But when?" she cried aloud, surprising the child who almost fell from her shoulders. Catching him, she held him close. "Look, Little Sun." She pointed to a small meadow filled with garlic and alfalfa. She gathered the roots of the garlic and alfalfa for her medicine bag, split a clove to chew, and offered the remainder to the boy. The strong fresh taste of garlic filled her mouth.

"Momma, we home." Little Sun yelled, wiggling and pointing at the village below. The village lay above the waterline along the banks of a lazy turn in the great river. At the water's edge, many canoes were pulled up on the beach, indicating that traders were gathering for market. Snow Pine could see clusters of people moving among the trading stalls. Each merchant built a shelter to keep out the sun and afternoon rains and displayed their goods on blankets. Noting the stacks of smoked fish, squash, cloth, obsidian, shells for knives, and furs for winter, all piled and awaiting trade, She smiled to herself and thought, *Yes, it is good to be home.*

Chapter 4 ~ The Find

Daniel French looked up at the Piasa Bird cliff painting. Across the parking lot he could see his wife Lauren, and the two kids, Cassie and Frederick, making their way toward the picnic area. It was going to be a great morning. After breakfast here, he planned to check out some artifacts that had been found by a road crew widening the highway a few miles outside of town. It would be good to spend the day in the field rather than the office. The university archeology department was often called upon to investigate unusual artifacts found during construction. Given that Alton was his hometown, Fred Eldrege, his department head, and man for whom his son was named, asked him to check it out. *Unusual artifacts,* he thought. More likely a forgotten garbage midden left over from some homesteader at the turn of the century.

These common sites were not particularly unusual but fun to poke around in and a good excuse for a day outing with the family. As an associate professor at the university, autumn was a busy time for teaching, research, and doing the write-ups on the work the team was doing at Cahokia Mounds. It would be nice to get the summer's findings organized into several abstracts, perhaps even a major article for presentation at the spring Chicago meeting. But this morning, the teaching, research, and writing could wait, and he stretched, enjoying the crisp autumn air. He remembered the many mornings he'd come here as a child, climbed the bluff face, and stared up at the creature painted above him.

Although wild and garish-looking with its long teeth, demonic face, wings and antlers, the Piasa painting stirred no unease in Daniel. In fact, it seemed to him that he'd spent some of the best moments of his childhood standing in this place. He could almost smell the aromatic pipe tobacco his grandfather used, and hear his stories of the ancient petroglyph, the Piasa, the bird that devours men. Whatever the thing was, creature or creation, it had been there a long time. The old man told him that the original painting was once located further upriver and that the first white explorers to the region mentioned it in their diaries. People said the one currently on the cliff face was much like the original, but who knew? It also looked like the label of a local pre-prohibition beer popular at the turn of the century.

Daniel smiled, thinking that perhaps his favorite memories spent under the Piasa were those with his wife, Lauren. As graduate students they'd explored the caves along the bluff. He remembered showing her the skeleton and artifacts he'd found, a mystery so astounding, so unbelievable, and so crazy, it cemented their desire to study archeology, and bonded them together personally and professionally. *How time flies,* he thought. *Seems like yesterday.*

Roused by Lauren's call from below, he turned and saw her waving to him from the picnic table. It was time. He walked toward the parking lot, looking into the tall caves that were cut into the cliff face below the painting. Originally these caverns were cut into the cliff for storage and cooling of local beer. As he walked by the caves he saw the old signatures scrawled on the walls. Several generations of Alton teenagers had left their messages of love, lust, and life. Finally the City Council fenced off the openings for safety concerns, but the old messages were still there. Daniel wondered if the Daniel loves Polly inscription could still be seen?

As he walked across the parking lot, he watched Lauren setting out breakfast. How right she looked, almost classically Turkish, strong nosed, olive complexioned, tall, broad shouldered, wide hipped, and surrounded by her two kids, Cassie, a miniature of her mother, and Frederick, more like Daniel, thin, freckled, scruffy haired and blue eyed.

"Mmm, smells good!" he said catching the aroma of coffee.

"Daddy, can we go climbing?" Frederick asked, pointing across the parking lot to the far wall of the bluff, still covered with scrub trees and bushes. "The caves are not fenced off there."

Daniel looked at Lauren, remembering when they'd done the same thing and climbed above the large caves and then along the bluff overlooking the river. It was during that trip he'd shown her the shallow cave with the skeleton and small strange coin necklace she still wore as a lucky piece. "Nope, too dangerous. Stay in the parking lot. We'll be going as soon as we finish eating."

Lauren smiled her 'do as I say, not as I do' look. "What did they find at the highway site? Anything fun?"

"Dunno really. Fred only said that they called saying they'd found some unusual Indian artifacts and could we send a team over. Since we live close by, he wants us to do a preliminary look-see, to determine if we need to send a team. I'm sure they want a quick 'all clear' so they can get on with their road widening business without being accused of asphalting over cultural history."

Daniel knew that tribes had lived in the area for thousands of years, but outside of the mound builders, centered at Cahokia which was several miles away, there were few significant local sites. Weighing the possibilities, he said, "Probably just some isolated relics, nothing big enough to stop 'progress.' We should be able to do the preliminary, and if it's nothing, call Fred and see if he wants us to sign off on their paperwork, and give them the go ahead."

They finished breakfast while the kids played. Reaching over, Lauren placed her hand on his, and asked. "Do you suppose we'll ever go back to the cave?"

Daniel didn't need a clarification as to the identity of 'the cave.' "It's been such a long time," he said. When first discovered, the skeleton seemed to be all they could think about. The find was fantastic, a great mystery: a skeleton and coin, the stuff of mythology. He thought again of the strange set of coincidences that brought an ancient manuscript to him, which tied the skeleton to ancient travelers who'd made their way to the new world.

When they told the story to their professor and now colleague, Dr. Fred Eldrege, he warned them against wasting time on a career-killing fantasy. He argued that the whole thing was probably a hoax and that graduation was their time to put away the things of childhood and get on with the business of adult life.

It was a good career choice. Both he and Lauren graduated and Eldrege, as promised, took them under his wing and brought them into the department, nurturing and mentoring their advancement.

Because Eldrege warned him to never attach the SIUE Archaeology Department or his name to such a bizarre story, Daniel anonymously published the find as fiction. He smiled. How strange, if it had been published as an academic article, from a grad student, it would have been forgotten years ago, but as the novel Flight of the Piasa it was still selling in the local bookstores, and was required reading at Southwestern High School.

When Eldrege found out what he'd done, it was touch and go for awhile, but finally the older scholar had seen the humor in it, and said, "Some people are too smart for their own good," referring to Daniel's use of a nom de plume, thereby technically not attaching his name or department to the work. But, in the end, they'd become friends, and now ten years later, he and Lauren had two children and successful academic careers. Daniel was second only to Eldrege in the department. He squeezed Lauren's hand, remembering their time in the cave. "One of these days we should visit the skeleton," he laughed. "And when we do, let's not tell Fred."

They cleaned up the trash, gathered the kids, and drove toward the construction site, which was located in a small valley inland from the floodplain. Arriving, they found construction suspended. The crew stood waiting for the foreman's go ahead.

Getting out of the car, Lauren touched his arm. "Daniel, do you know what's over that ridge?" She pointed toward the river.

"Yep, skeleton man. I was just thinking about him. But he's not today's problem. Our contact here is a man named John Cavanaugh." Daniel walked toward a man in a Carhartt coat who appeared to be in charge. "Mr. Cavanaugh? John Cavanaugh? My name is Daniel French, from SIU. Dr. Eldrege said you called."

Cavanaugh smiled and reached out his hand. He was a middle sized man with sandy brown hair, gray-blue eyes, and an open Irish face, lined from years in the sun. "Thanks for coming. Not wanting to hurry things along, but ..." His smile faded, turning into a grimace. Leaving his statement incomplete, he waved at the number of men standing idle at the work site. He looked at Lauren and the children standing by the car. "Your missus?" he asked.

"Well, yes. Actually we live nearby, but she's also a member of the SIUE Archeology Department and will assist with the initial inspection." He turned to Lauren, "Honey, come meet Mr. Cavanaugh."

Introductions complete, Lauren asked about the artifacts. Cavanaugh pointed to a small trailer, set off to the side of the construction zone. "Gathered them up and placed them in there. It's just a few Indian arrow heads, small decorative pieces, and bowl shards. Probably not enough to make this a protected site."

"Lauren, why don't you take the first look? Your eye is better than mine in categorizing isolated artifacts. I'll watch after the kids." Daniel turned, "John, is it alright for the kids and me to walk around the site and look at the heavy equipment? Promise, we won't touch."

Nodding his agreement, Cavanaugh pointed to a stack of yellow helmets on a side table "Be sure to use those. I think we have a couple of smalls." Stepping to the trailer, he opened the door. Lauren preceded him up the metal steps and entered the small room. In the center of the area was a round table, with papers and drawings strewn across the top, and a crook-neck lamp. A small section at one end was cleared for about twenty artifacts. Lauren pulled up a chair, adjusted the light, and began to examine each item.

Even with a cursory examination, Lauren could tell that the objects were common pieces, much like artifacts any farmer in the area might find after spring plowing. The bowl shards had the distinctive incising and stamping marks commonly used for decoration during the Middle Woodland Period when trading villages were spread over much of the Midwest. She fingered a small mica object. It was hard to tell exactly what it had been, but the mineral itself added to the probability that this was from an early trading group since mica was not found in this area. The artifact had probably come from the Appalachian Mountains region.

She turned to Cavanaugh. "I wouldn't bet my degree on it, but this seems pretty common. I wouldn't expect this to delay your construction. I need to have Daniel look at it though, because the forms take two signatures."

Cavanaugh smiled and blew air from between his lips in relief; he hadn't relished the idea of delaying construction for an extended archeology dig. Had it been his decision, he would have just looked the other way as his men reburied the stuff. However, he'd been in the business too long to believe in secrets, once you found artifacts, it was best to report them and get the official clearance.

"Well, I appreciate this," he said.

The door banged open, and Daniel with kids in tow came into the trailer. "You will not believe this. We found a skeleton, or at least Cassie did."

Cavanaugh's face lost its smile.

Chapter 5 ~ Beaver Lodge

Coming into the valley, Snow Pine could see the women tending their herbal gardens and fields of squash and beans. She looked back toward the path which led to Sun Kai's cave, shaking her head, and steeling her resolve. *Move forward,* she thought. "Little Sun, we're home," she said laughing and tossing the boy above her head.

The most prominent feature of the village was the great earthen burial mound at its center. Each year the mound grew higher as those who died were buried at ground level and dirt placed over them. A ceremonial temple built for gatherings of the Council of Elders stood at the top. Fanning out from the mound were rows of communal clan lodges. The housing was divided between the two major clan groups. Badger Clan, under Beaver Lodge was responsible for harvests and trade, had their huts closest to the river. The communal houses outward toward the fields and woods were for the Eagle Clan, led by the War Chief, Eagle Feather. In a tight circle surrounding the mound itself were the lodges dedicated to the Council of Elders, whose duty was general stewardship and direction of the tribe. The Elders were drawn equally from both the Badger and Eagle Clans. The housing and ceremonial areas were surrounded by a wooden wall, which only allowed entrance by the main gate.

Fawn Heart looked up as Snow Pine came into sight across the field. The foreign woman and small child made their way toward her and she waved welcome. At first she'd been upset when Beaver Lodge brought the woman to her lodge and bed, but soon Snow Pine's kindness, her skills with medicine, her love for children, and her willingness to share the hearth's labor erased the thoughts, and Fawn Heart came to view her as a sister. "Welcome, Dear One." She stood and embraced Snow Pine. "You have been away too long. We worried." She grabbed the small boy. "And you, Sun child. Have you been taking care of your momma?" Sun wiggled in her grasp as she kissed his neck. "I missed you also, little one." Fawn Heart linked her arm in Snow Pine's, "Your return gives me an excuse to finish work early for the day. Beaver Lodge will be pleased. You must tell me where you went for these several weeks." The two women swung the little boy between them as they moved toward the village gate.

That evening the family gathered by the cook fire, the air filled with the pungent smells of wood smoke, venison and boiled beans. Breathing in the smell from the various nearby fires, Snow Pine recognized a variety of meats and vegetables. It was a good time for the people. None would go hungry. Finishing the meal, the family sat in the dying light, smoke curling around them, keeping the insects away. The women laughing together, watched Fawn Heart's son, Blue Feather and Little Sun at play. Little Sun captured a lightning bug, but as the boys wrestled for it, Sun squished it in his hand.

"Look at me! Look at me!" he squealed, wiping a bright green stripe across his chest that glowed in the dark.

Beaver Lodge laughed at the boy's excitement, and said, "You are even greater than your name, little one. Not even the sun that warms us by day glows in the dark." He reached out and tousled the boy's hair.

"You may glow in the dark, but your clothing is filthy," Snow Pine said in remonstration. Yet she was pleased with how Beaver Lodge treated her son.

When she returned from the cave after a two week absence, Beaver Lodge welcomed her and hadn't questioned her absence. Yet, since her return, he seemed always to be near, as if her absence changed something between them.

"The Council of Elders has met regarding our trade mission to the south. I will be leaving next week for the gulf coast," Beaver Lodge said, generally to the family, yet looking at her.

Fawn Heart watched the two but said nothing. She was comfortable with Snow Pine's place in her husband's mind, and knew that as his first wife, Beaver Lodge would do nothing harmful to her or her children. "What would you have me bring you?" he said.

As first wife, Fawn Heart answered first. "Shells for beading would be nice, and perhaps that sweet stalk the boys like to chew." She looked at Snow Pine. "What do you think?"

Snow Pine held out a dried plant she'd taken from her medicine bag. "Perhaps more of this. I have not found any in our area and remember seeing it on the coast. It is good for dispelling the cold of winter."

Blue Feather, hearing the conversation, rushed to Beaver Lodge followed by Little Sun. "Can we go with you," the boy pleaded? "Can we go?" He stood on his toes increasing his height. "We could help."

Beaver Lodge appeared to consider the offer, and finally sat the boys down in front of him. "It would be good to have you with me, as I can always use additional traders; however, Eagle Feather also goes on the mission. Who would take care of your mothers? I need you here."

Beaver Lodge brought both boys into his lap to quiet them before bed. "Let me tell you how I gained my special name" he said. Although the boys had heard the story many times before, both grew quiet and listened intently. "As you know, every young man performs a vision quest to seek his totem animal. An animal that is a special cousin of the wild, whose heart he shares, and upon whom he can call whenever he is in trouble." He paused to place emphasis on his words before he continued. "The village elders determined that it was my time to go into the wilderness to gain my new name. It was a great honor, and I could not wait to go."

"My best friend, Spring Otter had gone the previous autumn. He climbed the great cliffs above the river and began to fast and pray. One day while he sat meditating and fasting, a great flock of Eagles landed in the tree above him. When he stood to look at them, they flew into the sky, but as they went they showered him with feathers. When he returned to the village and told his story to the elder's council, they gave him the name Eagle Feather, to honor the time when the Eagles recognized one of their own and loaned him their feathers. The blessing and promise he received that day told of a time when he would be a great warrior and would lead his people in many battles."

"I remember how I envied my friend, and how I too wanted to be a great warrior, perhaps even a war chief." Beaver Lodge laughed at himself, and pulled the boys closer. "Spring came early that year as I set off from the village. Although I did not know where the vision quest would lead me, I walked toward the western mountains."

"On the second night I came into a high valley with a dammed creek at its center. In the waning light I watched as a family of beavers worked the trees along the shoreline of the small pond they'd made. I made camp without a fire that evening and lay watching the stars that burned brightly above. That night I dreamed that I could fly and my body began great circles upward, even to the very heavens. There I moved among the stars and visited with the ancestors who watch from above and guide the Elder's Council. I saw my father, the greatest war chief of my childhood, and then came to land in what appeared to be the village of my youth. Here I saw all the great warriors of my childhood, but they were all still and did not move. Among the lodges, however, one chief did move. It was the Civil Chief of harvest and trade who took care of the families. As I watched him he reminded me of the beavers who I'd seen working the pond, moving from place to place, always cutting, storing and preparing for their families."

Blue Feather turned in his lap. "But Father, tell us about your name." Beaver Lodge touched the boy's nose, and began again. "In the morning I awoke to find myself covered by several inches of snow that had fallen during the night. Before I could get up and shake my furs free of snow, I heard a sound that froze my blood. Within twenty-five feet of my sleeping place, several Osage warriors stood looking at the pond and talking. As you know they are a tall people, fierce looking, with shaven heads, save for a small lock of hair in the back. Although I did not know their language, I knew they were talking about the beavers in the pond."

"Were you frightened father?" asked Blue Feather.

Beaver Lodge nodded, and said, "Yes, very frightened, and I knew I needed to find another hiding place soon before the sun melted the snow from my sleeping place and the warriors saw me. The men moved to the water's edge and one threw a spear at a beaver working the water. The spear missed but startled the beaver who made a great thump in the water with his tail to alert the other beavers and for a time the pond appeared empty. The animals all swam under water to the lodge they'd built near the center of the lake. Unlike our lodges, the beaver are very clever and build their doorways below the surface so they can come and go without being seen."

"The warriors worked their way to the other side of the pond and I decided it was time to leave. But where to go? Where to hide? The valley walls offered no cover and to go back the way I came would mean that I would pass the warriors. I was trapped and it was only a matter of time before our enemies would have me."

Both boys squirmed and looked into his face, knowing the answer but willing him to tell them. When he saw the tension build in their faces, he continued. "Finally, it occurred to me that the only way I could escape capture was to enter the pond. I slowly crawled with my sleeping furs toward the water's edge. I am sure that my leather vest looked like wood. When I reached the water I slid from beneath the furs and lying next to a log pushed off, kicking slowly underwater toward the beaver lodge at the lake's center. But now I was in new trouble, for the water was very cold. I could only stay in the water for a short period of time and if the warriors saw me, they could wait until I came ashore and grab me."

Beaver Lodge sucked in a deep breath. "When I got to the lodge, I held my breath, swam downward and looked for the opening. Finding it, I entered, praying that the beavers would not be there. But they were, a whole family of them, and they began to come toward me."

"Do they have teeth?" squealed Little Sun. Blue Feather put his hand in his mouth with fingers extended and pretended to bite Beaver Lodge.

"Yes, they do have teeth, but not for biting little boys. Just as I thought they were going to attack me, the mother beaver snarled at her mate, as if to tell him that I was just a boy who needed help and not an enemy. After that, the adults left me alone, although the kits came over to play."

"For several hours I sheltered in the lodge with the beavers, waiting for darkness so I could leave. Finally, I left the lodge, swam ashore, and made my way back to the village. Upon hearing my story, the elders told me that I'd found my totem animal and named me Beaver Lodge."

The boys had fallen asleep and Fawn Heart and Snow Pine stood and gathered them into their arms. "That is a fine story," Snow Pine said.

Beaver Lodge smiled. "Yes it is. When the elders gave me my blessing and promise, they did not talk about wars and fighting but rather about families and harvests. Before the quest I would have been hurt, but something in the beaver lodge changed my heart. I no longer wanted to be a great warrior; I wanted to be like the village chief, who was always on the move helping families. I am proud to be called Beaver Lodge." Both women nodded their agreement and moved to put the boys to bed.

Chapter 6 ~The Telling

The next morning Snow Pine heard Beaver Lodge quietly putting on his clothes, trying not to disturb the others in the hut. Following him into the predawn light, Snow Pine could see he was checking the fish traps placed the previous day.

Approaching him she said, "Beaver Lodge, I would speak with you, if you have the time."

He grunted his assent, thinking she would follow him to the river's edge. Instead, she touched his arm. "No, I want to take you to the place where I spent the last several weeks. It is but a short distance from here. I want to explain before you go." At first he thought to tell her that perhaps he did not have the time, but as he looked into her eyes, he could see that this was not a casual request. He turned to put the baskets back in place. *The fish can wait,* he thought, and followed as she led the way.

As she moved along the trail toward the rising sun, the light outlined her shape before him. She was tall, with a full body, and as the early light caught her hair there appeared glints of gold and red. How different she is from the others, he thought. All the women of his experience had raven colored hair, and none had the strange green-yellow eyes. She appeared as solid and strong as a man, yet her step was that of a deer. He was glad walking behind her as he could look upon her without notice. He thought of her often since she arrived at the village, and during her recent absence, his feelings had deepened.

Snow Pine did not take him to the valley with the hidden cave entrance but rather to the riverside where they could look up at the large painting of the demon bird. The creature scowled down upon them, a formidable horror, part demon, part bird, part elk.

Beaver Lodge was a brave man, but the painting above him always brought feelings of unease. He had heard many stories of the creature, how it hunted at night, taking small animals and children. When possible, it was a place avoided by the tribe members, and he felt uncomfortable standing below the thing. He placed his hand on his knife.

Snow Pine placed her cape on the ground and touched his arm indicating they should sit. "It is all right," she said, "it is not as you believe." She pulled him down beside her. "You are a good man, and I owe you much." Beaver Lodge shook his head, whatever debt there had been was long gone. "No, I owe you much, and as your wife I owe you the truth, and part of the truth comes from the creature above."

Snow Pine wanted to look him in the eyes but focused to the left instead so that she would not offend. She pushed up the sleeve of her jacket and laid her bare arm next to his. Even after these many seasons in the sun the color contrast was striking. "I am not from your land. We come from a place beyond the sea."

"Are there more of you?" He looked around, feeling unsettled sitting under the painting. "Is the great beast yours?"

"The great beast is but a picture. Nothing like it ever existed." She saw his tension ease. "I do not believe that there are any of us left beyond myself." Snow Pine wanted to tell Beaver Lodge the whole truth, but did not wish to betray Sun Kai's gravesite. She began to tell him about the land of the Chin'in, of the liquid-silver drink that induced madness in the emperor, the destruction of her people, the forced labor on the wall that did not end, the voyage of escape, being lost at sea, coming ashore, and finally the battle on the coast that took the lives of her companions. Indicating the creature above, she said. "Only one warrior survived the battle that day on the coast. It was he who painted the creature to keep others away." She looked down at her lap, gaining control of her voice and emotions. "The last of our warriors, he who painted the creature, has died."

Beaver Lodge placed his arm on her shoulder. "There are many things we could learn from such a people. If they come back, will they come in peace? Should the Elder's Council be warned?"

With all her heart, she wanted to tell him that the Chin'in would come soon and in peace but she did not know when or with what intentions they would come. "I believe they will come again, but not soon. You have time to prepare."

Beaver Lodge shifted his position, putting his hand to his forehead formulating the next question. "Do you want to go home?"

"No, my place is here with you. I will never leave." She again looked down to hide the tears that welled in her eyes. "I will never leave," she repeated quietly to herself.

Sensing her sorrow, Beaver Lodge pulled her into his arms, and she turned toward him. Snow Pine had previously felt a hesitation in their coming together, as if something remained undone. Today, she felt no barrier and warmed quickly to his touch. She loosened the strings that bound her robe, opening herself to him.

As she heard his breathing quicken and felt him tense for climax, Snow Pine smiled; tonight she would not use the powders that kept her from conceiving. There had been too much death of late; it was time for new life. Hooking her ankles over his and locking her fingers at the small of his back, she held him close. Finished, he began to move away, and she tightened her grip, her own body needing fulfillment, she rocked against him, a keening sound escaping her lips. The sun was warm as she slid from beneath him to lay by his side. *A girl child would be nice,* she thought laying her head on his chest. She began to wet his chest with tears. This time they were from joy, not past remembrances.

They spent the morning and early afternoon under the painting, laying together and talking. Beaver Lodge was relieved that the creature above no longer made him uneasy. His curiosity in regard to the Chin'in people overcame his normal quiet taciturn nature, and he asked many questions regarding Chin'in culture and how they approached problems. Many times as she explained how the Chin'in would handle a situation, he felt that while they might be more advanced, the solutions were not better or could not be adapted. He was surprised that even though the Chin'in seemed to know many things, they did not know of the one God who created the earth and gave man his spirit. Instead of trying to appease the gods of nature who controlled the winds and seasons, the Chin'in seemed most worried about the feelings of those Snow Pine called the ancestors, who to Beaver Lodge seemed more like troublesome neighbors than reliable gods.

Although primitive in comparison to the people of Chin'in, the Trading People were prosperous. They lived at the joining of two great rivers and traded with those to the north and south. For Snow Pine, the site under the great creature seemed a fitting place to begin her new life. If she was to carry out Sun's final request to wait, watch and remember, she could think of no better place. The village traders would hear if any new or strange people walked the land. *I am she who waits, watches, and remembers,* she thought. *And they shall be my ears and eyes.*

The afternoon sun touched the trees as they gathered their things and walked back to the village. Snow Pine touched his arm. "I will follow you, but accept my help."

Beaver Lodge grunted his assent, and again began the climb back to the trail. "I know the way," he said, but as he walked away he knew she was not talking about the path to the village.

Chapter 7 ~ Welcome to Archaeology 101

Daniel opened the classroom door and flipped on the light. He smiled, thinking about the many classes he'd taken in this room. *Yesterday, I couldn't spell archaeologist. Now I is one.* He liked teaching the early morning survey classes for undergraduates. They were still wide-eyed and in awe at the thought of becoming archeologists. Daniel put his overheads in order and flipped the screen light on and off. Nothing like beginning a lecture and having the bulb burn out, he thought to himself. He placed a stack of study guides for Tools Used in an Archaeological Dig on the first table so the entering students could pick them up.

Daniel nodded to Josh Green, the grad student he'd asked to assist him that morning. Josh came to stand beside him. "Heard you found a skeleton at the construction site the other day, anything exciting?"

Daniel shook his head. "Dunno. Exciting, yes. Important? Who knows? By the way, thanks for helping this morning. After you begin the demonstration of the dig site tools, I'll probably bail out to my office. Got some paper work to get done."

Noting that the students were in their seats, Daniel thought, *Show Time.* He placed the first film on the overhead platform and turned on the light. "Class, last year I was fortunate enough to be in Northwest China, in the Uyghur Autonomous Region. For me, the most exciting place I visited was Dun Huang. Here, you can see it on the map." He placed his second overhead showing a map of the Silk Road area on the screen. "Today, the city is just a small oasis on the edge of the Taklimakan desert. But, two thousand years ago, Dun Huang was a strategically important city." He placed the third overhead on the stage showing a desolated cliff face pock marked with caves. "The reason for my trip, and the thing that excited me most, was visiting the ancient Buddhist center known as Mogao Grotto. For hundreds of years and several dynastic cycles, Buddhist monks came to this place, carved caves into the hillside, meditated, and then in their spare time filled them with some of the most spectacular frescoes and statues in the world." The next overhead slide showed a fresco of colorful angels flying about a meditating Buddha. "Although earthquakes have closed many of the caves, about 500 are still open for viewing. Can anyone tell me what's interesting about this picture?"

Several students raised their hands. Daniel looked at the seating chart. "Miss Brent?"

"Well, I guess I'm surprised by the fact that what looks like angels with trumpets are included in the picture of Buddha, and even more so because they seem to have halos."

"You're right. There seems to be some cultural diffusion taking place here. This might be expected, given that at this time the Silk Road was perhaps the most international of all places." The next overhead showed a room labeled number 17, which was filled with stacks of old documents. "This was a hidden sealed off room discovered at the end of the 1800s. It's a treasure trove, a library of documents, about 40,000 in all: Jewish, Nestorian, Manichaean, Persian, Chinese, Roman, Arabic, and Tibetan."

"For a time, the finding of the secret library created a literal traffic jam of western explorers who came and scooped up the documents, many of which later turned up in museums in the west. The word 'theft' is used often in the Chinese guide's presentation."

Daniel placed the next overhead. "This brings me to one of the points I want to make." The projected picture was of a cave wall with several beautiful frescoes but in the middle was a blank square, where something had obviously been removed. "Museums in the U.S., France, Germany, and England all have artifacts taken from the grotto. The blank spot is where the American, Langdon Warner, used chemicals to remove the painting from the wall. First, who is Langdon Warner?"

None of the students raised their hands. Finally, Josh Green answered. "Dr. Langdon Warner is Indiana Jones."

Daniel smiled. "Josh is almost correct; Langdon Warner was one of several archeologists who were used as models for Indiana Jones. In Japan, Warner is a hero, a member of FDR's Monument Men who were sent out to preserve important historical sites and artifacts. The Japanese credit him with saving the two shrine capital cities of Nara and Kyoto from bombing during WWII. To honor his services, Japan posthumously awarded him the Order of Sacred Treasures, and citizens of Kyoto built a memorial shrine in his honor. The people of Nara placed a table in the Buddhist Horyuji Temple dedicated to his memory. It's clear that if the people of Japan had a book titled Saints of Science, Langdon Warner would be among them. But what of Mogao Grotto in China?" He paused, letting the rhetorical question hang in the air. "There he would be listed only in a book on Chinese demonology."

Daniel pointed again to the fresco's blank square. "So what is the correct response? Is this science or desecration? How are archeologists any different from grave robbers of the past? Is

Indiana Jones a hero or villain?"

Several of the students raised their hands. Daniel checked the seating chart and selected a large football-player-sized Hispanic youth from the back row. "Hugo?"

"Hey, he's a hero, man. If it wasn't for him, I wouldn't be here today. I remember running around the house as a kid with my whip, knocking furniture over."

Daniel laughed. "Which is why the whip is not generally listed as part of the archaeologist's tool kit." He selected another student. "Betty?"

"I think he was a hero. You said many of the caves were closed due to earthquakes, and, besides, would a grave robber or treasure hunter have placed their loot in a museum? One of the functions of archaeology is preservation, isn't it?"

"You're right; preservation is one of our functions, and the fresco that occupied that blank spot on the cave wall now resides in Harvard's Fogg Museum."

Daniel switched overheads. "I found this entry in Warner's field journal that speaks to his taking the fresco to preserve it. Apparently the cave was earlier occupied by White Russian deserters who'd made their way over the mountain only to be interred in the caves by the Chinese."

"It was with shock that I traced, on the oval faces and calm mouths, the foul scratches of Slavic obscenity and the regimental numbers which Ivan and his folk had left there. Obviously some specimens of these paintings must be secured for study at home and more important still, for safe-keeping against further vandalism.

Feeling validated, Betty laughed. "See, he's a hero."

Daniel smiled. "Well, maybe yes and, then again, maybe no. Before we give him full credit, we should note that he brought the chemicals for removing the frescoes with him on the expedition, prior to any knowledge of the vandalism." He paused, brushing his fingers through unruly hair. "But, the argument can still be made that in Warner's time the Chinese possessed neither the ability nor disposition to protect the ancient treasures of places like Mogao Grotto and that their loss would be a loss to all humanity. But, and maybe this is a whole new question. Today, China has both the ability and disposition to preserve and protect their ancient treasures, and they want them back. Should the artifact be returned to China? After all, surely along with preservation, appropriate disposition is also a function of archaeology."

The class broke into a buzz of side discussions with most students expressing the view that if the fresco belonged to the Chinese, then it should be returned.

Finally, Josh Green interjected. "Hell no! The Chinese don't deserve it." He stood, raising his voice. "Those guys are raping the planet. They don't care about history, unless it brings in tourist bucks. Look at em. They have air you can't breathe, water you can't drink, and lead-tainted toys you can't play with. There're the worst polluters on the planet. And we're suppose to give them art to take care of? Whatta fricken joke."

Daniel was somewhat taken back by the intensity of Josh's outburst. "You're right, Josh. The Chinese do have environmental problems, and you forgot to mention the contaminated milk. But before we're too quick to criticize, they do sort of remind me of the United States, say in about 1865. Developmental capitalism is not pretty to watch. But, that still doesn't speak to the issue of disposition. And this is important for us in the U.S." He placed a slide on the overhead which outlined the Native American Grave

Protection and Repatriation Act of 1990.

"What do we say to Native Americans when they come and ask for the return of our collections of bones and grave goods that we've been digging up for the last three hundred years?" Daniel raised his palms outward, signaling that this was only a rhetorical question. "Actually, I don't want to go there yet. Let's save that discussion for another class. But preservation and disposition are important archaeological subjects. Before Josh has you marching off to picket the Chinese Embassy, I've asked him here to review with you the tools used at an archaeological dig. As he goes over each device, make notes on the study guide you picked up as you came in. Josh, don't forget to show Hugo where we keep the whips."

Daniel stood for a moment watching Josh review each of the tools. He liked the way Josh went about the instruction. *Clear and concise,* he thought. *Josh has a real knack for this. A bit intense, but he has the makings of a fine teacher.* Daniel looked at his watch and whispered. "Josh, if you need me I'll be in the office. Oh by the way" he said in a loud voice. "Once you finish the guide you're working on, look at this and tell me what it is." He placed a new film on the overhead. The film showed a picture of a dodecahedron object with pentagonal ends. "One of the great functions of archaeology, somewhere between preservation and disposition, is interpretation. I will tell you that it's made of bronze, and all known specimens of this artifact have been found north of the Alps. Have your answer by next class."

Chapter 8 ~ Fruits of Knowledge

On the morning before Beaver Lodge left on his trade mission to the coast, Snow Pine approached him. She laid out a blanket, sat down and pulled a small device from her pouch. The thing was a wooden block which contained a set of strings upon which she had strung rows of beads. "My husband, perhaps you would look at something?"

Joining her on the blanket, Beaver Lodge picked up the strange thing. He shook it to see if it gave a pleasant sound. The beads rattled, but not in a musical way. He sat silently, waiting for her to explain. Snow Pine arranged differing numbers of trading goods on the blanket. When finished, she again picked up the thing, and talking to herself, numbered the items and shifted the beads. "It is a counting thing; it will help you as you keep track of what has been traded and how many are still left." She removed several items from the stacks and shifted the beads over to show the loss. Removing more of the items, she handed him the device. "Recount them now."

Beaver Lodge, following her example, moved the beads and counted the remaining items. "It is good," he said. "The counting thing will be useful in our trade. Thank you for this gift."

Snow Pine looked at her lap, repeating her request. "I will follow you, but accept my help." Beaver Lodge nodded, and without a word, stood, placed the device in his pouch, and walked away.

The next morning the women and children of the village gathered on the beach to watch the men leave. The clear warm air cleared the early morning mists. Snow Pine, Fawn Heart, and the children stood at the water's edge, watching the lead canoe carrying Beaver Lodge and Eagle Feather drift into the current, and turn southward toward the coast. Several moon cycles would pass before their return.

Snow Pine knew she would miss the conversations with Beaver Lodge, but now other things occupied her mind. Upon awakening that morning, she felt a twinge of nausea and smiled in recognition. The day was warm, the gardens promised a plentiful harvest, and a sufficient number of men protected the village. *It will be a good year,* she thought. She turned toward Fawn Heart. "Dear One, yesterday I saw turtle markings across the sandbar, perhaps indicating a nest. Would you like some eggs? I am truly famished."

Snow Pine and Fawn Heart sat with the children, eating freshly cooked turtle eggs. Fawn Heart watched as Snow Pine used many of the same herbs she collected for medicine to prepare the dish. "Dear One," Fawn Heart asked, "Why do you use medicine in your cooking?"

Snow Pine wondered how to explain that good food and good medicine were the same. Then it came to her. "Let me tell you a story of two brothers from my homeland who were known as great healers. The first brother could heal the most serious problems and was greatly honored among my people. Yet, when someone asked if he was the greatest of the healers, he said no, that honor belonged to his oldest brother. The difference he explained was that while he could provide medicines that would return someone to health, his older brother recommended herbs, teas, and food that kept people well."

Thinking about the story of the two brothers, Fawn Heart said, "So you added the herbs to keep us healthy?"

Snow Pine nodded. "Sometimes, cold, heat, dryness, or dampness can invade our bodies and we get sick. By adding good food to our bodies we can restore health, or like the older brother, prevent illness before it begins."

Fawn Heart finished the last bite of the turtle eggs and asked. "Is this something that could be taught?"

Pleased at Fawn Heart's interest, Snow Pine laughed. "Of course, perhaps we could go together when I am collecting herbs, and you can help me with the names. We can teach each other."

For the next several weeks Snow Pine, Fawn Heart, and the children roamed the woods seeking out herbs. On one outing, Snow Pine pointed at a small stand of wild plum trees. "In my land the flowers are single rather than double. Hopefully, it works the same for healing."

"What does it do?" Fawn Heart asked, as Snow Pine carved small pieces of bark from the trunk of the flowering plum and placed them in a collecting bag.

"Remember when Kestrel, smallest son of Eagle Feather, was so sick in early spring, complaining that something was crushing his chest? We will dry the bark and use it in a tea for when the tightness comes again. It will ease his breathing." Snow Pine hoped that what she said was true, even if the flower was double, rather than single. *Ancestors please guide me,* she thought.

The two women and their children had moved off the trail into a small grove of plum trees. From below came the sound of cracking twigs and soft murmuring voices, coming from the trail. Snow Pine grabbed Little Sun close and placed her hand over his mouth, and indicated to Fawn Heart that she should do the same with Blue Feather. The Trading People were not at war with any local tribe, but they were far from the village and the protection it offered.

Standing frozen they strained to see who was approaching. The silence deepened, as if those below sensed their presence and were also standing still, listening. After what seemed an endless time, a commanding voice sounded from the trail. "It is nothing. Move on."

Hidden among the flowering trees, the two women watched a line of men move into view. The tall, fierce-looking men had shaved scalps, leaving only a small lock of hair at the back of their skulls. Their faces were painted red and black. The painted faces and lack of supplies told the women that this was not a trading mission but a raiding party.

"Who are they?" Snow Pine whispered as the men passed from view.

Fawn Heart released her breath. The fear on Fawn Heart's face told the answer before she spoke, "Osage, our enemies. We must warn the others."

Snow Pine nodded and pointed to an animal trail that ran upward toward the ridge. The trail paralleled the path taken by the warriors. Leaving the baskets, the women gathered the children and ran along the path, trying to remain unseen. *Ancestors, please let us arrive before it is too late,* Snow Pine thought.

Although she'd never seen Osage warriors, Snow Pine had heard stories. They were known to be a fierce, violent people who lived on the fringes of the prairie lands. Although she knew the raiding party was too small to capture the village, they could, if the village was not warned, raid quickly and be gone before the warriors could provide a defense.

Arriving at the ridge overlooking the village, the women stopped. Below they could see the enemy warriors fanned out, silently making their way toward the outer sentry guards who protected the women and children in the field.

Screaming warnings, Snow Pine and Fawn Heart ran toward the village, but they were too far away to be heard, and too late. They watched in horror as the Osage emerged from cover, first attacking the guards, then moving into the fields, rounding up women and children. By the time the villagers became aware of danger; the raiders herded captives into the woods and were driving them back up the trail.

Snow Pine and Fawn Heart realized they were in eminent danger as the Osage warriors fled back toward them. Turning, Snow Pine pressed Little Sun into the arms of Fawn Heart. "Hide. I will try to draw them away." She turned and ran down the trail toward the warriors. "Ancestors, please help me." Moving off the trail she selected several rocks.

several rocks. When the enemy and their captives came into sight, she hurled the first stone, striking the closest warrior in the face. The man stumbled and bolted off the trail toward his unseen adversary. Breaking cover, Snow Pine yelled and began to run upward toward the ridge with the warrior in pursuit. The man who was young and strong soon closed the distance between them. "Leave her. There is no time," the leader of the raiding party commanded, and the warrior turned back, screaming in frustration at losing his prey.

As the warriors moved from sight, Snow Pine saw men from the village moving upward along the trail, pursuing the raiders. She breathed a sign of relief as Fawn Heart and the children came from cover and ran toward her. Snow Pine grabbed Little Sun, and the two women ran toward the village.

Reaching the edge of the squash field they saw groups of villagers gathered around the fallen guards. Snow Pine reached the first guard but could see from the head wound that there was no hope. The warrior was dead. There was nothing further to do but mourn, which she could leave to the others. As she approached the next group surrounding a fallen warrior, she could see that the sentry guard was still alive. Breathing a sigh of relief, she knelt beside the young warrior from the Eagle Clan. His face, tight with pain, was pale and beaded with sweat. She touched his cold, clammy arm. At first she could not see the extent of his wounds, but as she pushed the loin cloth aside, a small deep puncture on his lower abdomen wept clear liquid. *Oh ancestors, no,* she thought, wiping away the liquid seeping from the wound. Although there was very little blood and the external wound was small, the clear liquid indicated that the stabbing thrust had perforated his bowel. Tears began to well in her eyes as she reached up to touch the young man's face. "I will get you something for the pain," she said.

The young warrior nodded in appreciation, and said, "The wound is small. It hardly bleeds."

Snow Pine selected several powders from her pouch and dissolved them in water. Given his abdominal puncture, she worried about allowing him to drink but the medicine in the water would ease the pain and allow him to sleep. He drank greedily, as if parched in thirst, and winced as the fluid moved into his stomach. She reached into the pouch again and removed a compress that would serve as a bandage. People around her smiled, thinking that the wound was small, yet Snow Pine knew she could not change his future. Soon the wound's seeping contents would poison the flesh internally and lead to his death. Snow Pine placed the compress over the wound and secured it with ties. "Try to sleep now," she said. She smiled, touched his hair, stood, and quickly walked away. *Ancestors, why must he die,* she thought? But no answer came. "Ancestors, why?"

Once away from the sight, her tears flowed freely, and she

stumbled and fell as muscles supporting her gave way. In her mind's eye, the young warrior's face was that of Little Sun. So soon his time would come. *What then*, she thought? *What then?* She'd done all she could for the young warrior, but she knew it was not enough; tomorrow, the infection and temperature would begin.

Later that afternoon Snow Pine visited the young man's lodge and found him sleeping. She turned to the waiting family. "Mother, I will give you powders to mix into his drink, it will allow him to rest. Give him water and food sparingly as I fear that his injury is deep." Her words brought fear to the woman's eyes. "I am truly sorry," she whispered. "You might ask the Council of Elders to organize a prayer vigil. Keep him comfortable. He is in the hands of the gods now."

At first light the next morning, Snow Pine went to the wounded warrior's lodge. She heard the low murmurs of prayers as she entered. Approaching, she saw that the young man was awake, but his skin had a light sheen and his eyes were bright with fever. He smiled and beckoned her to sit beside him. Her heart ached at the sight of him. *His youth and strength will now betray him,* she thought. *It will take him a long time to die.*

Turning to the boy's mother, she said. "Brew some of the powders I gave you last night into a tea. He appears too warm." The woman moved away, happy to be given something to do for her son. Snow Pine moved the compress and saw the red lips of the small wound. She gently pushed on the wound, causing the boy to wince and clear fluid to seep. From her bag, she took an ointment that would assist in the healing of the outer wound, but she knew nothing would heal the deeper cut in the bowel. *What is best,* she thought, *to slow this process or to allow it to move quickly? What is right when there is no hope?* She smiled at the young warrior, reaching up and brushing hair from his face. "You look better this morning."

The boy introduced himself in a formal manner usually reserved for elders. "My name is Brown Falcon, and my family and I thank you for your kindness." Snow Pine was shaken by his words; he looked so young and strong. Perhaps her dread was unworthy. However, as the day progressed, the boy's temperature spiked and he had extreme pain and tenderness at the wound site that generalized across his lower abdomen. He slept fitfully and when awake, his eyes did not focus but looked beyond them, as though seeing something beyond the walls. Snow Pine sat with him, wiping him with cool cloths, giving small sips of medicines that eased his pain.

The hours blurred into an endless vigil of waiting. The boy slipped in and out of consciousness, and the pain which for a time could be held back by the medicines, became constant. The boy was bathed in sweat, his face twisted. Only fierce determination held back cries of pain. "Ancestors, help him," Snow Pine prayed. "Show me what is to be done."

The boy opened his eyes, "Help me, please."

Snow Pine held his hand tightly, and began to cry. She spoke to the anxious mother. "Please come. I must leave for awhile." Before leaving the lodge, Snow Pine whispered to the father, "You may wish to call the Elders, for the time is short."

Thinking of the boy's request, Snow Pine walked quickly from the village. She remembered seeing the great tree with the deep-green leaves and pods on previous trips, but hadn't collected the pods for her medicine bag, for in them was not life, but death. Now they contained the only help she could offer.

When she returned to the boy's lodge, the Elders had arrived. These were the oldest and wisest men of the village. Their faces were grim as they gathered around the boy, and each reached out a hand to touch him. The oldest of the group led the chant of healing, but the sorrow on their faces bespoke of knowledge that this was not to be. The boy regained consciousness, but his face was pulled into a grimace of pain, and he was unable to speak.

Snow Pine again sat down at the side of the boy's mother. She leaned toward her. "Perhaps, you would prepare a tea. I am going to give him something that will ease his pain and make him sleep." Snow Pine was grateful as the woman moved away. *No mother should be part of this,* she thought. She moved to the head of bed and lifted the prepared cup of liquid to his lips. "Drink this. It will help the pain." He drank the liquid. His eyes closed, his breathing deepened as if in sleep. When the mother returned with the tea, Snow Pine moved, allowing the mother her place at the boy's side.

Snow Pine left the lodge and made her way toward the river. The great water which moved slowly toward the south seemed to pull at her. She waded in to her knees, feeling the coolness. "Why ancestors? Why?" she cried. A vision of the boy floated before her, then grew fainter in the light. Finally, the image became one with the river and slowly moved downstream beyond her sight. Behind her she heard the cry of the mother as her child breathed his last. Bending, Snow Pine washed the pod husks from her medicine bowl.

The next morning Snow Pine slept late. It was near mid-morning when Fawn Heart touched her shoulder. "Dear Heart, I have made you tea." She placed a pillow under Snow Pine's shoulders and handed her the cup. Fawn Heart's face was somber. "You did the best you could."

Snow Pine's hands shook as tea and tears spilled on her gown. "My best was not good enough. Oh, Dear One, my best was not good enough, and all I could think of was how much my Little Sun would look like him one day."

Fawn Heart placed her arms around Snow Pine, hugging her

close like a mother to child. She took the cup from her hand, touched her hair, and stood. "You are a wonderful healer. No one could have saved him." She handed Snow Pine her robes. "Dear one, it is time."

During the night the clouds moved in, hanging low in the sky. A dark heaviness marked the day, and the air felt full with rain. It was suitable weather for the morning's activities. As Snow Pine left the lodge, she could see the families gathered at the burial mound to honor the young warrior. The Elders took the body to the prayer mound which dominated the village center. There, they washed him and chanted his story, so that the gods would know how valiant he'd been in this life. The boy, clad for burial, was carried to the burial mound where the families were gathered. A high keening sound came from the women as the boy's body passed through the crowd. Snow Pine stood at the back of the crowd while the body was laid on the mound. The boy was placed on his back with his legs bent upward and arms crossed at his chest. His family placed small possessions around him so he would have familiar things to comfort him on his journey. Finally, dirt was placed over him and the village burial mound imperceptibly grew.

As if on cue, as the last of the dirt was placed over the body, the rain began, and the family huddled together, their tears joined by the falling rain. Snow Pine moved toward them, but as she approached they huddled closer together, as if fending off her presence. Understanding their pain and unable to offer comfort even to herself, Snow Pine bowed her head and walked away.

That afternoon the warriors who pursued the Osage raiders returned to the village without the captives. They'd followed the trail onto the plains, but lost the signs where the enemy moved among a vast buffalo herd, making it impossible to track them. There would be no celebration this night, only the heavy quiet of despondence and loss dampened by the gentle rain.

That night Snow Pine lay awake rethinking all that had been done for the boy. While she knew she could not have done more, it did not seem enough. The next morning she awoke and gathered Little Sun. Turning to Fawn Heart, "Dear One, I must leave for awhile."

Fawn Heart nodded. "It was not your fault. You did the best you could. No one can blame you."

Tears came to Snow Pines eyes. "My best was not good enough," she said. She turned and left the lodge. At first she hadn't thought where to go, but as the afternoon sun touched the trees, she found herself sitting below the great painting that marked the cave of Sun Kai, with Little Sun asleep on a nearby blanket. She'd not been back to this place since the day with Beaver Lodge. She remembered her declaration in regard to beginning a new life, but now she was not so sure. Perhaps her place was here with the dead. *My best was not good enough,* she thought. "Sun Kai, what shall I do?"

Little Sun awakened and sat looking at her. "Momma, you alright?" His voice sounded small and unsure as he watched tears run down her cheeks. "Momma, you alright?"

Snow Pine stood, walked to the boy, and swept him into her arms. "Yes, little one. Momma is alright." Snow Pine picked up her blankets and moved upward along the trail and crossed into the small valley on the other side of the cliff face. Stopping at a nearby spring she gathered water in a leather bag. She moved to the cave entrance and prepared camp for the night. From her food bag she took dried meat and a grain bar made from ground venison, honey, and seeds gathered from a variety of prairie grasses.

With darkness falling, she moved her blankets into the cave and prepared their bed next to the wall that hid the body of Sun Kai. His nearness gave her strength. She listened as Little Sun's breathing slowed and deepened and she too closed her eyes. That night she dreamt of Sun Kai, not as he was at the end, broken and bent, but as he was in Chin'in, young and strong. He stood before her holding out his bamboo breastplate that provided him protection from chest wounds. A light appeared at the cave entrance, and the young warrior wounded in the Osage attack came to stand beside Sun Kai. He fitted the flexible armor to the young man's chest. The boy smiled in appreciation and as rapidly as he'd come, faded from her vision. "But we have no bamboo." She protested. "I did the best I could." Sun Kai did not appear to hear her but leaned forward to place his hand on her hair. His touch gentled her mind, and she turned to kiss his hand then slipped again into dreamless sleep. She awoke hours later, the sun entering the cave. Asleep but restless, Little Sun lay twisted in his blankets. *But, we don't have any bamboo,* she thought.

Snow Pine lifted the boy from his blankets and kissed him awake. She broke the remaining venison and grain bar into bite-sized pieces and gave the boy the last of the water. After repacking her possessions, she touched the wall that hid the body. *How tempting to remain here with you*, she thought, patting the wall. *But not today!* Snow Pine called to the boy to follow and made her way into the daylight.

Fawn Heart was waiting for her when she arrived at the lodge. The woman's hands moved quickly over a vest of leather covered in beads and shells. The effect was like a night sky across the garment. She held out the vest. "Dear One, this is for you."

Taking the vest, Snow Pine marveled at its beauty. Each bead and shell seemed to cling to the leather as if suspended above the material without attachment. Snow Pine reached forward and touched Fawn Heart's face. "You are a marvel." She said. "This is truly lovely." Brushing her hand slowly down the other woman's face, she changed her statement. "You are truly lovely, and I thank you."

Over the next several days Snow Pine busied herself around camp. The deep despondency that had lain upon the village slowly seeped away as life's small duties intervened. There were crops to be taken in, boats to be mended, food to be stored, ducks and fish to be taken; and all of these conspired to move the people's thoughts forward beyond the tragedy. Although Snow Pine received no criticism for the boy's death, she did notice his family's quietness in her presence. It did not feel like blame, but rather painful remembrances. When they looked at her, they thought of him. *Only time will heal this*, she thought. *Only time*, and her mind again slipped to thinking about her life with Sun Kai. Tears welled. "With enough time, this too will heal."

The next morning Snow Pine awoke and walked to the river's edge to watch the men checking fish traps and lines. The river ran smooth and quiet in the morning sun. Wisps of fog moved across the surface in the shaded areas. Ducks bobbed in the grasses that grew along the sides, periodically spreading their wings to catch the morning sun. The morning catch of carp and catfish was plentiful. *This is a favorable place*, she thought. She noticed a commotion as a man untied his line and pulled it from the water. Suddenly, he stopped moving forward and was jerked backward. The line tightened and he yelled for help as he was pulled toward the water. Several of the other men grabbed the line and stopped his slide. A great churning of water appeared just beyond where the line touched the river. For a period it seemed the men would all be pulled into the water, but as others grabbed the line, the creature in the river could not drag them about. Each time the men pulled the fish toward the shore it would be seized by a new burst of energy, and the line gained would be lost. The whole village now alerted, came running to watch the contest.

Fawn Heart came with Little Sun and Blue Feather, spreading a blanket where the family could sit. "It is an old man of the river," she said. "We rarely catch them." She pointed to the water where a dark body could now be seen below the surface. The creature was the size of a trading canoe. Snow Pine had seen such creatures at sea but hadn't imagined they would inhabit inland waters. Thinking of the many hours she'd spent bathing and swimming at that very spot, she shivered. Fawn Heart reached out and hugged her. "Dear One, it only looks fierce, the old man of the river, is as its name, and like the old, it eats only soft foods." The struggles of the fish grew less violent as the creature tired. Some men rushed into the water to stab at the thing with their spears, and Snow Pine could hear the clunk of spear-heads against the fish's body, but none seemed to find the mark and all bounced off.

They drug the creature into shallow water, where it lay in plain sight. The fish, dark grey, longer than the height of a man, and as wide as a canoe, made a raspy sound. Instead of scales, the thing was covered in hard plates. It was a frightening sight, but as she watched the great thing die, Snow Pine felt sadness.

The men pulled the fish from the water and arranged themselves around the creature, each telling his story. The women and children backed away from the thing and waited. It would soon be their turn. They gathered baskets and knives to render the fish into steaks that could be smoked and stored.

Fawn Heart and Snow Pine joined the women in the gutting and cleaning. Regular knives would not pierce the plates along its back, and the meat could only be taken by finding an opening between the plates and skinning the armor from its back and sides.

Other women cut vines and wove wooden racks, arranging them along the river's edge. They then scooped out sand below the racks to open a space for a low fire. Fish steaks were hung on racks above the flames. They placed green boughs of hickory on the fires to slow the burning and create smoke. It was late afternoon before the last steak was cut from the fish, and its skeleton lay in the sand.

Throughout the evening Snow Pine tended the fires and assisted the families in smoking the fish. From the skeleton she picked a dozen small sharp bones for use in medicine. As she stood looking at the carcass she picked up a plate section that had been cut off to reveal the meat. Her mind wandered to the dream of Sun Kai in the cave. *If not bamboo, why not these?* She quickly removed the remaining meat from several plates and placed them over a fire to dry.

The next morning Snow Pine sat watching Fawn Heart sleep, willing her to wake up. Impatient, she touched the woman's arm. "Dear One, it is time to wake. I have something to show you," She handed her a cup of tea and arranged the blankets so Fawn Heart could sit. Placing the section of fish plate over her own chest, she said, "Do you think that this could be sewn onto a jacket as you did the shells? In my country men wear something like this as armor to protect them from stab wounds."

Smiling, Fawn Heart took the plate section and examined it carefully. "Have you been waiting for me to wake up to show me this?" she laughed. She then looked at the plates carefully; "I think we could hook them to leather in much the same manner I work with shells."

Snow Pine placed another section along her arms and legs. "See, if the young warrior had worn such protection, the spear would have slipped to the side rather than piercing him."

Fawn Heart placed her hand over Snow Pine's. "I will help you Dear One. But remember, this is your idea. Men do not always like women to have ideas. Hand me my sewing kit."

Later that afternoon Snow Pine went to the guards and showed them the plated garments. At first the men would not try the garment on but finally with persuasion they pulled them over their shoulders. They stood before her embarrassed until she took a spear and jabbed at a clad guard. The spear struck the plate and slipped to the side. "It will protect you in attack," she said. Though recognizing the purpose and benefit of the garment the men still did not appear comfortable.

When Snow Pine made her way back to the lodge, Fawn Heart was preparing a meal. Snow Pine told of her meeting with the young men and how the plated garments protected them from spear thrusts. "I think it would do the same for arrows," she said.

Fawn Heart nodded. "How did the men like the armor? Were they happy?"

Snow Pine thought for a moment. "I don't know. They seemed embarrassed. But they were still wearing them when I left."

"I am sure it will be all right," Fawn Heart said. "You took them by surprise. They will understand the great benefit of the body armor and be appreciative."

Snow Pine smiled. "I will never understand the men of your people. They never look one in the eye. How can you know what is in their heart? They never seem happy if they have been given a gift or made to feel special. Even dear Beaver Lodge becomes quiet when I give him something."

"It is just our way," Fawn Heart responded. "We are members of a clan. We never feel comfortable if separated from the others, even if it is a good thing."

Snow Pine shook her head. "I know, I know; I won't tell anyone it was your sewing that made the garments." The women laughed together and embraced. Men would always be men, but sisters did not hold to such foolishness.

Over the next several days the women dried and cut more

sections from the fish plate for garments, continuing on until all the guards were fitted. Snow Pine hoped that when they were all wearing the same armor it would lessen their embarrassment.

One night Fawn Heart and Snow Pine sat with the children around the lodge fire. "Tell us the story of the ancients," Blue Feather begged. Snow Pine pulled Little Sun to her. Fawn Heart began.

"This is a story from long ago, even before the buffalo roamed the land, before time itself. In those days our people lived under a great lake. There we farmed and lived but there was very little light. One season a plant grew up into the lake and disappeared above the water. It seemed to some that this would be an opportunity to reach the world above the lake. So one by one the people began to climb the vine upward into the sunlight." Fawn Heart made the signs of someone going hand over hand up a vine. Blue Feather and Little Sun mimicked her. "Then a very pregnant woman began to climb the vine. It was very hard for her, and suddenly just as she neared the top, the line broke under her weight, and she fell back among the people." At this Fawn Heart fell back among the blankets, and the boys laughed. "You should not laugh," she said, "for all those who remained behind were trapped forever below the lake. Those people who made it to the surface began to move apart and disperse across the land, but two great mystical beings, First Creator and Lone Man found us. They taught us that someday a great flood would come and only those who stood on high ground would survive. It was then that we gathered tightly in our villages so that we could build the mounds to bury our dead and pray for guidance. First Creator left the people, Lone Man stayed among us to teach the rituals of life. It was Lone Man who established the Elder's Council to guide our chiefs." Fawn Heart reached out and tapped Blue Feather's forehead. "And that is why we are the people of the mound, and live in villages, rather than following the buffalo across the plains like other tribes."

Snow Pine looked down at Little Sun who'd fallen asleep. *It is a good story,* she thought. *People should stay together.* She smiled in appreciation at the telling: Glancing at Fawn Heart across the fire, she said. "Good night, Dear One." She carried Little Sun to their sleeping area. "It was a good story."

Chapter 9 ~ Return to The Valley

As was her custom, Snow Pine left the lodge early while the others slept, making her way to the river. Finding a comfortable bank, she sat and watched the sun peak over the horizon, light the river and bring into focus the dark shapes from the other side. An otter made its way among the fish traps taking its share of the harvest. "Little Cousin, don't be greedy," she called, startling the creature, making it duck beneath the surface. A great grey heron, which had only been a dark shape across the water, squawked its annoyance at hearing her voice and flapped its wings, slowly rising above the mist to move further down the river to land in a quieter place.

Snow Pine waded into the water, and began to wash. Down stream she heard the sound of paddles thrust into the water and she hid in the brush. She breathed a sigh of relief as the first boat came into view. It was the trading mission. As they came closer she saw Beaver Lodge and Eagle Feather in the first canoe. Snow Pine moved quietly backward from the beach area, not wanting to be the first to spot the arriving boats. *Eagle Feather would be displeased if his village guards were not alert enough for that honor.*

As she thought this, a voice called from above. "Ayee, they come. The traders are home."

The village moved from slumber to joyful sound as families

quickly came to welcome the travelers' home. Snow Pine joined Fawn Heart and the boys at the back of the crowd. As Eagle Feather stepped from the boat he spied the village guards and saw the plated vests. A frown quickly replaced his smile. "What is this? You look like turtles. No wonder you did not see us until we were almost upon you." His frown increased as the embarrassed men slipped out of the garments.

Suddenly, it was as if the whole village was looking at Snow Pine. Fawn Heart grabbed her hand and squeezed it. "See," she whispered, "we never feel comfortable if forced to stand out from the others."

Stepping from the boat, Beaver Lodge moved quickly to his family. "It is good to be home," he said loudly, "the mission was successful. We bring many gifts to the village." He turned and called for a bag to be brought forward. The previous moment's tenseness was quickly lost as families pressed forward to see what had been brought. Beaver Lodge distributed goods generously, and all received something, especially the old and young. The very young received a sweet root to chew, that was found only in the far south.

Eagle Feather stood in the back of the crowd, for the moment forgotten. "Wah," he snorted and walked away.

Laughing and joking with the older members of the crowd, Beaver Lodge continued to hand out gifts and tell stories about how they out-traded all the tribes along the river.

The people soon made their way back to the village, and Beaver Lodge stood before the family lodge. Smiling, he stepped inside. It was as if the shade of the lodge changed the day from summer to winter, and Beaver Lodge's face went from laughter to dark anger. "What have you done?" he demanded. "It took almost all the gifts I had to not bring the council down about our ears. They still may not be satisfied once Eagle Feather tells of our trade mission."

His anger was clearly directed toward Snow Pine, and she turned to face him, her face a caricature of defiance and determination. "I have done nothing except try to help."

"Well, stop before we are all ruined." Reaching into his pack he took out the counting machine and shoved it toward her. "Even this," he said. "When I used it, those we traded with called it witchcraft and cheatery. Eagle Feather needed to use his warriors to save us. A man died because of this thing."

Snow Pine took the counting tool from his hands. "That is not fair," she said. "I cannot be made responsible for the ignorance of others."

Beaver Lodge's face grew angry and his hands shook. Fair or not," he said, "it gave Eagle Feather the right to counsel me in regard to your actions. He reminded me that you are a foreign woman who does not know her place and suggested that if I were more of a man, you would spend more time on your back and less time in the affairs of others. And what do we find upon our return? You have put the guards in silly costumes where they move like turtles."

Fawn Heart reached forward to touch Beaver Lodge. "Be fair, husband. She meant no ill."

He shoved Fawn Heart away. "And you, why have you not taught this woman her place. You are as bad as she." Fawn Heart shrunk under his displeasure and moved aside.

Snow Pine's anger now boiled beyond control. "You are such barbarians," she taunted. "How could I have hoped for you to understand?" She moved toward him and he reached for her, but before he could grab her arm, she turned sidewise, sweeping her foot under him, spilling him to the floor. At first she was so astonished by her action that she didn't know what to say. Kneeling before him, she said, "I am so sorry, husband. I did not mean to bring you shame, not here or before."

As Beaver Lodge fell, rage filled him. But, as he saw her kneeling before him the impossibility of the moment stunned him. Partially sitting, Beaver Lodge said, "Woman, you will be the end of us all. Get out before we say more. What am I to do with a woman who seems destined to make me look foolish?"

With tears filling her eyes Snow Pine stumbled from the lodge. She quickly wiped her eyes not wishing to feed the curiosity of those who might have heard their angry voices. Fawn Heart and the boys caught up with her and together they walked from camp. Fawn Heart placed her hands to her temples. "Dear One, how could you have done such a thing? If anyone heard or thought, we would be shamed. He could not recover."

"I know, I know. I am so deeply sorry. I did not mean to hurt him. I was just so angry."

That evening Beaver Lodge was summoned to council. Inside the darkened lodge the elders sat about the central fire. Others sat along the outer walls. The flickering of the fire highlighted and shaded the faces of those present. The faces of the elders were lined and weathered from seasons of life, and in the shifting light they appeared to move even though all sat motionless. These were the elders, the wisest of village, and they had summoned him to council. Glancing about he kept his face calm. He'd been to council many times but never to explain embarrassing personal failures. He took the offered pipe and breathed deeply, drawing the smoke into his lungs. He waved his hand above the bowl washing himself in its smoke. Then he passed the pipe onward. *Let this go well,* he prayed.

No one spoke as the pipe made its way around the circle. Finally, White Otter, eldest of the council, broke the silence. "Beaver Lodge, it is good to have you back. We have missed you and Eagle Feather. How was the trade mission?"

"It has been better," Beaver Lodge admitted, "but was generally successful."

Eagle Feather interrupted. "We had to fight our way out of the Hidatsa camp, because of the foolish tool the woman gave him. What am I to tell the family whose man did not come home?"

White Otter held up his hand for silence. "We have heard you, Eagle Feather; it is now time for Beaver Lodge."

Beaver Lodge spoke. "It is true, what Eagle Feather told you. The tool was misunderstood, and we fought over it. This winter, I will watch over the dead man's family, so they do not want. He fought and died well. We will honor his loss."

One of the younger warriors shouted, "It is not enough; the foreign woman should be punished. It is she who is to blame and him for not keeping her in her place. We should…" Several of the elders turned to face the young warrior, and he stopped in mid-sentence.

White Otter continued. "Often the young are like boiling water, hasty in what they say, but perhaps we should discuss the woman." He faced Beaver Lodge. "We have heard that there is a problem in your lodge, and the woman is at the center of it. Even this morning loud voices were heard from your home. Should she be placed with another family? Perhaps, Eagle Feather would be willing to take the burden."

The color drained from Beaver Lodge's face. "I am afraid that is not possible. She now carries my child. I will be responsible for her."

White Otter spoke again. "Then it is settled. Our village chief will continue to shelter the foreigner, but will limit her to women's work; she will not again intrude upon the affairs of the men." The circle of elders nodded in agreement.

Turning to Eagle Feather, White Otter continued, "We must

also talk of the Osage raid and our losses."

As War Chief, Eagle Feather rose and addressed the assembly. "We are not sure which Osage clan family was responsible. I sent warriors to each of the local groups to see if we can learn of the captives. It will be weeks, but we will not forget."

The elders nodded agreement then turned their attention to White Otter. He stood and waved the younger men out of the lodge, leaving only the elders, Eagle Feather and Beaver Lodge. "Soon it will be time for the great hunt," White Otter said. "This problem between you must cease, it is unworthy. Beaver Lodge, come back with plans for the hunt at our next fire. The elders have decided that the village will travel upriver to flint cliff; you can focus our hunt at the nearby salt licks. Eagle feather will organize the warriors to provide a safe trip for the families." Chastised, Eagle Feather and Beaver Lodge turned to leave the council. White Otter reached for Eagle Feather's arm. "About the young man who spoke out—counsel him with kindness, as his mouth still smells of mother's milk. Teach him that it is not wisdom to repeat the words of others, as an echo does the thunder." Nodding, Eagle Feather lifted the flap and left the lodge.

Once outside the council, Eagle Feather and Beaver Lodge faced each other. Each knew that a problem existed between them, but this was not the hour. The elders were right; the needs of the village family were too great. They embraced as brothers and went their separate ways.

That night as the family gathered for the evening meal, a heavy silence smothered the conversation. Neither Snow Pine nor Beaver Lodge looked at the other. Untouched, the prepared venison and vegetable dish turned cold. Snow Pine broke the silence first. "I am sorry. I meant only to help."

His face somber, Beaver Lodge related the counsel he'd received.

"I know you meant well, and you may continue to help. But not me. You must stay out of the affairs of men."

Snow Pine looked down at her food. *What a mess I have made of this,* she thought. "The elder's are right," she said. "I am obliged to be held by the ears and instructed. Thank you." She stood and left the lodge.

Fawn Heart started to rise and follow, but Beaver Lodge's hand blocked her way. "She must face this alone," he said. "It must be so, if we are to live in the village. The elders have spoken."

"But…" Fawn Heart began.

Shaking his head, Beaver Lodge cut her off. "There is no but. It must be so."

Late in the night Snow Pine returned to the Lodge. Her eyes were dry, her resolve certain. *It is my mistake,* she thought. *There is no new life for me. I am only she who watches, waits and remembers.* She patted her stomach, the new life within was beginning to swell. "It will be you who has the new life." Trying not to wake the others, she packed her belongings.

Snow Pine intended to leave before the others awoke, but as the sun brightened the sky, she knew that this would not do. She needed the others: the swelling in her stomach bound her to them, the needs of Little Sun bound her to them, her love for Beaver Lodge and Fawn Heart bound her to them.

Fawn Heart first to awaken, was startled by the pack sitting by the doorway. "Dear One, no!" The women silently embraced.

Snow Pine backed toward the door. "Please ask Beaver Lodge to meet me at the valley of the winged thing. He knows the place. And, Dear One, watch over Little Sun for me." She turned away, tears dripping down her cheeks. But, before her resolve could lessen, she hoisted the pack and stepped through the door.

Snow Pine barely reached the valley before Beaver Lodge

arrived. "Woman, this will not do," he said. "You cannot live here alone—you belong with us, with me."

Snow Pine turned toward him putting her hands before her, pushing away his argument. "No, my place is here," she said. "I was wrong; I do not have a new life." She spread a blanket and sat down. "Please sit; there is much we need to discuss. I carry your child and am leaving another in your home for your safekeeping." She reached for him, pulling him down beside her. "Sit. We have much to discuss this day."

"But."

She placed her hand to his lips to end the words. "There is no time for argument. We have much to discuss, and our time is short. I will not return to the village."

"You cannot live here alone," he protested. "The Osage."

She smiled. "The Osage are like all men. They will think any woman crazy who chooses to live alone. They would not harm such a touched woman. But that is not what we need to discuss. We must speak of Little Sun and our child to be." Though she knew it would make him uncomfortable, she took his face in her hands, looking directly into his eyes." I will need your help with this. You are right. I cannot do this alone. The elders told you they do not wish me interfering with the world of men, but I can still help you with the women. They could come here to learn of medicine and other women things my people have to offer. Fawn Heart can take care of Little Sun for me and bring him for visits. She could also help when it becomes my time." She looked down at her swelling belly.

They sat talking throughout the afternoon. Although unconvinced, in the face of her resolve, Beaver Lodge ceased to argue for her return. As the Civil Chief he could arrange for the women to come to the valley for instruction. It would keep Snow Pine attached to the village. He knew Fawn Heart loved the boy as her own; she would take care of Little Sun. She also loved Snow Pine, and would bring the boy to the valley so that he did not forget his mother. Perhaps as she neared her time to birth, she would relent and come home. *Such a hard headed woman,* he thought. He looked at the clouds moving across the afternoon sky knowing that after this day he, like them, would be a man unsettled. Snow Pine noted how his thoughts filled his face with sorrow, and reached to touch his hand.

He stood and pulled her to her feet, starting to say goodbye, but she stopped him, pressing her fingers to his lips. "Don't say it. Goodbye tastes bitter. I know that you love me and I you. That must be enough. I will always try to help, but I can no longer follow."

Chapter 10 ~ Ancient Queens of Alton

Daniel sat at the breakfast table reading the Alton Democrat. They were having a heyday with the story of the two female skeletons found at the construction site. The Democrat referred to them as the 'Ancient Queens of Alton.'

He handed the paper to Lauren and said, "Good picture of you though." He got up to get more coffee. "I can just hear Fred." He mimicked the department's head nasal accent. "I send you to do a preliminary site investigation, and you turn it into a circus."

"Well, it's not like we could forget we found them," Lauren offered defensively. "Ancient Queens of Alton. Where do you suppose they get this stuff? It feels like every newspaper in the country is a tabloid."

"I suppose 'Ancient Queens of Alton' is better than 'Ancient Murder Most Foul,'" Daniel said, laughing. He thought of the cottage industry that developed around the supposedly haunted houses, hotels, churches, schools, and graveyards of Alton. No less of a literary figure than Mark Twain once noted the darkness of the city, describing it as a 'dismal little river town.' Daniel shook his head. "I wonder how soon the spook tours will add our grave sites to their itinerary. It's not as if the town's history, replete with murders, epidemics, abolitionist mobbing, Civil War prisons, Underground Railroad stations, and prohibition gangsters and molls needs another attraction."

Lauren smiled at his grousing, knowing that if given the chance to live anywhere else in the world, he would pass. "Come on. You know you love this place. For all its spookiness, it's still the land of Tom Sawyer."

"Well, Tom Sawyer or not, Eldrege isn't going to like it. We might as well go see what he wants us to do." Daniel picked up the lunch she'd packed for them.

They arrived at the university early, and no one was in the department. Daniel looked at the clock, 7:30 am. "We have 15 minutes before Fred gets here. Let's get the coffee started." Dr. Frederick Eldrege was notoriously punctual. One could actually set a watch according to his movements: 7:45 through the department door, 8:00 a cup of coffee and review of the day's schedule with Betty the department secretary, 8:30 a catch-up of the e-mail, and 9:00, meetings with the various department heads.

"Daniel, I need to stop by my office before we meet. When Fred comes in, give me a call. I'll get some coffee then." Lauren moved down the hall toward her office.

Daniel knew that Eldrege was a man of routine and focus. For him the finding of the women might be interesting, but off subject. *I can hear him now*, he thought: '*Those damn women don't feed the bull dog.*' For Eldrege, the bull dog was his Cahokia Mound research. He was the foremost authority on Mississippian Culture, and the grants he obtained funded his research studies allowing him to build the department and stipend a dozen graduate students. Daniel was sure that the two female skeletons, regardless of how ancient, would not be appreciated, especially if they distracted from what Eldrege considered to be the 'real' work.

He poured the first cup of coffee; Jennifer Rausch, one of the department's graduate students, walked in. She was young, fresh, and very attractive, in a female graduate-student way. Several of the younger male faculty had made comments about her cuteness and wondered about her availability, but in Daniel's classes, she worked hard, and hadn't tried to charm her way out of assignments.

"Hi, Dr. French. You're here early this morning."

"Morning, Jenn. Lauren and I are here to see Dr. Eldrege about the gravesites we found near the construction site. Just fortifying myself with some coffee. Want some?"

"Sure, thanks." He handed her a cup. "That gravesite find is so exciting," she said. "Did you see the write up in the papers? You think you'll need any help?"

"We saw them. Don't know yet about the need for help. Depends on what Dr. Eldrege wants. It's a bit out of our focus, so he might want to leave it in the hands of state people."

"Well, I hope he lets you do the investigation." She smiled. "If he does, please keep me in mind. I'd love to work with you on it."

"Sure, although I can't promise you anything. We're awfully busy cataloging the summer Cahokia material. More than likely he'll not want us to not take our minds off getting ready for the Spring Conference. You plan to do an abstract?"

"Hope to," she replied. "Well, anyway, let me know if you need help."

Daniel looked at his watch, 7:45. "He should be in by now. Think I'll take him a cup of coffee and see if we can meet before he talks to Betty. See you later."

Daniel, two cups in hand, saw that Betty was gathering her notebook to meet with Dr. Eldrege.

Betty smiled. "Is that for him? When he came in this morning, he asked if you and Lauren could meet him in his office at 9:00.

Here," she took the cup from his hand, "I'll make sure he gets it."

Daniel smiled. *I'm too late,* he thought. *It was Betty's turn.* If nothing else Dr. Eldrege was a follower of routine. The finding of two graves would need to wait their time on the schedule. Walking back to the faculty area, he got another cup for Lauren.

At 9:00 am, Daniel and Lauren were waiting in the department office for Eldrege to finish his morning routines, when his door opened and he waved them in. "Betty, get me another cup, will you please? Also, call Josh Green and see if he can meet with me at 9:45."

Once Lauren and Daniel were seated, Eldrege pulled his chair from behind the desk so they were sitting together. He leaned forward, elbows in his lap. "So, what do you think?"

Lauren started first. "Well, not much to think yet. Two skeletons so far, both female, seemingly ancient. Not much by way of grave goods, but the skeletons seem old, maybe around a thousand years, maybe even a bit more."

Breaking into the conversation, Daniel said, "Yeah, it's really hard to tell. There they are two skeletons, buried side by side, both females. The artifacts we've found seem a bit strange, but I wouldn't want to comment until we get a real chance to look at them."

Straightening in his chair, Eldrege frowned. "Any chance we're dealing with those damn Creative Artifacts Society nuts? This sounds like them, artifacts that don't make sense, found at construction sites, so that work stops. Damned anarchists." He shifted his gaze from Lauren to Daniel.

Lauren looked at Daniel, not sure how to respond. The CAS was one of Eldrege's pet peeves. According to department lore, the CAS had cost him a prized department head position at an ivy league, exiling him to a Midwest state school instead.

Eldrege could not abide the anachronistic efforts of this radical student group. They hurt not only him, but made a laughing stock of archeology, treating his science as a game to stop what they denounced as materialistic progress.

Daniel responded, "God, Fred. We don't know. I don't think so. The graves appear genuine, and untouched. I've heard the CAS use artifacts stolen from university archeology departments to seed their sites, but I don't think they're this good. The site looks legitimate. Besides, we're the local university archeology department and our graduate students wouldn't get involved with this nonsense."

Lauren nodded in agreement. "Fred, I won't swear to it, but the graves don't seem to have been tampered with. Maybe one of the schools in St. Louis, or perhaps in Chicago, might have CAS problems, but who cares whether a road is built in Alton?"

Eldrege looked relieved. "I guess you're right. It's probably not those bastards. But that takes us back to my original question. What do you think?"

"Well, the grave sites are interesting. They fall under the Illinois Grave Robbery Act of 1989, which prohibits the disturbance of any unregistered graves over 100 years old without a state Historical Preservation Agency permit. That stops construction for awhile until the site can be evaluated." Daniel put his hands behind his head and leaned back. "Of course, I'm interested, given that Alton is my home town. Yet they might not be anything, just two women. Who knows? Maybe the fact they were both women is just a coincidence? Then again, what if there are more? Who is to say we only find two. It's not as if we're not busy enough already, but, if you want me to take a look at it, I'll make the time."

Lauren smiled at Daniel. He was in one of his, maybe yes, maybe no, reasoning on both sides of an argument, moods. She knew Eldrege held Daniel in high regard for his intellect, but the 'maybe yes' 'maybe no' part of his thinking style drove the department head wild. She could see the muscles in his neck tighten.

Lauren intervened before Eldrege became exasperated. "Fred, I think it's worth looking at. Perhaps, put together a small team—say me, a couple of other faculty, and one or two graduate students. Who knows? Maybe we'll find it's nothing and be done in a couple of weeks. Besides, I've just about done all I can on the summer finds, at least for now. What do you think?"

Looking at his two junior colleagues, Eldrege smiled. "Lauren your thinking is going in the same direction as mine, although I was thinking of Daniel as the team leader, but if you want it, take it. In fact, I was going to ask Josh Green if he would be interested in an extra credit project."

Daniel interjected. "You know, Jenn Rausch expressed an interest. Maybe you could also ask her?"

Eldrege looked back at Lauren, "What do you think? Josh and Jenn? Both are near graduation, and both have experience at the Cahokia dig. Any problems?"

"No," Lauren said, "they would be fine. I've worked with both."

When Lauren and Daniel stood to leave, Eldrege frowned. "Lauren, keep a low profile on this. No tabloid paper stuff and certainly no Ms. Science talks on how we examine bones. We don't need a delegation of Native Americans showing up, reminding us of the Native American Graves Protection and Repatriation Act and demanding immediate possession of the bones for reburial." Eldrege called after them and they paused in the doorway. "Ask Betty to invite Jennifer to my meeting with Josh Green."

Chapter 11 ~ The Child

Though alone in the valley, Snow Pine was rarely lonely. Small animals she cared for became her constant companions. Often her cave housed young raccoons, possums and birds that lost their mothers or were too hurt to survive in the wild. The village women regularly came to the valley to ask for her help regarding a sick child or family problem. They marveled at how the wild creatures accepted her as their mother. It seemed the distance between animals and man appeared suspended in this place, and like in the early legends, all were again part of the same family. She taught the women the uses of herbal teas and talked of the need for balance and harmony, which she described as the light and dark side of the mountain. Opposites such as light and dark could only be understood in relation to one other, and so it was with men and women, night and day, winter and summer, each needed the other to complete and explain itself.

Regarding her safety in the valley, Snow Pine had been right, for although the Osage knew that a lone woman occupied the valley, they believed she was a mindless one, touched and therefore untouchable.

Of late she dreamt of Sun Kai and their past life together. She saw not the deformed Sun Kai of the cave, but the man she loved back in their homeland. During these visits he taught her to fly, and they followed the winds to far away places in this new land. They soared west over the high mountains to a land of dryness, over great salt deserts, and finally to a bountiful land bordered by a warm blue sea. She remembered tales of her childhood, of the warm sea bordering the home of her ancestors. Could this be the place?

On other occasions they flew east across great forests, to inland oceans where the blueness of the water seemed to draw her downward into the depths, and where the fish and fowl were so numerous it seemed that one could walk across the great waters without getting wet. Then onward they flew, beyond the great inland seas to a rocky coastline embraced by a colder ocean. *This land is so great,* Snow Pine thought, *even if Sun Kai's people come again, how will I know? How will they find me?*

Snow Pine knew that Beaver Lodge often came to watch over her. Sitting at the evening fire she could sense his presence. Although she could not see him beyond the fire light, she could feel his love, his concern, his frustration, and at times she almost bade him join her, but that would be unfair. She would only hurt him again.

Often Fawn Heart came. The children spent hours playing with the small animals that shared Snow Pine's valley. During these visits they discussed the village, the family, and the problem between Eagle Feather and Beaver Lodge. Although she thought her absence would heal the wounds between them, somehow it had not.

Some nights her senses picked up a presence beyond the light of the fire that was not Beaver Lodge, but rather a darker, harder, colder spirit, that emanated no warmth, but great hunger. On those nights she built the fire high, keeping the spirit further from her. She never heard or saw the dark presence but felt him. Often, she would move her blankets into the cave, closer to the wall that protected Sun Kai's burial chamber, praying he would watch over her.

Snow Pine loved when village women visited and she spent hours teaching them herbs and therapies they could use in their homes. She listened to their traditional stories that were so different from those of her homeland, yet so very similar. The women often brought word of trading missions that crossed the land. She was especially interested in the coastal area where she and Sun Kai landed so long ago, and the two lands, one to the east and one to the west, bordered by the oceans she had seen in her dreams. If Sun Kai's people were to come, they would land there. *Yet how will I know?* She pondered. *What if they came and left without my knowing? How am I to keep my promise to wait, watch and remember? How?*

As seasons passed the child grew inside her. When the day drew near, Beaver Lodge strode into the camp. "Woman, it is time for you to come home."

Struggling to rise from her position near the fire, Snow Pine faced him. "No," she said quietly. "This changes many things, but not that."

"Yes," he demanded. "It is time for you to come home."

Snow Pine smiled, tears filling her eyes. She moved to embrace him but her belly held her at a distance. "Husband, this will not do. We can not spend the day with you yelling yes, and me no. Please sit and join me for tea."

Beaver Lodge felt his frustration rise. "Can't you just once obey?"

Snow Pine placed his hand on her belly. "I cannot thank you enough for this new life. I will always try to help you, but I will no longer follow." She felt a deep cramp form in her back with finger-like pressure spreading across her abdomen. "Now, let me sit down, or it will be you who helps me with this baby."

After helping her down to the furs, Beaver Lodge joined her. She reached for the warming pot near the fire, poured him herbal tea, watching as he drank the honey sweetened liquid, and said, "Now tell me of Fawn Heart and the children."

"They are behind me on the trail. I wanted to see if you ceased being hardheaded and would come home and join us." He waved his arm, and Fawn Heart and the children came into camp. "If you won't come home, we will come to you, we are here until you have the baby, now don't disagree."

Snow Pine reached for his hand, bringing it to her lips. "Thank you."

That night as she lay listening to the sleep breathing of the others, she smiled, rubbed her belly, and thought how the little one would grow to love this family that surrounded her in the darkness. She never thought of the baby in any terms other than she. It was a girl. She was sure of it.

When she awoke the next morning, Beaver Lodge and Fawn Heart were already up, but Little Sun sat next to her. Looking into his dark eyes, Snow Pine was reminded how much he looked like Sun Kai.

The boy reached out and touched her belly shyly. "Momma, why doesn't the baby come out?"

Snow Pine smiled. "She will soon, and when she does, you will be her older brother, and she will look to you for guidance. You will be her best friend." She reached out and patted his face. "It is a big responsibility to be an older brother, but I am sure you will be a great one." How much he reminded her of Sun Kai, the seriousness, the thoughtful concern. She knew it was time to join the others, as the smell of onions, and meat from the morning fire filled the air. Her mind and stomach moved in different directions. Her mind registered hunger, but her stomach turned momentarily queasy.

"Help Momma up. It is time for breakfast."

As they left the cave entrance she could see Fawn Heart at the fire. Fawn Heart smiled, stood, and embraced her. "Dear One, it is so good to be with you. Sit down. Food is almost ready. Here, have some tea."

Taking the cup, Snow Pine breathed in the smell of mint, honey and sage. She sank down on the furs that lay spread near the fire. "Mmm, smells good. Where is Beaver Lodge?"

"He heard noises last night and has gone to see if he can find the animal sign. He had the impression that it was something large. He said to call when you awakened."

Just then, Beaver Lodge stepped from the tree line that surrounded the camp, scowling as he came forward, "No sign of anything. You have so many wild friends. Perhaps, it was one of them."

Fawn Heart handed him bowls of food and tea. "Sit. Let's eat together."

Crouching by the morning fire, Beaver Lodge looked about the camp. When he moved a fur aside to become comfortable, a small raccoon stuck its head out, yawned, and pulled itself back under the covers. "Wah, woman. What magic you do with these creatures. At the village they say you are a witch."

Reaching into the furs, Snow Pine scratched the young raccoon's belly. "No, not a witch, just someone who loves little ones." She reached over and scratched Little Sun's belly. "Especially this little one. How I miss you." She smiled at the notion of being considered a witch. "How is the village?"

Beaver Lodge threw the last of his tea into the fire, the liquid sizzling in the heat. "Well enough. We still do not know which Osage clan made the attack. Our scouts came back with no news. Eagle Feather and some of our young warriors want to find any group of Osage and take retribution. The Elders Council is having a hard time keeping them in check. But Eagle Feather argues that a people who do not defend themselves are inviting further attacks. I argue that our village lives by trade. A war that involves our people against all the Osage is not good. Fight if we must, but only against those who have offended us. So far the Elders Council has stood with me, but many of our young complain, saying my advice is but cowardliness dressed in trade goods."

Snow Pine thought of the wars that had raged throughout her homeland of Chin'in, resulting in the final destruction of her people, the Praxen. Shaking her head in remembrance, she wondered how anyone could wish such a thing. "I am sure the elders will be too wise to listen to the hot headed ones. You are right in your counsel. So they say I am a witch do they?"

Fawn Heart smiled. "Not exactly a witch. They have begun to call you Pregnant Woman, after the ancient one who could not climb from the underworld. Your knowledge of the healing herbs is considered a great blessing in our village. You are not thought of as a witch but as a gift from the ancients."

Snow Pine looked at her swollen belly. "Pregnant Woman is a good name."

They spent the day around camp, Snow Pine resting and Fawn Heart making preparations for the coming baby. After the evening meal, they sat under the stars and watched the fire burn low. "What shall you call the little one?" Fawn Heart asked.

Using a stick, Snow Pine drew the symbols for the moon and sun in the dust. "In my homeland we take these two characters, this one for the sun and this for the moon, and place them together to form the word ming, our word for brightness. She will be called Ming."

"But what if it is a boy?" Beaver lodge protested.

"Our child will be a girl. I promise you." She reached out, took his hand, and placed it on her belly. "A beautiful girl child."

That night as the stillness gathered about them, Snow Pine felt the first pains. She lay quietly at first, feeling the pain gather in her back and move across her belly. For several hours she lay thinking of the new gift that was working its way toward her. Then, the contractions increased in hardness and frequency. Finally, the pain was such that it took her breath away. "Fawn Heart," she said quietly, "Ming is becoming impatient. It is time."

Chapter 12 ~ Let the Games Begin

Josh Green arrived at the Department Chair's office fifteen minutes before his meeting with Dr. Eldrege. He sat in the outside waiting area, rubbing his fingers across his stubble, wondering what the 'Old Man' wanted.

Eldrege could be a tough nut sometimes, but as he considered it, he couldn't think of anything that might have brought him to the Department Chair's attention. He'd worked hard to fly under the radar. *Christ, I even scrubbed my MySpace Page; I'm a fucken boy scout.* His sense of dread heightened when Jenn Rausch came in and took the chair beside him, a worried look on her face. "How could they know?" she asked.

He put his finger to his lips. "They don't know shit."

Before Jenn could respond, the door opened and Betty, Eldrege's secretary, told them to enter. Jenn shot Josh a worried look then led the way. They entered the office and Eldrege pointed to two chairs. "Well, how do you like the program?" He paused, waiting for their answer.

Both students mumbled "fine," smiling and nodding their heads.

"I like to ask students that," Eldrege said. "It's kind of like asking diners how they like the meal. You always get a more truthful answer than asking the cooks." He smiled broadly, appreciating his own humor. "I'm glad you like it because I'm hearing great things about you. In fact, I've assigned Drs. Daniel and Laura French to do the evaluation on the gravesites that are getting all the local press, and they've asked if you two could be added as assistants for the team evaluation." Eldrege watched the strain leave their faces. They broke into smiles. *Couple of nice kids*, he thought. "I've spoken to the other department faculty, and they've agreed to allow this work to take the place of class projects this semester."

Jenn responded first. "That would be great. I'd love to work for them. I especially like Lauren." she paused awkwardly. "Ah ...I mean Dr. French"

Josh nodded in agreement. "What would they want us to do?"

Eldrege paused. "You need to talk to them personally. Leave a number where you can be reached this afternoon, and we'll call and set up an initial meeting to discuss details."

Josh looked at Jenn before answering. "Sure, why don't you call my apartment? Jenn and I were planning to study together this afternoon anyway. If we're out, just leave a message."

Eldrege stood, signaling the end of the meeting. "Well, it's been nice talking with you, and thank you. I'm sure the faculty will be pleased that you've agreed to assist."

Outside in the hall, Josh turned to Jenn and said mockingly. "No, No, let me thank you."

She replied, "No, No, No, Let me Thank You!" Then both broke into laughter.

That afternoon they lay in bed together, the smell of love-making filled the room. Jenn's short brown hair was matted, and without her glasses, she appeared boyish and younger. "You know," she murmured happily, "we should patent that smell, such a good smell. We'd make a fortune."

Josh turned to kiss her neck. "What shall we call it? Funky Spunky?"

"So common, let's give it a bit of class," Jenn teased, her hand playing with the hair on his stomach. "How about Eau de Funky Spunky?" She leaned forward and kissed his belly. "Wanna make some more?"

Josh slapped her hand away, laughing, "My God, the girl's insatiable!" He rolled out of bed and headed to the bathroom. "But I have promises to keep, and miles to go before I sleep."

Jenn watched as his hairy back and short legs retreated toward the door. *Who would imagine,* she thought. *I'm in love with a hairy cave man.* She looked at her watch. *He's right. Gotta get a shower, and clean this place. Aaron should be here in a couple of hours for the meeting.*

Later that afternoon, waiting for Aaron's arrival, Jenn concocted something called "Walk the Plank" from spiced rum, vodka, Hot Damn, and fruit juices. Josh was pleased with the turnout, mostly graduate students, some from the Archaeology program, some English majors, and a few from Poli-Sci. He'd carefully selected the group from the radical fringes of the university. As the deceptively easy to drink cocktail worked its magic and tongues loosened, he knew he'd chosen well. *Let the Games Begin,* he thought.

Aaron arrived at five-thirty; he was thin, tall and blond. He wore jeans and a t-shirt on which was emblazoned UNABOMBER for PRESIDENT – *If Elected, He Will Not Serve.* With his light blue eyes, blond hair, and pale complexion he seemed almost to glow in the darkened room.

After introductions, Josh rose. "I invited you here this afternoon to meet with Aaron and to discuss the creation of a Creative Artifacts Society cell here at SIU. Aaron joins us from the CAS Kaczynski Cell of the University of Chicago."

He handed out a packet of bumper stickers Aaron had given him. *FED UP WITH PROGRESS?' Write in UNABOMBER for PRESIDENT.* "Look, this is an in-or-out meeting. As you know, the CAS is outlawed in all universities, and exists only as an underground society bound by silence. Hell, most people think that the CAS is some kind of urban legend that doesn't even exist. If a CAS cell is not of interest to you, if you are not interested in protesting the existing hierarchy through eco-anarchism and radical environmentalism," he paused, letting the words sink in, "fill your glass with a little more Walk the Plank and take a walk."

No one spoke or got up to leave. "Aaron?"

Aaron rose. "Look, Theodore Kaczynski wrote his manifesto, Industrial Society and Its Future, now commonly known as the Unabomber Manifesto in 1995. The media and all their lemmings tried to make a joke of it. But the truth is, it's not the Manifesto that's a joke, it's the fricken political system that's the joke."

Several students in the group murmured approval.

Aaron continued. "The CAS seeks the end of the industrial-technical society. As humans we've gone down a blind alley of materialism, the effect of which has been a narrowing of human potential and freedom. The industrial technical society inevitably leads to the end of individual humanity. What we need is a revolution against technology!"

"But," one of the group interrupted, "Aren't you calling for a new form of Luddism? You sound anti-science, for Christ sake"

"Don't know about Christ's sake," Aaron replied. "Yes, we're calling for the end of science as we know it. Hell, think about it. Scientific research is directed toward an artificial goal that scientists have set for themselves merely for the sake of the fulfillment they get from pursuing the goal. It's a personal masturbation thing."

"But," the same student broke in again. "You can't be against human progress."

Aaron took a deep breath, sighed, shook his head, and looked at the guy as if he were talking to an idiot. "First I have to deal with

Christ's sake and now human progress. Gimme a break." Others around the room laughed. "The thing is KIDDO, it ain't progress. Oppenheimer is quoted as saying 'Now I have become death, the destroyer of worlds.' The bastard said this as his new and improved H-bomb turned a part of the southwestern desert into glass. Who the hell hired him to become a destroyer of the world?" Aaron hit his forehead for effect. "Science marches on blindly, without regard to the welfare of the human race or to any other legitimate goal, obedient only to the psychological needs of the scientists seeking to fulfill themselves, and to the corporate executives, or their political hirelings who provide the funds for research. Science is not the solution. It's the problem."

Josh rose to support Aaron's argument. "Read Jacque Ellul's _The Technological Imperative,_ and you'll see it. Every technological advance leads to new societal problems which require a new technological fix, which leads to new technical advances, which create problems that require even more dramatic technical fixes." He paused looking at the group, "Who here thinks that autism, ADD, and all the rest is normal?" He added rhetorically, "Do you suppose it's caused by all the fricken garbage that science pumps into our environment?" Several heads nodded. "And what is the great technological fix, for the problems that the last technological fix created? A Brave New World, a society of numbness caused by psychotropic pharmaceuticals." He raised his glass in salute. "Here's to progress. The techno-industrial society is aimed at taking away our creativity and eating our souls. Hell, read Ray Kurzweil's _The Age of Spiritual Machines,_ if we keep going in this direction, the future won't need us humans anymore."

Silence filled the room. Aaron rose and continued. "Look, everyone knows that the shift from hunter-gatherer to agricultural subsistence gave rise to social stratification, coercive governments, and alienation from self. We in the CAS call for anarchic-primitivism, a return to non-civilized ways of living through deindustrialization, abolition of the division of labor, and abandonment of technology. What we're saying is, Screw the Man and the Hummer he rode in on! Our goal is nothing less than a return to a feral state of being. We're going to climb into the machine and throw a wrench into the system's guts."

Many began to speak at once. The room echoed with "Screw the Man." Several raised their fists in assent. In the other room the phone rang. Josh looked at Jenn, "Let it ring. The answering machine will get it." They heard Jenn's voice on the machine. "Hi, this is Jenn, Josh and I aren't here right now. If you're selling something, Hang up and Go Away! If not, we'd love to talk to you, leave a message." They could hear Lauren French's voice respond.

Josh raised his hands quieting the group. "Can I take that as a yes to forming a CAS cell? Along with talking with us, I asked Aaron to bring along some wrenches to throw into the gears of progress." He pointed to a bag.

Aaron reached into the bag and began removing artifacts stolen by the Chicago cell. "I like this one best," he said, unrolling a winter count buffalo skin on which the Mandan Indians had drawn symbols, indicating the number of buffalo seen. He held out the skin. "Nice thing about this item is that it's authentic, yet it comes from so far away, no one will recognize it. I stole it myself during a summer seminar at Oxford England. You bury this baby at a construction site or new housing development, and I guarantee all work will stop." He looked at his watch. "Speaking of stopping, I gotta go. Got other wrenches to deliver to the cell at UMSL in St. Louis." Putting his hand to his forehead, he said sarcastically, giving a big sigh. "A revolutionary's work is never done."

Later, after the group left the apartment, Jenn pushed the

blinking red button to retrieve the message. 'Hi Jenn, this is Lauren French, getting back to you and Josh about the meeting. Let's make it Wednesday at five in Daniel's office. If that doesn't work for you, give me a call. Oh, and thank you guys for agreeing to work on this."

Jenn laughed. "No, No. Thank You."

Chapter 13 ~ Ming

Snow Pine warmed herself in the sun and watched her daughter play. *How the seasons pass so quickly*, she thought. Ming had grown fast, first a helpless bundle that captured her heart and made the strong Beaver Lodge quake at the thought of holding her, next a wobbly unsure toddler of two summers, and now the whirl wind of movement that went everywhere. Snow Pine smiled, watching an orphaned fawn she nurtured through winter, nuzzle about in Ming's pockets for sweetened grain, and a baby raccoon, which sat perched on the girl's shoulder, play with the hair about her ears.

"Momma, watch," Ming called, throwing a stick for a young wolf cub to fetch. The valley was peaceful, a place where all enmities could be forgotten. Outside in the world beyond the cave and valley, the tribes fought and men died, but here, protected by the spirit of Sun Kai and the winged beast, peace prevailed.

Beaver Lodge came often, telling of the raids on the Osage, and the counter raids which had become a veritable storm so that none could live peacefully. Sadness molded his face and shoulders. "You would not recognize Eagle Feather. He has become a changed thing. He thinks only of hate and revenge. The longer the war, the more who die, the less likely we can find an ending to the killing."

She reached out and touched his arm. "I am sorry for Eagle Feather, although we did not agree; he was a good man."

"Come into the village where you will be safe," he pleaded. But she knew in her heart this was not so. The violence between the people had taken a life of its own and no one was safe. She did not blame Beaver Lodge since he'd done all he could to preserve the peace. This was his war only in as far as he had to deal with its consequences.

"Here, they leave us in peace," she said. "There, they raid the village. We are safer here under the protection of Sun Kai and his demon painting. Besides, why bother with a crazy witch and her spirit child who talks to animals?" Beaver Lodge was torn. He knew she spoke the truth. He could not protect her, and, in fact, his very presence might bring enemies.

As the war continued Snow Pine taught Ming the writing characters. Since she had neither silk nor ink, they used charcoal and flattened pieces of wood or leather. Not every character could be made in this manner, and there were many new things in this land for which no Chin'in words existed. She and Ming made new marks to indicate new words, like buffalo, or Osage, or Trading People. "Daughter, you are indeed like your name." Snow Pine drew characters for the sun and moon. "Such a bright one you are." Ming smiled. She loved this secret game, in which messages could be passed between herself and her mother that no one else understood.

One day, when her brother Little Sun came for a visit, Ming whispered to him that the young wolf cub who lay resting on the other side of the fire thought that he'd grown since the last visit. "Wolves don't think such things," he said. "Don't be a silly girl."

"Yes he does," Ming laughed. "I can prove it." She drew a few characters on a stick and threw it toward the young wolf. "Take to Momma" she commanded. The young animal, who loved this game of fetch, picked up the stick and carried it to Snow Pine. She looked at the stick and called to Little Sun. "He thinks you have grown since your last visit, and he is right. You are growing into a man. Soon I won't be able to call you Little Sun." The boy stared at his sister with something akin to awe. *Maybe the tales of his mother and sister being witches were right,* he thought.

Often by the evening fire, Snow Pine told Ming of the ancient homeland, of Sun Kai, and their voyage to the new land. She told how Sun Kai painted the great bird on the cliff, and now since his death, how his spirit protected them in this valley. She fingered her small coin necklace. "See, this is a token he gave me when we were separated. I wear it to remember him." Snow Pine slipped the necklace from her neck and handed it to Ming.

Ming looked at the coin with the profile of a man in a feathered cape on its surface. "Is this Sun Kai?"

"No, little one, that is not Sun Kai. The man on the coin in the feathered cloak is a great chief of Sun Kai's homeland. He had a group of special warriors, who all wore coin necklaces like this to remember him. It was this chief who sent Sun Kai and me on our voyage." Snow Pine smiled, and reached out to hug the child. "If it were not for him, you and I would not be here tonight." She replaced the necklace around her neck. "Both Sun Kai and I always wore these about our necks, but it was not for the chief, it was for each other. Sun Kai is buried with his." She pulled a small green stone from her pocket and handed it to Ming. "This is known as jade, and it is very special. The great seal of the land of Chin'in is made from this stone. Some believe that if you wear this stone on your clothing it will grow darker over time because it collects good luck and good health. Then if you ever get into real trouble or get sick, the stone breaks apart and returns its collection to the wearer."

Ming looked at the small jade piece. "This looks like a cricket."

She turned the piece in her hand. "Why is it shaped like a cricket?"

Snow Pine smiled again. "This is a very special piece of jade, designed for an important purpose. In our land we don't call this thing a cricket, but a cicada. It is a strange creature, which appears dead for a long period of time, and then comes alive. People in our homeland believe that if you place a small jade cicada in the mouth of someone who dies, they will live again, just like the creature. Perhaps when I die, you will place this jade cicada in my mouth to help me live again and find Sun Kai."

Afterwards, Ming sat considering the remembrance necklace and jade cicada. With a stick she drew a small circle with a profile of a man in a feathered cape.

Chapter 14 ~ Buffalo Woman

Later that season, a group of Osage came into the camp carrying a young wounded warrior. They were tall, well-formed men who scowled and waved their weapons at Snow Pine. At first she thought they might hurt her or the child, but soon she understood the threats were born in fear of her, the witch woman. She also knew they would not have come if not for great need. Only their concern for the young warrior and his needs kept them from fleeing. She went to her medicine pack and gathered a handful of minerals that when hot gave off a green and red flame. She tossed these into the fire along with seeds that popped when heated. She remembered the Chin'in war cry: *'Make Them Fear,'* and smiled to herself. Raising her hands above her head, she waved her fingers, beckoned at the clouds, and sang one of Chin'in's street operas in high falsetto. All heads looked up fearing she might be calling the great flying demon from the cliff. *Sun Kai would be proud*, she thought. The fire burned an eerie red and green, and hissed with the popping seeds while Snow Pine's movements and song held then entranced. The scowling bravado of the warriors was now replaced by fear and awe. *Enough magic*. She called Ming to bring the medicine bag. The wounded warrior's eyes widened with fear at Snow Pine's approach. She sat next to him and placed her hand upon his forehead. It was hot to the touch. *Yang excess*, she thought.

I must somehow return the balance of yin and yang to his body. She handed Ming herbs from the medicine pouch. "Place these in the boiling pot. It will release the medicines he needs." She moved his cloak aside, exposing a small puncture wound in his left chest wall. With each breath frothy bubbles gurgled to the surface. She closed her eyes, and said, "Oh ancestors, let this end soon, before we have no young men left."

Snow Pine put her ear to his chest and listened. The sounds across much of the surface seemed diminished. She timed each breath, leaned over him and said, "On the next breath, breathe all the way out." Snow Pine took several green leaves, placed an ointment on them, and covered the wound when the chest was at its emptiest. "Now, breathe in deeply," she commanded. The young man struggled to inhale. She felt suction under her hand as the open wound tried to bring in air but she covered the wound with the leaves before that could happen. She leaned forward again, listening to his chest; it seemed as if the sounds were more pronounced and regular. With her free hand, she spread a sticky resin across the outside of the leaves, hoping to seal them in place so she could remove her hand. The boy gave a weak smile as his breathing became easier and less painful.

Ming brought the herbal tea to alleviate the excess yang, and Snow Pine added powders to help the boy sleep. She cushioned his head, and he drank the draft. Closing her eyes, she appealed to the ancestors, "Please do not let him die. Help me." *He will need rest if he is to return to health,* she thought. *A puncture wound into the lung is a dangerous wound indeed. He will need to stay, but his fellows must leave if war is to be kept from the valley.*

Snow Pine stood, gathering a handful of minerals and popping seeds from her bag. She smiled; it was again time to make them fear. "Hear me!" she yelled, pointing at the young warrior. "He must stay if he is to live, but you must go."

The men began to talk at once, frowning and nodding in disagreement. The leader stood towering over Snow Pine. "No. He stay. We stay."

Snow Pine threw additional minerals and seeds into the fire, throwing up fresh sparks. "Hear me! This is a sacred place, home of the First Ancestor who dwells in the cave. Home to his great bird that overlooks the river and devours men."

The man pointed his spear at her. "We do not fear you, Witch."

Snow Pine batted the spear aside and looked contemptuously at the man. "Would you threaten me? I have only to look you in the eye for First Ancestor and his Great Bird to see you and mark you for death. They do not want you here. They will not have you here! Be not afraid of me, but if you stay, they will hunt you at night and kill you in your sleep." She raised her arm, indicating the whole valley. "This is a place of great power and magic."

Snow Pine could see resignation and indecision in their faces. She turned to the leader. "You must go!" She pointed to the trail leading out of the valley, "I will not have you bring the war between the Trading People and Osage into my valley. I will tend him, and if you must come here, do not come with warriors, better yet, send me someone useful, send me his mother." She made a gesture of dismissal, turned her back on him, and went to tend the young man. The men stood, momentarily indecisive, then without speaking, slowly filed out of the camp and up the trail.

"Wah," Snow Pine muttered at the worthlessness of men. She placed her hand upon the sleeping young man's forehead. He was still warm to touch, but his pulses were regular and his breathing easier. Gesturing to Ming to sit by his side, Snow Pine said, "Watch, daughter, and tell me if anything changes. Do not be frightened though, he is strong." The next hours would be crucial in his recovery.

Snow Pine smiled at Ming who had remained sitting at the young warrior's side, watching him intently. "Mamma, is Young Wolf going to die?"

Snow Pine looked at her daughter. "Young Wolf? Is that his name? How do you know?"

"He told me." Ming giggled as if she'd been entrusted with a grown-up secret. Her face saddened with concern at the thought of the young warrior, "But will he die?"

"I do not think so, Little One. Such a wound is serious, but only the Ancestors know." Later, Snow Pine brought her daughter bread and a piece of meat. "You are such a good watcher. I am sure the Ancestors will be pleased by you and will try to help Young Wolf."

Over the next several days Snow Pine and Ming nursed the hurt warrior. Slowly, the wound sealed and she removed the leaves that covered the puncture. Snow Pine placed her hand on the young man's chest and ordered him to, "take deep, slow breaths." She watched, but no air seeped in at the wound site. The lips of the puncture itself were still somewhat inflamed, but the boy was not overly warm, indicating no internal infection. She turned to Ming, and hugged the girl. "See, the Ancestors watched you watching over him and made him well."

Looking up, Snow Pine saw a woman standing at the edge of the camp watching them. The woman was tall, even taller than Snow Pine herself, and appeared to be middle aged, with long straight black hair, clear black eyes, a full mouth, and firm chin. While the woman was not beautiful, she was somehow remarkable, perhaps commanding. She was wearing a snow white buckskin dress with jewelry and markings of the Osage People. "The men said you sent for me. I am Buffalo Woman. I am his mother."

Chapter 15 - The Pledge

Snow Pine raised her hands, beckoning the woman forward. "Please, come. He is doing well. I think the danger is past."

Buffalo Woman moved to the boy's side. "Well, Young Wolf, I send you to war, and now find you resting among women."

They boy smiled shyly. "It is nice to see you, Mother. This is Snow Pine and Ming. They have been kind to me."

Buffalo Woman's face relaxed as she sat beside her son. Snow Pine imagined how she might feel coming into a camp, knowing her son was wounded, but not knowing the severity. How hard it would be to remain composed under such circumstances. Snow Pine admired the woman's control. She thought, *perhaps that is what I saw in her countenance, not beauty, but strength of will.* She pulled Ming toward her. "Let's give them time alone, Little One." Addressing the woman, she said, "Thank you for coming. Ming and I will go and prepare the meal."

Under the close watch of Ming and Buffalo Woman, the young warrior returned to health. Within the week, he was able to leave the shelter to sit by the fire and play with the animals. Ming was his constant companion, and he would often allow her to ride on his shoulders around camp. In the evenings, as the fire burned low and Ming and the boy slept, Snow Pine and the woman sat and talked about their children and the war between the two peoples. Pointing to the scar on Snow Pine's forehead, Buffalo Woman asked, "How did you get such a thing?"

Snow Pine spoke of her life. She told how she and Sun Kai made the journey across the great water, how their group landed and built homes, intending to stay. She told of the natives living nearby. They had considered them friends, and traded with them. She used her skills with medicine to care for them. Her smile faded when she told Buffalo Woman how the natives got sick and when her medicine failed to heal them; they blamed the sickness on the newcomers. "One night when they came into camp as friends, they turned against us, and attacked us. The last thing I remember was the local shaman laughing as he tried to crush my skull with his bludgeon." She pulled back her hair, revealing the scar, which stretched from hairline to eyebrow. "That is how I got this."

Buffalo Woman leaned over, put her arms about Snow Pine, and kissed the scar line. "I am sorry. But how did you get to this place?"

Snow Pine continued. "When I awoke, I was trussed up in the bottom of a canoe filled with trade goods, heading up river. The Trading People bought me and took me to their village. She pointed down river. I thought all my group were killed that night, but my husband, Sun Kai, although wounded, survived. After many months he found me. He is the one that painted the great bird on the cliff."

"Where is he now?" Buffalo Woman asked.

"The wounds he received were very deep and he could not be restored to health. I tended him as best I could, but he died." She pointed to the cave above them. "He is buried there. It is why I live in this valley, to be near Sun Kai, to watch over him and to have him watch over me." Snow Pine began to cry softly, and Buffalo Woman pulled her into her arms to comfort her. She began to sing the creation song of the Osage, how the people came from the sky, how the great Elk blew the water from the land, helping them find a new home.

Young Wolf grew stronger, and Snow Pine worried Trading People warriors would come and find him there. *What will happen then,* she thought. *Will they see the young man for what he is? Or will they see an Osage Warrior, and bring the outside war to the valley?* She could not bear where her thoughts led, and rushed to find Buffalo Woman, "He must leave. Your son must leave now."

Upon hearing that Young Wolf was leaving, Ming was inconsolable. Snow Pine took her daughter into her arms and sat rocking her. "Little One, it is time for him to return to his people. One of these days, men from the trading village will come, and they will not see him as our friend, but as an enemy warrior. He must leave before then." When Ming offered to protect him, Snow Pine replied, "Hush now, Little One, he is our friend, but he must leave. Perhaps you could spend some time making him a gift, a gift that he will remember you by." That seemed to mollify the girl, and she left Snow Pine's arms to think about what to make.

Young Wolf was only slightly less agreeable to leaving. Snow Pine listened as he argued that his presence offered protection, that he could not leave his mother so near the enemy.

Snow Pine smiled at the thought that he was protecting them. "You may be right," she said, "that your mother should leave, and she may if that is her desire. I would miss her, as we have much to learn from each other. But, that is her choice." Snow Pine turned toward Buffalo Woman.

Buffalo Woman stood considered the idea. "I agree. Young Wolf must leave, not only for his protection, but for ours," she then paused. "But I think I will remain for a few more weeks." Young Wolf turned to protest, but Buffalo Woman raised her hand ending the debate. "When you get to our camp, tell your father I will be there before the clan moves to the high meadow hunting ground."

The next morning Young Wolf prepared to leave. After breakfast, he gathered his pack and weapons. Buffalo Woman took him into her arms, giving motherly advisements as to conduct and safety. Snow Pine watched, thinking how she'd seen this scene between mothers and sons before. How similar we are, she mused. *For all the differences between the tribes, or for that matter, even between the people of my ancient homeland and this land, we are all so very much alike.*

Ming approached Young Wolf. When he looked down and smiled, she raised her arms to be picked up. In her hand was a necklace she had made for him. When he pulled her into his arms she placed the piece around his neck. On the leather thong was a small flat sandstone the size of a small coin. Etched into the surface was the torso of a man in profile, a man with a rather pronounced nose, and feathered cape. Snow Pine gasped in recognition. Ming had fashioned the boy a necklace much like the gold one Sun Kai had given her in Chin' in. Snow Pine fingered the coin she wore round her neck. It was her connection to Sun Kai, a token of their love and trust. Ming in her most serious voice said, "Someday, when I grow up, you will come and ask for me in marriage. Until then, this necklace will protect you and remind you of me."

Young Wolf's face became crimson, and he looked helplessly at the two watching women whose faces were distorted in their attempt not to laugh at his discomfort. Snow Pine thought that he might drop Ming and run from the camp. But he finally smiled, kissed Ming on the cheek, and said that she was his favorite sister. Buffalo Woman and Snow Pine looked at each other. Ming was six summers. Young Wolf sixteen. Given time, it was possible.

Chapter 16 ~ White Buffalo Calf Woman

Following Young Wolf's departure, the valley returned to its normal routine. Fawn Heart and other women from the Trading People village made their way to the valley to ask for assistance regarding family problems, or to obtain healing herbs. At first they were hesitant in front of Buffalo Woman. "She is an enemy!" they whispered. "What if she tells the Osage about you, about us coming here?"

Snow Pine shook her head. "This war between our two peoples is not a war of women. Do not Osage women cry over their husbands and sons, as you do?" She could see the women nodding in agreement. "Take Buffalo Woman into your heart, you will find her like us. If matters were left to women, would we be at war?"

Following this exchange, a slight change occurred. Often the camp contained women from both tribes. Although the women remained separated by tribe and did not reach out to the others in friendship, no animosity stirred between them, rather an understanding of mutual suffering and sameness.

During this period Snow Pine had reoccurring dreams. In the dream, she and Sun Kai climbed upon the great winged beast and flew out into the evening sky. They would sail far to the west, south, north and east, all across the great prairie. Everywhere they went, she could see the herds of buffalo, and following behind them, the camps of the Osage.

She remembered the dreams in great detail and related them to Buffalo Woman. When she described certain rock formations she'd seen, which rose like lonely watchers from the prairie floor, Buffalo Woman knew them and gave their clan names. "You have truly seen these places?" Snow Pine asked. Buffalo Woman nodded, adding that the clan followed the buffalo, and they passed those great stones each year.

Snow Pine's mind raced at the possibility of the nomadic tribes seeing things that the Trading People never viewed. If Sun Kai's people came to the coast, or anywhere along the rivers, the Trading People would hear of it, but what if they came across the land, from the west or east? They could pass by and she would not know. She took a deep breath. "Buffalo Woman, do you think the Osage women would keep a record of what they see along the hunting migrations? I fear that if my people come, they may pass without my knowledge."

Buffalo Woman turned, her face drawn in thinking. "How would they keep a record? What would you want to know?"

"Here, let me show you." Snow Pine knelt down and pulled a piece of leather from a pouch. "One woman among the traveling families could carry a piece of leather like this and mark it with things they see. They could draw a map of the area, perhaps indicating some of the great stones markers we spoke of. They could indicate the season, and moon phase. If it were the time of the full moon and they saw a large herd of buffalo, they could mark the leather like this." She drew a full moon and several of the buffalo characters. "And this would be a special sign." She drew several stick figures and an arrow pointing toward the great river. "This would be our sign for strangers coming. If it were on a map, I could know of their presence and from what direction they came."

Snow Pine pondered as to how the messages could be carried. Suddenly, she said, "I could give each woman a medicine bundle to carry, which would help your people remain well during their travels. The leather map could be carried inside. When the women returned, the pouch could be sent to me, and I would provide another medicine bundle with fresh herbs and a new piece of leather."

Buffalo Woman frowned. "I am not sure that such a thing could happen, but I will think on it.'

Over the next several days the women talked of the medicine bundles. Snow Pine taught Buffalo Woman the use of each herb and several more writing characters to indicate mountains, forests, lakes, rivers and streams. Buffalo Woman, quick to see the power in the writing, learned eagerly. "This power of sending words through these marks should be kept just for the women," Buffalo Woman said. "It will allow us to communicate among ourselves." Snow Pine nodded in agreement. She had tried to share information with men, and she knew their resistance to women's knowledge.

Buffalo Woman lingered in the valley, talking and listening to Snow Pine. They spoke of their families, the medicine bundles, and the histories of their people. Of all the stories Buffalo Woman told, Ming's favorite was that of White Buffalo Calf Woman, the ancient one whom Buffalo Woman was named after.

"Please, once more" Ming begged. Snow Pine smiled, knowing Buffalo Woman would not refuse the child's request, although she'd told the story many times. Rising, Buffalo Woman began the tale:

One summer, before the counting of time, our people came together to camp. This was a time in which all our people were one. There were no tribes. The sun shone brightly and there was no night, but the people could not find food. They were very hungry and sent scouts out every day, but no food was found.

One morning the chief sent two young warriors to hunt for game. They searched everywhere but could find nothing. Finally, they came to a great mountain and decided to climb it, so that they could see the whole land. Halfway up, they saw something coming toward them from far away. As it came closer, it appeared to be a person, but instead of walking, the person appeared to be floating.

As the figure came closer, they saw that it was a beautiful woman dressed in white. The woman was beautiful. She had red dots painted on her cheeks and wore her blue-black hair loose, except for a strand on the left side, which was tied up with buffalo fur. Her eyes shone dark and sparkling, and the men warmed to her gaze.

Struck silent by her beauty, the two men stood with mouths open. One was awed recognizing her sacred nature, but the other looked upon her with lust, desiring her body. He reached out to grab her, but she was too sacred to be disrespected in this manner. Before he could touch her, he was struck by a mighty bolt of lightning, which burned him so completely that only a small heap of blackened bones remained.

Turning to the good warrior, White Buffalo Calf Woman said, "I bring good things for your people. Go tell them I come and prepare me a medicine lodge." So the young warrior ran back to camp and told them of his meeting, and how they should prepare.

After four days, White Buffalo Calf Woman approached. Her white buckskin dress shone from afar, like a beacon of light. She carried a sacred medicine bundle filled with gifts of power. The most powerful was the sacred pipe. She held it out to the people to let them look at it. She grasped the stem in her right hand and the bowl with her left. Buffalo Woman paused in the telling of her story, "Even to this day, that is how the pipe is handled," she said.

The chief thanked White Buffalo Woman for instructing them and offered her food. However, they had no meat, so they offered water into which sweet grass had been dipped. The woman took the offering and drank deeply. "Even now, our people dip sweet grass or an eagle feather into water, and sprinkle it on a person to be purified." Buffalo Woman explained.

White Buffalo Calf Woman spoke to the women, telling them that it was the work of their hands and fruit of their bodies which sustained the people and kept them alive. "You are from Mother Earth. What you do is as sacred as what warriors do."

Buffalo Calf Woman taught the people many things. Finally, she again addressed the chief: "Remember, the sacred pipe. Respect it and it will take you to the end of the road. I am the four ages of creation and will visit you again in every generational cycle. I shall come back to you."

With that she turned and walked away in the same direction from which she came, her form outlined in the red ball of the setting sun. As she went, she stopped and rolled over four times. With each roll she took the appearance of a buffalo, first black, then brown, then red, and finally a white female calf.

Completing the story, Buffalo Woman smiled at Ming. "That is why the white buffalo is sacred. That is why we honor the pipe in our ceremonies. Before she came to us, the people did not know how to live. She put her sacred mind into us." Buffalo Woman pointed to her dress. "That is also why I wear white."

"Could you make me one like yours?" Ming begged.

Buffalo Woman agreed to the request but Snow Pine shook her head no. Finally, Snow Pine acquiesced and agreed to help prepare a white dress for Ming. "It will suit your name, Little Bright One," she laughed.

The leaves turned colors; the time had come for Buffalo Woman to return to her people. Yet she lingered.

One afternoon as Ming lay sleeping in the shelter, Buffalo Woman gathered her sleeping furs, "It is so hot today; perhaps a wash in the creek will refresh me." Snow Pine smiled in agreement. "It is warm. I'll come with you." The two women walked hand-in-hand to the stream a short distance from camp where a rock formed a deep pool. Buffalo woman dropped her sleeping furs, shrugged out of her clothing, and waded into the cool water. Snow Pine reached into her pouch and found herbs that when wet produced a slippery soap scented with lavender. Dropping her clothing, she joined the older woman in the pool. "Here, we can use this to clean and refresh ourselves. Turn your back, I will scrub you."

Snow Pine washed the other woman's back, her hands moving across her well-muscled shoulders and arms, down to the smallness of her waist. The woman seemed both strong and soft at the same time. *Such a beautiful form,* she thought. Buffalo Woman laughed. "Here, let me." She took the herbal soap from Snow Pine and scrubbed her. Snow Pine felt Buffalo Woman's strong fingers kneading her back and shoulder muscles. Buffalo Woman leaned forward, smelling the lavender scent. "Turn and I will wash your front."

After bathing the women lay in the warm sun, cleansed and

bonded by the intimate familiarity. When they were dry, they gathered their clothing and sleeping furs and returned to camp. That afternoon, both went about camp duties laughing and talking with a closeness only sister share. As evening approached and Ming lay asleep in the shelter, the women pulled their sleeping furs together and disrobed for the night.

That night Snow Pine dreamed of Sun Kai. They again went sailing on the back of the great beast across the night sky. She saw the sky land where the Osage people lived before coming down to Earth Mother. She saw the buffalo herds and Osage move across the great prairie. When she awakened, Buffalo woman was up and when she saw Snow Pine wake, she smiled.

Seeing the woman's pack set against the door, Snow Pine asked, "Are you leaving?"

Buffalo Woman moved toward her, "Yes, I have been too long away from my husband's bed, and my time with you is too lovely. I will send you the information you seek." She leaned down, kissed the scar on Snow Pine's forehead, turned, gathered up her pack, and left the shelter. Snow Pine lay back upon her furs, smelling lavender.

Chapter 17 ~ The Dig

Dr. Eldrege looked around the conference table. The team members were there except for Lauren French, who was ill that day. He originally planned to delay until she could be there, but she'd asked him to assume leadership for an initial meeting.

He stood, looked over the group, and began. "One of the things I like to do before beginning any dig is to tell the story of Augusto Jandolo. If the name is unfamiliar, he was a Roman antiquarian. As a boy Augusto was with his father at the opening of an Etruscan sarcophagus. Let me read to you his description of that event."

> *It was not an easy matter, moving the cover, but finally it was lifted upright, then allowed to fall heavily on the other side. And then something happened that I have never forgotten and that will remain before my eyes as long as I live. I saw resting within the coffin the body of a young warrior in full military panoply, the helmet, spear, shield and greaves. Observe it was not a skeleton that I saw, but a body complete in all limbs, and stiffly outstretched as if freshly laid out in the grave.*

Eldrege stopped reading. "Who can tell me what comes next, and why I'm reading you this note from Augusto's memoirs?" Those around the table looked at each other, but none answered.

Finally, Josh Green whispered to Jenn Rausch, "Maybe the body moved. Oooh." Several in the group laughed, and then stopped when Eldrege scowled. He stood silently, looking at the graduate student. "I suppose in a sense the body did move. Not particularly funny, certainly not scary, but it did move. Let me finish reading you the section."

This apparition endured but a moment. Then every thing seemed to dissolve in the light of the torches. The helmet rolled to the right, the round shield fell into the now sunken breast-piece of the amour, and the greaves suddenly collapsed flat on the ground, the one to the right, one to the left. The body that remained untouched for centuries suddenly dissolved into dust when exposed to the air ... a golden dust was suspended in the air and about the flame of the torches.

"In that sarcophagus lay a member of Etruscan society. Think of it, an Etruscan, a people whose origin and descent remains to this day a mystery. Just a passing glimpse and it was gone." He stopped his face pensive, as if pondering a personal loss. "And what caused this incredible loss? Gross carelessness!" He looked directly at Josh. "And that, Mr. Green, is not a matter for humor at all."

Josh's face grew red but he did not respond; rather, he looked down sheepishly.

Eldrege continued, "Each archaeological site is like a chapter in a one of a kind rare book. There are no other copies. When you study early Indian remains in Illinois, you study a people without written records. The arrow heads, pottery, vessels, pits, houses, burial sites, animal bones, charred vegetables, and even the soil in which these things are encased are as important to the interpretation of the site as are the words on the pages of a book.

The people we are studying were not literate; all you have is their mute testimony, left unintentionally, while they went about their daily life." Again, Eldrege paused, letting his words sink in. "Artifacts alone are like words out of context. Unless the excavation is done carefully, and the associations of the artifacts with all the various features of the site recorded well, the people's story is lost. Once excavated, all information not recorded or saved is destroyed by the process. If the excavation is not done right, it should not be done at all. In archaeology, we get no do-overs."

"Yet, if we do our jobs well, record and catalogue each item, faithfully placing each bit of information in its context, then, even if we don't get the interpretation right the first time, others in the future may solve the puzzle."

"Well enough of history and philosophy, and on to the work. And work it is." He looked at the graduate students. "The site investigation is but the tip of the iceberg, for every hour on the dig, you will spend at least four hours in the laboratory." Eldrege smiled for the first time. "I've asked Dr. Lauren French to oversee the excavation. As you can see she was not able to be here for the initial meeting. She asked that her husband stand in for her to update you on the current status of the dig. Now, if you will excuse me, I will be off and let him be at it." Several in the group stood as he gathered his papers and rose. In the Department, there was a lot of honor paid to the 'old man.'

After the door closed, Daniel stood to give the update. "Well, what we have is a site where two female skeletons have been uncovered. All road construction has been suspended pending our evaluation. We've taken pictures and noted all the important features of the site. We've also plowed the area to remove the surface vegetation." He nodded at Jenn Rausch. "Jenn and I have been at the site, set up the controls for the horizontal area, and staked it out in a one meter grid aligned along the cardinal coordinates of north and east." He handed out a grip map showing the location of the two skeletons. "We laid out a rather large area, to insure that we capture whatever's there. The site presents us with two different dig situations. About half of the area has been torn up by the earlier construction work with considerable earth removal, and the remaining area appears to be in an undisturbed state. Fortunately or unfortunately, depending how you look at it, we found an obsidian knife which we believe is associated with the first grave. We think this because it was in dirt recently removed from the area by a backhoe. With all the earth removal it will be hard to really determine a precise datum line for the disturbed area."

Jared Davidson, one of the faculty assigned to the dig, interjected. "Well, the obsidian knife is interesting. Probably means the site is associated with early Mound Culture and arrived as a result of trade, since there's no obsidian in these parts."

"Probably," Daniel agreed. "But you heard Eldrege. We better be careful with our opinions. After all," he changed his voice to mimic that of the Department Chairman's nasal accent, "a lone artifact is like a word from a book taken out of context."

Jared laughed. "He's right, you know. Tell you what. If Jenn and Josh are available tomorrow, I'll take them out and establish a hypothetical datum line." Both of the students nodded eagerly. "Josh, perhaps you could gather up a transit, a farmer's level, and an alidade from the storeroom. That should be all we need; I'll bring a camera. Let's meet at the site, say ten o'clock?"

Later that afternoon, on different sides of town, there were two conversations regarding the meeting. The first occurred when Daniel caught Lauren up on what had taken place. "You should have seen the 'Ol Man' stare down poor Josh Green when he tried to make a funny. Josh grew so red. I thought he was gonna burst out crying. He'll know after this that Eldrege takes his archaeology very seriously. I actually felt sorry for the guy."

"Anyway, the work got off to a fine start. Along with the graduate students, we'll be working with Jared Davidson. He knows his stuff. Good man. Easy to get along with."

Lauren blew her nose, snuffed and coughed. "I hate colds. Sorry about Josh. I'm sure he meant no harm. Fred can be such a bear sometimes." She yawned. "Don't know whether I hate a cold or the medicines more, they make me so sleepy and woozy." She yawned again, "It will be nice to work with Jared, he's a nice guy. Mormon, I think. Maybe we can have him and his wife over for dinner sometime. Right now I think I'll go back to bed."

"Yeah, get some rest. I'll order in pizza for dinner. You want some soup later?"

The second conversation occurred across town in Josh's apartment. "I can't believe the bastard acted like that" Josh seethed. "All I did was poke a little fun. You'd think I made fun of God or something. Christ!" He slammed his fist into the wall leaving an indentation. "Son-of-a-bitch," he snarled, shaking his injured hand. "Fricken thing hurts. He'll pay for this too."

Jenn stood silent, waiting for Josh to calm down and become rational. "What did Aaron want when he called this morning?"

Rubbing his knuckles, Josh took a seat beside her. "He said it was payback time for the CAS wrenches he left the other day. Aaron gave us a buffalo hide he stole while doing an internship at Oxford. Then we're supposed to send back to him artifacts taken from here which he will send on to Cells at other schools. In that way, those using the wrenches are widely separated and the CAS members who plant them are not connected with the department they came from. Pretty smart." He tapped his head, wincing in pain, "and in this way when they're tested, the artifacts are authentic."

Jenn laughed. "You love this cloak and dagger stuff, don't

you?" She mussed his hair. "Now you look like the mad anarchist you really are." She put her arms around him and squeezed, there was something thrilling and dangerous about his wild intensity. "I just love crazy men. By the way, if the Chicago group is the Kaczynski Cell, what are we going to call our little team of anarcho-primitivists?"

"How about the Berenger Cell, after Professor Berenger of Wurzburg Germany?

"Professor Berenger?"

"You remember, Professor Beringer, the guy from the 1700s who wrote a popular textbook about petrified frogs, insects, and spiders. He claimed to have found a spider and fly petrified simultaneously. Anyway, the book was well accepted in early archaeology circles until it was found that the good professor had been victimized by students who manufactured the *'fossils'* and planted them where they were sure the professor would dig."

Jenn giggled, kissing him on the neck. "So, we're the Berenger Cell. I love it."

"And, as for that pompous bastard Eldrege, one of these days I'm going to Berenger his ass."

Chapter 18 ~ Daughters of White Buffalo Calf Woman

In spring Snow Pine tended her gardens. In summer and fall she gathered, and as winter approached, she mended, stored, and planned for the new year. Now, in camp she and Ming maintained a continuous fire to keep warm as the seasons changed. Beaver Lodge visited regularly with Fawn Heart and the boys. Snow Pine loved these times, as the children played and she and Fawn Heart caught up on the news from the village. The war continued. Men and boys died, women and children were kidnapped. Beaver Lodge was quiet about the war, but she knew that he had no heart for the dying, mourning each family's loss as his own.

Often when she and Ming were alone, she felt the presence of a dark spirit watching from beyond the camp fire. She would draw Ming close to her, not allowing her daughter to venture from camp, or beyond the fire light. When it was time for sleep, they moved their furs into the cave to lie at the foot of Sun Kai's wall. Though Snow Pine felt the protection of Sun Kai's spirit, her dreams were restless.

One morning as Ming lay sleeping, Snow Pine came out to kindle the fire, and begin preparations for the day. She was startled to see a warrior squatting with his back to her tending the fire.

His clothing was that of the Trading People. "Hello Brother," she called. "I did not hear you come in."

He turned and watched her approach. Although something about him was familiar, she did not immediately recognize him. The warrior looked angry, his face deeply lined, his eyes burning fierce and cruel. "I have watched you. Why do you harbor our enemy? Why are you not in the lodge of a man? I saw you with her."

She recognized the dark presence of the watcher in this man. "It is you who watched from the shadows." Snow Pine stood straight, hoping to appear confident. "My home is in this valley, and we are protected by First Ancestor, he who controls the winged beast. I have no need to live in a man's lodge. In this valley, we have no enemies." She stopped and gasped. "Eagle Feather?"

He did not acknowledge the recognition. "Why did you live with the weakling Beaver Lodge? You should have chosen a warrior. I would have taken care of you."

Snow Pine started to tell him that Beaver Lodge was a greater man and greater chief than he would ever be. But, his look told her he was not a man in possession of his passions. Instead, she demanded he leave. "You have led the young men to their deaths. You stink with it. This valley is under the protection of the great winged beast. Here we live in peace with all. Your presence is neither wanted nor welcome."

He reached out to grab her, but the young wolf behind her growled, showing his teeth. Eagle Feather stepped back. "You should have chosen me," he insisted. "I am a man. You should have chosen me!" He turned to leave, kicking the pup as he passed. His moccasin-clad foot struck the animal on the side of his head, causing it to howl in pain.

Snow Pine stood shaking in the cool morning air. She took a deep breath clearing her mind of Eagle Feather's visit. *How different he is,* she thought. *The killing has changed him almost beyond recognition. He is a man possessed.*

Ming came from the cave. "Momma, did I hear a man's voice? Why did wolf howl?"

"Yes Dear One. A visitor came, but he could not stay. He was an old friend."

The Osage women's information trickled into the valley. Buffalo Woman and Young Wolf came several times each season, with medicine bundles which had been brought back from Osage hunting trips. Overjoyed, Ming would squeal and laugh, launching herself at Young Wolf, insisting he ride her about on his shoulders, or admire her white deerskin dress, which was similar to Buffalo Woman's.

Ming never again mentioned the special relationship with Young Wolf. For all appearances they seemed like brother and sister, or best friends, but Snow Pine did notice the young man still wore around his neck the small stone necklace with the image of the feather cloaked warrior.

Often when Buffalo Woman and Young Wolf visited, Snow Pine and Ming sat with them by the night fire and listened to the creation tales of the Osage People. Ming still loved the story of White Buffalo Calf Woman, and how she brought the sacred ceremonies to the people.

When the small pieces of leather began to arrive, Snow Pine took the information and placed it on a large roll of buffalo hide. As new information was added she found her map extended from the great inland oceans in the east to the great mountains in the west. Information she received from the Trading People allowed her to extend the map along the great river systems to the north and south and finally to the coast where she and Sun Kai first landed. *Such a vast country,* she thought. *It would be wondrous to see, but how will*

I know if they come? Sometimes when she examined the map, she found details that did not make sense. To the far north and west in the high mountains, women watchers always reported large groups of animals, even in deep winter.

During Buffalo Woman's next visit, Snow Pine asked about the strange gathering of animals in the high mountains during the winter season, pointing to the marks on the buffalo skin.

"Oh," explained Buffalo Woman, "that is a land of steam, hot mud, and boiling water pools. I have not seen it myself, but I am told it is a place where the spirits are strong and the land moves under your feet. It is a place where winter never comes, and animals shelter among the heated pools. It is from there we gather the black stones for our best knives, scraping tools, and arrow heads." Buffalo Woman reached into her bag bringing out a long, thin reflective blade made from black stone. She pulled the knife across a piece of leather, cutting it smoothly. "Here," she said, handing the knife to Snow Pine, "a gift."

During the sixth summer cycle of recording, Snow Pine discovered that when she added seasons and moon phases to the map, the information regarding movement and numbers of buffalo were repeating. She beckoned to Buffalo Woman. "Come, see this."

Buffalo Woman leaned over to study the map. At first she did not see the significance of the patterns. Suddenly understanding, she said, "So, each year, during the same seasons, the buffalo are found in the same places? Then the women who watch can predict where the hunters should go to find buffalo!" She sat back, excitement draining from her face. "But would men listen to the women?"

Understanding her concern, Snow Pine nodded. She remembered her past attempts to introduce new methods to improve the lives of men. She smiled; even Beaver Lodge at times seemed oblivious to the obvious. When Little Sun was seven summers, she carved for him a small wooden buffalo and attached a set of wheels for the toy. Even as the child played at their feet, pushing the buffalo about making grunting noises, Beaver Lodge hadn't seen the possibilities. She finally gave up. *Perhaps it is because they have no large animals for pulling,* she thought.

"They will not listen to women," Buffalo Woman said, her voice resigned. "I can hear them now." She lowered the tone of her voice sounding more masculine. "Hold your tongue woman. Hunting is the work of men."

Both women laughed at the general foolishness of men. "You are right," Snow Pine conceded. "They will not listen to the advice of women, but what about Daughters of White Buffalo Calf Woman?"

Buffalo Woman looked startled. "White Buffalo Calf Woman? The ancient woman in white, who taught the people the seven great ceremonial truths? What does she have to do with our watchers?"

Snow Pine laughed. "Nothing actually. But if our women watchers were Daughters of White Buffalo Calf Woman, men would listen. The medicine they carry could be in memory of the great healing ceremony and sacred bundle she brought to the people. Each woman could carry a white deerskin dress such as you wear, and when dressed for ceremony, she could read the sacred markings sent by White Buffalo Calf Woman herself to guide the hunt. I could give them minerals to burn in the fire during the ceremony to provide additional persuasion."

"But these tricks dishonor White Buffalo Calf Woman," Buffalo Woman protested.

"No sister, it does not," Snow Pine argued. "I am sure that White Buffalo Calf Woman would want us to share this information. It will give the men reason to listen." She leaned forward, taking Buffalo

Woman's face in her hands. "Look at Young Wolf, and Ming, must they be enemies? Must Little Sun and Young Wolf fight? White Buffalo Calf Woman taught peace. Perhaps her Daughters can help end this war."

Finally, Buffalo Woman nodded her agreement. "Yes, but how do we start? How do we become the Daughters of White Buffalo Calf Woman?"

Snow Pine considered the question before answering. "Could you get women from the Osage clans to come to a meeting with women of the Trading People? We could share information about the movement of the great beasts and begin the Daughter's of White Buffalo Calf Woman training."

"I think so," Buffalo Woman replied. "There are many women who've tired of this endless war. If they thought meeting with other women would end the killing, they might come. When should we meet?"

"We need time to prepare. The conference should be held on a special day. In my land our wisest men predict the shortest of days, the time when Mother Earth remains dark and cold, when for three days the sun does not move on the horizon. We call this time, sun-stand-still. In our homeland, families gather for feasts and dancing to celebrate the rebirth of the sun. Let us plan our meeting for the time of sun-stand-still."

Chapter 19 - The Gathering

Women from the Osage and Trading People clans gathered in the darkness. They came by ones and twos, answering the call of Buffalo Woman, Fawn Heart, and Snow Pine. They were twenty in number, the best of the watchers who marked the leather, all respected medicine women.

As the women came into the camp, they were greeted by Fawn Heart and Buffalo Woman. Snow Pine stood watching from the shadows of the cave. They were given new medicine bundles and directed by Ming to sit beside small vessels filled with burning grease and pitch. The vessels glowed gently in the darkness, forming a circle of lights. Taking a deep breath, Snow Pined closed her eyes, murmured a plea to her ancestors for assistance, then took up her small lamp and strode to the circle's center.

Raising her hands above her head, she called to them, "Sisters, hear my words. They come to you, through me, from White Buffalo Calf Woman. It is she who calls out to you. Her heart weeps at the deaths of your husbands and sons. The madness that has come is like this night in which the sun does not rise."

Snow Pine called upon each woman sitting in the darkness to tell her story. One by one they rose to speak of loss: mothers who lost sons, women of cold husbandless beds, fatherless children, of hunger amidst plenty. Though each story was personal, each woman recognized the pain as their own and when some began to sob in the darkness, those around them, regardless of clan or tribe, reached out and provided comfort.

Snow Pine stood silent, allowing the women's words to linger. "White Buffalo Calf Woman knows your heart, but she also knows, alone you are but a small voice, a small light in this long night. But, joined together we can be a mighty fire." Snow Pine threw her lamp onto a large pile of wood. "Add your light to mine and watch how together we become a mighty flame that pushes against the darkness." Each woman cast her small lamp into the fire. Snow Pine had sprinkled minerals on the wood, and now the fire burned blue, yellow, and green. "White Buffalo Calf Woman calls you to become her daughters, to take up her garments, and serve peace." As the fire spread, light and warmth covered the group. Snow Pine rose to speak. "We shall keep this fire alive until the great sun rises again. Sisters, White Buffalo Calf Woman has sent you a gift, a white dress, like the one she wore when she came among us. This garment will be worn as a reminder that you are one of her daughters." She reached down, took a dress from her medicine bundle, and put on the garment. Buffalo Woman, Fawn Heart, and Ming handed similar dresses to the others. The deer leather, whitened by the repeated addition of animal brains to the tanning process, glowed in the fire light.

The women returned to their seats around the fire, each taking her turn to add wood so that the fire would not wane. Buffalo Woman and Ming passed food and drink among them. Snow Pine addressed the women. She pointed to three bright stars at the horizon, and said. "This morning the sun will rise where you see the three stars, the earth will again be reborn, and the days will grow longer. Soon it will be time to plant and gather. Like the rising of the sun, the Daughters of White Buffalo Calf Woman, her Sisterhood, will also rise, nourish, and bring healing comfort to our lands gone mad."

Several women spoke at once: "What shall we do? We are but women. How can we help?"

Snow Pine looked over the group. "That is not given for me to say. It is a weak woman who must be commanded in all things. In your hearts you will know. When an enemy warrior is captured, see him not as an enemy but as the husband or son of your sister. Then you will know what to say and do. When your child asks you about the war, think of the fatherless children, and you will know what to say. When you do not know, ask yourself—what would White Buffalo Calf Woman have me do?"

While the women sat and sustained the fire, Snow Pine, Fawn Heart and Buffalo Woman taught each the use of their medicine bundle. One small section of the medicines was marked with the sign of two insects enclosed in a bowl. The women were told never to touch or open these since they contained great magic for good or harm. The herbs were in hollow shafts of eagle feathers, which were recapped and fitted into sleeves. When questioned by the women, Snow Pine promised that the use of these special ku medicines would be revealed at a later time.

Each woman was taught how to mark the new leather pieces showing what they saw in their travels, and record the sighting of strangers. Using the information from the great calendar, Snow Pine instructed each woman where the great herds would gather according to the moon phase and season.

As the first rays of the sun broke through the three bright stars, a hushed silence fell upon the group. Snow Pine again rose to address them. "A new day arises, a new season, a new sisterhood. Come with me, and I will tell you my story." She led the women into the cave to the burial place of Sun Kai. She told them of her homeland across the great sea, and how war, like they now faced, forced them to flee their land. She told how fear of strangers led the natives to attack them, and how Sun Kai painted the great bird on the cliff overlooking the river. She spoke of their last days together. "As he lay dying, I pledged to '*wait, watch and remember,*' for someday his people would come, and I would tell his story. He will not remain lost to them. I thank you for marking the leather; you help honor my pledge." Pointing to bowls of colored minerals, she said, "Come, let us again refresh the colors on the beast bird, as a sign to all women who pass that this is their sacred place. A place where any woman can find shelter and be guarded by the winged beast and Sun Kai."

Later that morning the women packed and prepared to leave the valley. Their white dresses were folded and put away. New medicine bundles hung from their shoulders. They left as they had come, in one's and two's, and to all appearances seemed the same, but they had changed.

Chapter 20 - The Jade Cicada

Daniel stood looking over the dig site taking pictures. He rubbed his back, easing the strain from bending over all morning. *Thank God it's Friday,* he thought. The excavation work was going slowly, as they methodically worked downward toward the strata where the first skeletons were found. Strings, tape measures, and line levels recorded the opening and closing elevations of each stratum. He watched as Jared Davidson opened the Munsell book, to compare a fresh soil sample to the book's reference color swatches, and designated numbers and names. *Jared's a good man,* Daniel thought. *Very thorough. The 'Old Man' will be pleased with the quality of this dig.* Thinking of the archaeologist's motto, he laughed. "When in doubt, write it down twice." Several other members of the team including Lauren, squatted over sections of the grid, slowly removing dirt with trowels. When they found something interesting they worked with brushes, spoons and dental picks to expose the small features. The removed soil was then swept into a dustpan, and kept for later screening.

Although the findings were preliminary, it appeared they were dealing with a group of graves, perhaps as many as several dozen. The team opened the first five graves down to the skeletal remains, leaving them in place for measuring and pictures. They found few associated grave goods with the exception of the obsidian knife, which having been moved by the construction workers, may or may not have been associated with the first grave. The primary feature that all the skeletons shared in common was that they were females. Unlike most gravesites Daniel excavated in the past, they were all buried in a row about a meter apart, rather than in a cluster. Another interesting anomaly was that the first two were together at one level along the grid, and then the others continued in the same direction but at the next lower grid level. Daniel wondered why the people started a second level. *Maybe they didn't,* he thought. *Maybe the earth shifted. After all this is New Madrid earthquake country. The quake in 1811 reportedly toppled chimneys in Cincinnati and rang bells as far away as Boston. Or maybe it was something as simple as a tree in the way that grew old and disappeared.* He shrugged his shoulders. *The Munsell soil color recordings will tell us something.*

Lauren was working in the area of the second skeleton. Daniel watched her carefully brush around the skeleton, measure it, and snapped a picture. He saw her lean down apparently attracted to something near the skull. She put down the brush and with her dental pick began to excavate something. From her tense posture, he could tell whatever it was excited her. She looked up and waved him over. "It's getting pretty late," she said. "Why don't we call it a day? Maybe we should pull a tarp over this; the weatherman said it might rain this weekend."

Daniel was a little surprised, as Lauren was someone who loved field work, to leave a site early was not in her nature. "Sure, you're the boss. I'm sure everybody will enjoy getting off early. Besides, it's Friday." He touched her arm. "What were you just digging? Did you find something?"

Lauren looked at him, her eyes shining with excitement. She shook her head no, not wanting to talk about it. "Later," she whispered.

Nothing further was said while each crew member completed their work and prepared the dig for the weekend. Lauren asked Josh to drop several bags of soil samples off at the lab for flotation testing. Finally the tarp was pulled over the excavation site to keep it secure and dry. They stood alone together, watching the last of the crew drive away.

Lauren laughed, put her arms around his neck, and kissed him. Putting her hands behind her back, she said. "Pick a hand"

Daniel picked the right. "No, not that one. Here." She brought out her left hand, which held a small green artifact the size of a finger joint, and gave it to him. "I found this between the teeth of the second skeleton. Daniel, it looks like a jade mouth amulet."

Daniel looked at the object, a small carving of a cicada, his mind and pulse racing. The carving looked like those used in ancient Chinese burial rites as a symbol of rebirth. He looked toward the river. Over that hill, inside a cave he and Lauren had found the skeleton and gold coin necklace. They were graduate students then, and got caught up in researching the possibility of an early Chinese landing in the New World. Their study led them to a copy of a manuscript purportedly written by an ancient Qin China warrior named Sun Kai and his woman, Snow Pine. Daniel and Lauren convinced themselves that Sun Kai had taken refuge in the cave and it was his skeleton they'd found. According to the manuscript it was Sun Kai who painted the original Piasa Bird. Unfortunately, their theory had several problems, not the least of which was how the manuscript of Sun Kai's journal got back to China. Even after exhausting themselves in research, they still had major unresolved problems. First, they couldn't prove the authenticity of the manuscript copy. Second, the original Piasa was destroyed in the late 1800s, and its original position was unknown, so they couldn't even say for sure the cave was related to the original pictograph.

And third, when they'd taken their findings and suspicions to Dr. Eldrege he was not convinced, telling them that if they wanted careers in academic archaeology, they would give up this obvious hoax.

In frustration, Daniel published their findings as a historical novel, *Flight of the Piasa,* under a pseudonym. Lauren still wore the coin necklace with the inscribed torso of a man in a feathered cloak as a good luck piece. Daniel smiled, remembering how irritated Eldrege was when he discovered they'd published their findings. But, given that they had not attached their names to the work, nor the SIU Archaeology Department, Eldrege finally came around. Still, the disagreement was an area Daniel avoided revisiting with his department chair, who was now also a colleague and a friend. He turned the small jade carving in his hand. "Jesus, Lauren. Do you suppose?"

Taking the jade piece from him, she giggled. "Do I suppose what? That over that hill is the skeletal remains of Sun Kai? That buried here," she pointed to the second grave site, "is Snow Pine? God, Daniel. I don't know. Do you suppose?" The laughter drained from her face and eyes. "If we tell Fred, he'll go berserk."

"That's why we're not going to say anything. Let's open the site back up, replace the cicada and you can find it again on Monday. That way it will be checked in as an artifact associated with this dig, and we will have time to think about what to do."

"But …" she protested.

He shook his head. "No buts. Until we figure this out, let's not say anything. You can just hear Eldrege—*A single artifact is like a word in a book taken out of context.*"

They drove home in silence, each running the implications of the jade cicada over in their minds. Lauren turned to him. "Instead of picking up the kids at your folk's house, do you suppose that your Mom would mind keeping them for the evening, and we could pick them up in the morning? I'd like some time to think about this."

"Sure. Let's give them a call. A little distracted, are we?"

Lauren laughed. "Not a little. A lot. Do you suppose that the second skeleton is really the remains of Snow Pine?"

"I dunno. But I'm beginning to feel like a graduate student again.

When they opened the door to their home, they heard the phone ringing. Lauren, picked it up. "Hi, Fred. We were just talking about you. No, nothing bad. What can we do for you this evening?" She listened for a moment, "Golly Fred, that's too bad, it's hard for me to believe. Sure, the kids are with Daniel's parents tonight. We'll come right over."

When she returned the phone to its receiver, Daniel asked, "What does Fred want?"

"He said that the department is missing some artifacts from the collection. He wants us to come over to discuss the matter. He seems excited."

"Why us?"

"I don't know, Daniel. He just asked if we could come over and discuss it. When I first heard his voice, I thought he somehow knew about the jade cicada." She laughed. "Funny how having your dissertation chair call you, even after all these years, brings out the fearful child response."

When they arrived at the Eldrege home, they saw Jared Davidson's Honda in the driveway. *Good,* Daniel thought. *At least this doesn't concern Lauren and me directly.*

Marge Eldrege greeted them at the door. Lauren and Daniel liked Marge. She was solid, her closely cropped white hair, clear blue eyes, and lined face told of a life well lived. Her saucy sense of humor reminded them of Barbara Bush. "Fred's in the front room with Jared. Just go on in. I was over in Grafton the other day and picked up a couple of bottles of a lovely red from the Piasa Winery. Would you like something?"

"That would be wonderful," Lauren said, "thanks." Entering the living room they found the two men sitting and talking.

Marge came in with wine. "Jared?"

"No thanks, Marge," Jared replied. "Perhaps some water with lemon?"

Marge smiled, "Sorry, forgot. One good glass of *Adam's Ale* with lemon coming up."

Eldrege held up his glass. "Á toast to Professor Winckelmann, father of scientific archaeology." Everyone raised their glass and sipped. Eldrege then launched into why he'd called them. "The Department has a problem; some of our collection is missing. I was preparing to give a short show-&-tell discussion on artifacts from the Mississippian Culture for the local Rotary Club dinner, when I couldn't find a few pieces."

Jared Davidson was first to respond. "What couldn't you find? Maybe it's just something one of us is using in our classrooms?"

"No, I don't think so," Eldrege replied. "What we're missing are things from the Piasa Creek area: a decorated bone hairpin, leptoxis shell beads, a small birdman tablet, and a green turtle effigy gorget. At least that's all I know is missing."

"Funny," Daniel said, "other than the turtle effigy, the rest seem pretty common, not much resale value. Now that the birdman tablet has been adopted as the symbol of the Cahokia Visitor's Center, it's famous, but not rare. Who would want to take them?"

Eldrege looked at them. "Any ideas?" When they shook their heads, he continued. "Well, one of the reasons I called you three is that you've been working with Josh Green. When I reviewed the videos from the security cameras for the last week, I saw Josh coming and going with some bags. I even have him in the lab at about 2:00 am."

Lauren laughed. "Poor, Josh. He was probably there doing 'poppy seed' tests on the flotation tank. Last week I purchased a bag of seeds, charred them in the oven, and mixed a hundred with a dirt sample. I asked Josh to do the flotation work from the grave sites, and come up to speed on the testing process and make sure our flotation tank worked properly." She paused. "He was able to retrieve ninety-eight out of one hundred, which is pretty good. Anyway, that's probably why he was in the lab at all hours."

Leaning back, Eldrege stroked his beard. "Okay, that makes sense. Thought that was to too easy an answer. But I'm concerned about the CAS. Several departments in Illinois, especially those around Chicago and Springfield have recently found they're missing artifacts. Those anarchistic bastards may be trying something."

Marge tensed when Eldredge swore, and then made a small hand gesture, rubbing one finger over her thumb. Eldrege seemed to stop his tirade in mid-sentence. "Anyway," he said. "I'm concerned about the CAS. Keep your eyes and ears open. Let's be sure it doesn't find a place to hide in our department."

"Since we started with a toast to the father of scientific archaeology, I think it would be appropriate to remember that even the great Winckelmann was hoaxed by the painter, Casanova." He stood, pushing back his chair. "If there are no further ideas, let's close. Sorry to bring you out in the evening. Thanks for coming over."

As the faculty walked to their cars, Jared stopped. "What was that hand thing about?"

Daniel laughed. "Marge and Fred have been married for forty-five years. They met at a North Africa dig where she was studying dung beetles. You know the little guys that you always see dragging the balls of fecal matter. Well, the way the system works is that the female builds a nest and the male goes out and brings back these little balls of dung to feed the hatchlings. When they gather enough to feed the larvae, the nest is sealed. The problem is, how does the male know when he has delivered enough dung?" He laughed dragging, one finger across his thumb. "The female signals with her front legs. Marge doesn't allow swearing in the house. I think she was telling him to stop bringing the shit."

Chapter 21 ~ Sisterhood

Ten winters passed since the first gathering of the Daughters of White Buffalo Calf Woman. Season by season the Sisterhood grew. Early lessons taught focused on the home and the five relationships. Snow Pine taught that most tribal and family problems could be solved if only a people could get five basic relationships correct: the relationship between a man and woman, mother and child, family to neighbor, friend to friend, and warrior to chief. If these relationships were healthy, a people would prosper. The women traveled in groups of three, two women, and a male protector. The women in white taught their lessons, and where they went love and service followed. No sister attempted to usurp the role of the men. They provided instead gentle guidance from the shadows. The medicines they carried brought health to their tribes. Their hunting predictions were not only recognized but requested. For many tribes, the medicine bundles became sacred objects, treated with deep respect as things of great power.

Among the Sisterhood none were greater than Buffalo Woman. Her bravery and acts of courage became legendary among both the Osage and Trading People. On one occasion even as a battle raged, she came between the two sides to nurse the wounded. Her commanding presence and white dress stilled the fighters. By the time she finished tending the wounded, the warriors from both sides had left the field.

Tears came to Snow Pines eyes as she thought about the successes and defeats. Change was slow in coming. Captive warriors and women were still ill treated, and the war continued. The worst defeat of all was that no returned leather piece carried the message of the stick figures and the arrow pointing to the river. No strangers were seen. *What if I die before they come?*

Snow Pine stood in the morning sun when a sound on the path to camp broke her reverie. Looking up she saw Young Wolf pulling a travois loaded with a large bundle of goods. Ming wearing the special white dress of the Sisterhood peeked from the hut.

Young Wolf unpacked the travois, putting down cleverly decorated bowls, blades of dark stone, buffalo skins, deerskin robes and blankets. Young Wolf piled a fortune at Snow Pine's feet.

Pointing to the goods, Young Wolf said, "I have come to ask for your daughter's hand. Please accept these small gifts as token of my respect for your family and my love for Ming."

Snow Pine was sorry that Buffalo Woman was not here to see how well he presented himself. *Any woman would want such a man for her daughter.* She knew Ming was a free spirit, and would make her own decisions in such matters, but in this case she did not turn to ask. Ming had long ago made her decision. Snow Pine smiled. "Yes, it will be good to have you as my daughter's husband." Young Wolf, who'd been holding his breath awaiting the answer, whooped and yelled with joy. Ming rushed from the hut to join him. The two chattered, jumped about and laughed like children. Snow Pine smiled. "We must get a member of the Council of Elders to come and officiate the wedding. Buffalo Woman and your relatives should be here. I know that Fawn Heart and Beaver Lodge will come from the Trading People village."

Almost before she said Fawn Heart's name, Fawn Heart burst

into camp. Stopping to catch her breath, she cried out, "Warriors have taken two Daughters of White Buffalo Calf Woman as they entered the valley. I had stepped off the path, and they did not see me. We must hurry to help them."

Snow Pine grabbed her medicine bundle, yelling to Young Wolf to stay and protect Ming. He began to protest, but her look told him this was not the time for argument. Grabbing Fawn Heart by the arm, the women ran toward the valley's entrance.

Nearing the place where the women were taken, Snow Pine heard men's voices and saw a curl of smoke from a small fire. She thought she recognized Eagle Feather's voice among the group. "Ancestors guide me," she prayed. She took a long deep breath, slowed her pace to a walk, and tried to shield her face and eyes from the emotions she was feeling. With Fawn Heart beside her, she pushed through the group of warriors and approached Eagle Feather. "What are you doing in my valley? You know this place is protected by the winged beast. How dare you attack Daughters of White Buffalo Calf Woman? You have no..."

Eagle Feather turned at her voice, raising his hand to silence her. "No! How dare you. You, who shelter our enemy. You, who betray our families. I warned you that you had chosen wrong. Now a man speaks. Be silent."

"Where are the women? What have you done with them?"

Eagle Feather laughed, turning to his men. "We have put them to good use." He bent down and tore the blankets off two women lying by the side of the fire. Snow Pine gasped, as she recognized Buffalo Woman. The woman seemed dazed, with bruises about her face and human bite marks on her upper torso. Buffalo Woman cringed in fear as Eagle Feather stood over her. Stained with blood, the bottom of her white dress was pushed up. The other sister did not respond, her neck obviously broken.

Snow Pine turned to Eagle Feather, "This will not do." She sneered in contempt. "Do our great warriors now attack women who travel in peace?" She turned to glare at the other warriors, who looked down unable to face her gaze. "This valley is protected by the winged beast. He is displeased with you. He is a creature of the night and you will be eaten from the inside."

Eagle Feather seemed to come to a decision. "Be silent woman. You never knew your place. You once belonged to our village, and many still believe in your nonsense." He laughed, slapping the shoulder of the man next to him. Turning to Snow Pine, he said, "It is you who should go while I am still patient. Or would you like to join your friends on the furs? Perhaps, you came here seeking a man?"

Snow Pine saw that Eagle Feather would not relent. He reveled in his power over her, and waited for her to beg. From the corner of her eye, Snow Pine could see Buffalo Woman's face entreating her not to leave her with him. Snow Pine lowered her eyes. "What would it take to buy the woman from you?"

Snow Pine knew Eagle Feather was enjoying her weakness. "Perhaps, you would exchange yourself for the woman?" He grabbed himself lewdly. The ever-modest Fawn Heart gasped and turned away at the gesture. Again, he laughed, and was joined by several others. "We are not particular."

A cold rage clouded Snow Pine's mind. "I would die before mating with something like you, but I do have something to trade. Those who say I am a witch are right. Let us sit and talk. Perhaps you would trade the woman for something more valuable, something that would make your warriors invincible in battle."

Distrustful of Snow Pine, Eagle Feather's eyes narrowed. He laughed. "Silly woman. You talk nonsense, but your story may entertain us." He indicated a place for her to sit.

Snow Pine sat. "Before we begin, I would like a drink of water." When the water was provided, Snow Pine asked for sweet grass to purify the liquid. When sweet grass was not available, she requested the water be purified using an eagle feather. Reaching into the medicine pouch, she produced a feather and dipped it into the liquid. Finished, she drank and offered it to him. When he finished, Snow Pine began. "What I have to trade is an ointment that stops a warrior from being hurt by arrow or knife." She brought from her bag an ointment container. "When this is spread on the skin, it will repel a blade. Neither arrow nor blade can penetrate this medicine.

Eagle Feather laughed at her, thinking, now he understood the trick. "And who shall we try the magic on? Me? Would you have me choose one of my warriors? You are such a foolish woman. You cannot trick us."

Snow Pine paused, as if in thought. "If you are afraid, perhaps you would be willing for me to prove the magic on the enemy woman?" Eagle Feather again laughed, this time less certain, trying to see the trap.

"Yes, the woman," he said. "Use the enemy cow. Let us see this magic."

Snow Pine walked over to Buffalo Woman and helped her to her feet. Looking deeply into her eyes, Snow Pine said, "I promise I will not leave you with him."

Nodding her understanding, Buffalo Woman straightened.

Snow Pine spread the ointment across Buffalo Woman's throat. She turned to the men. "Where the ointment is spread, no blade can enter." The men gathered around her, waiting to see the magic. Snow Pine reached into her medicine bundle and produced the obsidian knife Buffalo Woman had given her. The thin blade reflecting the light of the sun was beautiful. With a quick movement of her hand, Snow Pine pulled the blade across Buffalo Woman's throat. The men leaned forward gasping. The magic was working. The woman at first appeared unharmed. But, slowly a thin red line appeared where the knife had passed. Then a gaping wound opened, and blood gushed out.

Snow Pine pulled Buffalo Woman into her arms looking into her eyes. Red froth appeared at her lips. Buffalo Woman mouthed, "Thank you," and closed her eyes.

As she watched, the life went out of Buffalo Woman. Snow Pine took no notice of the men standing about or of the blood staining her white dress a crimson red. She called to Fawn Heart for assistance. Together, the two women lifted Buffalo Woman into their arms, and carried her away. Snow Pine called to the men, "I assume that you do not still desire this woman?" The men moved aside as they passed, ashamed to look.

Snow Pine and Fawn Heart carried the body into the camp where Ming, and Young Wolf waited. Young Wolf rushed forward, saw his mother and wailed. "Who has done this thing?" he demanded. "I shall fill my hands with his heart."

Snow Pine took the young man into her arms to comfort him. "It is done," she said. "He who caused this drank ku poison from the eagle feather. Your mother has already been avenged. Even now, he who did this dies badly." She took medicine from her bundle and quickly prepared an antidote for herself.

In Eagle Feather's camp at the entrance to the valley, the warriors were subdued, ashamed of their actions. Eagle Feather strode about in a terrible rage. "She tricked me. The witch tricked me." In the middle of a sentence, he stopped, grabbed his abdomen, and fell writhing to the ground, his fingers tearing red scratches across his belly. "The winged beast eats my stomach. The winged beast…"

The men were struck by fear as they watched him die. "She is a witch! What if she comes back? What if the winged beast comes?" Without plan or direction, the men backed away from the dying Eagle Feather, first turning to walk, then running.

Chapter 22 ~ Cult of Ku

Snow Pine beckoned Ming. "Come attend your betrothed. He is in need." Young Wolf stood with arms at his side, unable to move or look away from his mother's blood-stained body. "Stay here with him. Fawn Heart and I will prepare her." The two women carried the body into the cave where they washed her, painted her face and dressed her in a fresh white dress. They placed a sky-blue stone necklace at her throat hiding the bite marks and wound. Finally, Snow Pine stepped back. "She appears to be sleeping," Fawn Heart nodded. Placing Buffalo Woman's body on a blanket, they carried her to a place near the fire and laid her down.

Sitting at his mother's side, Young Wolf chanted the Osage mourning song. Ming sang, joining him in his loss. After asking Fawn Heart to prepare food for the evening meal, Snow Pine retreated into the cave. Alone, her mind went out to Sun Kai. "Why must evil win? Why? Why?" Unanswered and inconsolable, she fell to her knees, great rasping sobs shaking her body. When Fawn Heart brought her meal, she found Snow Pine sitting quietly, her head resting on the wall that protected Sun Kai's grave. Fawn Heart put the bowl down by Snow Pine and withdrew.

The next morning at sunrise, Snow Pine sent Young Wolf to prepare a grave in a nearby glen. It was a beautiful spot from where one could see the cave entrance. When he returned, the women had finished preparing the body, wrapping it in a buffalo blanket. Fawn Heart, Snow Pine, and Ming carried Buffalo Woman into the glen and placed her on a bed of flowers which lined the freshly prepared grave bottom.

One by one the group told the story of Buffalo Woman. Young Wolf remembered the love of his mother, but also her sternness in matters of honor. Ming related how she admired the white buckskin dresses that Buffalo Woman always wore and how she had looked forward to becoming her daughter. Smiling shyly, she linked her fingers with Young Wolf's. Fawn Heart told of the many sisterhood trips of service that she and Buffalo Woman made and how her wise counsel had bestowed blessings upon those they served. Finally, Snow Pine told of the first day when Buffalo Woman walked into camp to find her wounded son, and how noble and majestic she had looked. She related how Buffalo Woman changed within a heart beat from enemy stranger to beloved sister.

Snow Pine stood, then placed the long-bladed, black stone knife in the grave with Buffalo Woman. She lifted her hands and face to the heavens to pray.

Where you go, you will feel no rain.
The cold of winter will not touch you.
You will feel no pain or loneliness.
Soon, you will join all those who went before.
Go now to your high dwelling place.
Know that here you are loved – wait for us.

Snow Pine turned back to the group who huddled together, crushed by sorrow. "As Sun Kai lay dying," she said, "he told me that the only way one can remove pain from death, is to remove love from life and that is a bargain we must never make." She reached down, picked up a handful of dirt, and sprinkled it over Buffalo Woman's body. "I would now have you perform a last service for

Buffalo Woman. Place a handful of dirt over her body. This will become a blanket to shield her from the cold of winter and heat of summer." When each had done this, Snow Pine asked Fawn Heart to take the others back to camp, saying, "I will remain here for a moment, and complete the covering."

After the others left, Snow Pine reached into her medicine bundle, withdrew a small bag of the lavender-scented herbs, and placed these in the grave. "You take a part of my heart," she said. "You were the best of sisters." She pushed the remaining dirt over the body and placed rocks on top, discouraging animals. Finished, she sat back, and cried.

When Snow Pine returned to camp, she found that Beaver Lodge and Little Sun had come from the village. Beaver Lodge looked tired, his face lined with fatigue. Her heart reached out to him, but before she could speak, he confronted her: "Warriors from our village say you and the winged beast attacked them and killed Eagle Feather. They say you are an evil witch. They say something must be done about you."

"Tell them to leave us alone! Tell them to leave the Sisterhood alone as they travel!" Snow Pine stood before him, her hands on her hips, her eyes defiant. "The winged beast protects this valley, and he hates cowards who attack women."

Beaver Lodge raised his palms, as if to ward off this attack. "What would you have me do? I cannot have your winged beast killing our warriors."

Fawn Heart approached her husband. "They attacked unarmed women; Snow Pine did not use magic. The men lie."

Beaver Lodge sat down, attempting to defuse the anger. "I know, but you cannot kill our warriors. Many of the men call for revenge. They say she is a witch."

Snow Pine knew his heart did not follow his words. "What do

the women of the village say?"

Beaver Lodge looked down, "They say Eagle Feather led their husbands and sons wrong, that the fault is his. But," he paused and frowned, knowing his next words would be ill received. "It is not their place to guide our tribe. Women are to follow after men."

Resigned and defeated, Snow Pine did not respond. If Beaver Lodge, the best of men, could not be made to understand, what hope was there? She turned, and without looking back, walked toward the cave. Perhaps the spirit of Sun Kai would provide answers.

Beaver Lodge began to follow, but Fawn Heart held his arm. They stood in silence, watching as Snow Pine entered the cave. Shaking his head, Beaver Lodge spoke to Fawn Heart. "It is time, come home. It is time for you and Little Sun to come home."

Little Sun, who'd been watching the conversation without comment, rose and approached Beaver Lodge. "I cannot leave Mother here alone. It is too dangerous now."

Beaver Lodge looked at the boy, now nearly a man. He started to argue that Little Son's place was in the village, that there was no future with a witch woman. However, seeing the boy's determination, he relented. Turning to Fawn Heart, he said, "Get your clothing; it is time.

After they left, Snow Pine returned to the camp fire. She was overcome by loss, first Buffalo Woman, now Beaver Lodge. She regretted her angry words. *He is not to blame*, she thought. *He is not to blame*. She unrolled the buffalo skin upon which she placed the women's findings, took out a scoring tool and charcoal, and drew a small woman figure. She smiled, thinking of Buffalo Woman. *That is for you, dear sister.*

Ming brought Snow Pine a bowl of stew and sat beside her. "Mother, what is ku? And why do the women carry medicines they may not touch?"

Though startled by the question, Snow Pine realized the time for telling had come. She turned to Little Sun and Young Wolf. "Perhaps, you could leave us for a time. Ming has asked a question, and the answer, only a woman will understand."

Once the men left, Snow Pine began. "Long ago in our homeland across the sea, there was a group of women who practiced dark magic, who belonged to a cult known as Ku. Anciently ku was thought to be a poison that the women created by placing venomous insects into a container where they then fought until only one survived. The cult extracted their poisons from the surviving creature known as the ku." Snow Pine stopped, leaned over and picked up her medicine bundle. She pointed at the drawing of a small bowl with two insects painted on the inside. Just below the sketch were the eagle feather shafts with the medicines hidden inside. "These feather shafts contain ku."

"But," Ming could not contain her questions. "Why ask the women to carry these poisons? And why tell them never to touch them?"

Snow Pine continued. "Why is a good question, for ku is very powerful, and the ancients used the poison for evil and personal gain. They poisoned their victims and took their property." With a stick she drew a series of characters in the fire's ashes. "See these two characters? When placed together they make up the word ku, but this first one by itself means loss of one's soul. I gave the women the eagle feathers filled with ku because it is very powerful, and we may need it. But, remember, it is said the ancient women lost their souls because of its use."

Ming shook her head. "But our sisterhood would not use it for evil. We are not like the ancients."

"You are right, Bright One. Our Sisterhood is not evil. Yet, it is said that those things not desired need not be forbidden. Why do our teachings tell us not to kill? Is it because killing is desirable?" Snow Pine hugged Ming to her. "I have given the Sisterhood great power, but their lack of knowledge protects them from desiring its use." From her daughter's silence, Snow Pine could tell she had not been convinced.

That night Snow Pine slept in the cave next to Sun Kai's wall. Her dreams were restless and wild. She and Sun Kai again took flight, but the land was dark, and a terrible storm raged below. In the distance she could see Buffalo Woman standing by one of the great sentinel stones of the plains. Although she'd beckoned them to come, the winds always pushed them away.

When she awoke, she found Young Wolf, Ming, and Little Sun at the campfire. Little Sun arose as she approached. "Mother, while you slept, we talked. We decided that the three of us will stay in the valley with you. You need protection."

Snow Pine took her place near the fire, taking food offered by Ming. "Children, there is much to be done, a marriage to be sealed, lessons to be taught." She stopped for a moment savoring the spicy stew. Smiling in appreciation at Ming, she reached for more. "I understand your concern, and will stay here with you for awhile. But soon I must leave. A storm rages outside our valley, and somehow I must find a way to stop it." When Young Wolf protested, she put up her hand, ending the conversation.

Chapter 23 ~ A Legend Grows

Over the next several weeks Snow Pine prepared Ming to care for the valley and watch over the women who came for medicine and advice. She laid out the great buffalo skin of memory, on which the findings and history of the Sisterhood were being written. "When you give them a new skin, be sure they understand each sign, especially the stick figures, and the arrow pointing toward the great river." Taking Ming's face into her hands Snow pine paused, "Daughter, it is important to know if strangers come this way. Sun Kai's people will come. They must, and we must be ready."

Sorting though a medicine bundle, Snow Pine explained to Ming the placement for each herb and its use. When she came to the area of the eagle shafts which contained the ku, she paused. "I am sorry daughter, that I must teach you this. It is a great burden. Ku is powerful, and you must never use it. But someone besides me must know how to blend the poisons and use the antidotes. It is a secret that cannot be lost."

Messages were sent to the Trading People, and Osage clans. Friends and families gathered and the valley slowly filled with the tents of both groups. Although there was tension between some, all held their peace.

Finally the day arrived. Ming's father, Beaver Lodge, officiated the wedding. He walked with the wedding party to the small glen, which held the grave of Buffalo Woman, so she could be part of the celebration. Ming stood radiant in her white deerskin dress, and red flowers entwined her hair. Young Wolf, standing over six feet tall, his scalp shaved except for a small curl of hair at the back of his head, towered over his bride. The tall warrior and diminutive bride glowed as they stood before their families.

Instructing them to hold hands, Beaver Lodge bound them together with a red cloth. "The red cloth that binds you symbolizes love, good fortune, fertility, and longevity. May you always have these in abundance." He nodded to Little Sun to bring him the wedding vase. "I received this in trade from people of the deserts to our south, many summer cycles ago, and kept it in anticipation of this day." The vase, red and yellow at the base with a long curved blue neck and two spouts, was of beautiful design. "It is filled with water from where the two great rivers come together. Like you, it comes from two great streams to form one." He turned to the gathered family. "Sweet grass has blessed the water, and the mixture signifies deep love and happiness for both." He handed the vase to Ming, who drank from a side spout. She handed it to Little Wolf, who drank from the other side.

"Before I remove the cloth that binds your hands, know this. You are now one. Never imagine in the future that one of you can be hurt without the suffering of the other. Be kind and watchful of one another." He removed the cloth, and family and friends crowded forward congratulating them. They returned to camp where a group of Daughters of White Buffalo Calf Woman had prepared a feast.

The next morning, following the departure of the last guests, Snow Pine called Ming and Young Wolf to the campfire. "This is a good time for you to be alone" she said. "And it is time for me to go and confront the storm." Ming protested saying Snow Pine should stay and not leave them, that it was unsafe for her outside the valley. "Don't worry; I will take Little Sun and the wolf with me. For a time we will be traveling among the Trading People."

That afternoon, Little Sun, the wolf and Snow Pine, clothed in her white dress with her medicine bundle slung over her shoulder, left the valley. When they reached the ridge, she looked back toward the cave. "Sun Kai, watch over us," she prayed. "Prepare our way, for the future is uncertain."

When they reached the Trading People village, Snow Pine was startled by the changes. *How long has it been since my last visit,* she wondered. The wooden wall was taller, and the central burial mound was twice the size she remembered. *So many have died in this senseless war,* she thought. On top of the mound, the Council of Elders had built a large ceremonial lodge.

Snow Pine increased her stride, and straightened her shoulders, as she and Little Sun neared the village gate. She was soon recognized by the women working in the fields and the guards who had been assigned to watch over them. A small crowd formed around them as they moved. Those who came too close were confronted by the wolf, which bared his fangs, snarled, and kept them at a distance. In front of them, Snow Pine ascended the steps leading to the top of the mound. Nearing the top, the Council of Elders confronted her.

Snow Pine recognized White Otter, senior member of the council, standing in front of the ceremonial lodge. She knelt before him. *How old he has grown,* she thought. He beckoned her to rise, and invited Beaver Lodge to come forth and speak.

"The Council wants to know why you have come," Beaver Lodge stated. "Do you not understand you are unwelcome here? The family of Eagle Feather mourns his loss, and many wish revenge."

"Know that I am both mother and wife," she said. "I know

the pain that comes from losing family. I understand their feelings toward me, but Eagle Feather entered our valley and attacked and abused innocent women. I also mourn his loss, not only his death, but also the man he became. It was the war and the winged beast that killed him."

Beaver Lodge protested, pointing out—the creature was only a picture painted on the cliff and had no power to kill. Finally, he shook his head and said, "The Council decrees, that you are a witch. If you stay, you will die. You are not welcome among us."

Snow Pine breathed deeply, "I understand; but know this, the valley of the winged beast is a sacred place. No warrior may enter it unless he is one of the Protectors. You will know them by this symbol." She withdrew a small stone necklace inscribed with a torso of a man in a feathered cloak and hung it on Little Sun's neck. "Do not harm the sisters in white as they travel or their Protectors, and leave the valley of the winged beast in peace. Only women and Protectors are welcome in the valley." Facing Beaver Lodge she thrust the point home. "Not even you are welcome now."

Beaver Lodge's face reddened. "You do not give orders here. You never knew your place."

Snow Pine looked at him, knowing this was a final break between them. The words this day would be a river, which neither could ever cross. "I give no orders," she said quietly. "I only request that you leave us in peace. But," she paused, calculating her next words, "also remember the punishment of Eagle Feather who dishonored the valley of the winged beast."

Snow Pine stepped back. "I leave now and will not return. The Trading People are no longer my people. My family now is the Daughters of White Buffalo Calf Woman." Fawn Heart stood at the bottom of the stairs. Snow Pine descended, embraced her and walked toward the gate. Along the way, some in the crowd moved to confront her. However, as she passed, they gave way.

Snow Pine never again visited the village of the Trading People. In the valley of the winged beast, Ming and Young Wolf still received women of both tribes. The Daughters of White Buffalo Calf Woman still carried the medicine bundles and rolled pieces of leather.

During the winter conferences, the Daughters of White Buffalo Calf Woman restored the painting of the great winged beast, and Ming and Fawn Heart taught lessons in regard to medicines and the five great relationships that would heal the land. Although younger than most of the women and their protectors, Ming emerged as the central leader of the Sisterhood. She was especially attentive to any word of her mother or brother. Many women reported seeing Snow Pine and Little Sun. It was said that they now made their home far to the north, in the valley of steam, where winter never came. Some said her face appeared in clouds over a battle, causing both sides to flee. Others claimed she'd trekked to the far southwest, brought back new medicines, and then died attending the sick during a great illness. Some said her spirit now sat in the great councils on both sides of the veil, speaking against the endless wars. Strange deaths reportedly followed in her path. Men who beat their wives and children were found writhing in pain, scratching at their bellies. Those who urged war seemed most vulnerable, succumbing to the same strange malady.

Following the latest winter conference, Ming opened her medicine bundle and looked at the eagle shafts filled with ku. She remembered Snow Pines words: "Something that is not desired need not be forbidden." Ming's heart was saddened as she handled the poisons under the sign of the two insects in the vessel. *Mother now desires ku*, she thought. She looked down at the swelling of her belly. Soon, a new life would join them. "Mother, come home, before the ku devours you. Come meet your granddaughter. Come celebrate life."

Chapter 24 ~ Cahokia

In the early morning darkness Eldrege took a deep breath; the air was fresh and crisp. He loved this place, especially at this hour. He was standing on Monk's Mound, and although he could not see its contours, he knew them by heart. During this last hour of night, the sounds and smell of diesel from trucks on the highway disappeared, the lights at the Cheap Beer & Cigarettes Store turned off, and the last rifts from a band playing at Tops, the local nightclub, gave way to silence. In the early morning stillness, Eldrege imagined what it was like when the ancient Sun Born climbed the mound to stand and await the sunrise.

He brought himself back to the moment and watched as a small graduate class straggled up the slope and began to sit down around him. Eldrege had given each student a short Hindu verse to memorize and recite in unison as the sun rose. As instructed, at first light they stood, faced the rising sun, raised their arms in welcome, and recited the prayer.

We meditate upon the glorious splendor of the Vivifying Sun
May He Himself illumine our minds!

Eldrege laughed and applauded. "Okay, be seated. And that or something very much like it, is what might have taken place when early Mississippians came to pray as the first rays of the sun appeared. I chose a Vedic verse for you to recite because we sit upon an ancient religious holy site."

He turned, pointing outward in a circle. "Out there, the morning light will soon reveal a rather seedy sight of rundown buildings, abandoned cars, overgrown lots, and dusty roads. Your ears, nostrils, eyes, and minds will fill with what we call progress." He paused, "But, before it does, try to see this place as they might have. We stand on the highest mound, the Holy of Holies. Behind us, imagine their sacred temple. Imagine walls inscribed with powerful symbols depicting the three levels of the world. See? There they've painted the icons of the upper world, the swift falcon and the eagle. Over there, frogs, fish, lizards and snakes represent the dark lower world, unstable and chaotic. Look closely. Between the two lies our world, represented by beavers, raccoons, and cougars, animals with characteristics of both upper and lower realms. In this world, the people struggle to balance perfection and chaos. The Middle Realm, the world of man, is one of opposing forces, light and dark, order and anarchy. It's a world of good, which is its own reward; and evil, first to be avoided and if that fails, punished. The people of Cahokia recognized the natural order of the cosmos and tried to bring themselves into harmony with its forces."

He reached into his bag, pulled out small sandstone artifacts, and passed them around. "Cahokians found many symbols for these worlds in the animal kingdom. This is a copy of the artifact known as the Birdman Tablet. On the front is a warrior with feathered cloak and beak of a falcon or eagle, which symbolized both the upper world and this one. On the back, note the curved crosshatched ridges, which give it a snake-like appearance, representing the lower world." Eldrege gave them time to examine the small flat stones. "These are my gifts to you this morning; I was fortunate to be with the archaeology team that found the original Birdman Tablet on the east side of this mound in 1971. Since then, it's been adopted as the logo for the Cahokia Mounds Visitor's Center."

"Between Monk's Mound and the Twin Mounds, known as Fox and Round top, is the Grand Plaza. Here, early people came for ceremonies, recreation, and trade." He turned and pointed. "Over there is a sports complex where they played a stick and ball game similar to lacrosse. The game nearest and dearest to their hearts was Chunkey, a contest where two players threw javelins at a rolling concave stone puck, attempting to mark the place where it rolled to a stop. If the Cahokians had a 'national pastime,' it was Chunkey."

He pointed in the direction of the Twin Mounds. "Now, over there, we believe the two mounds functioned as a mortuary complex. Fox Mound was the site of a charnel house, where the bodies of the elite were prepared for burial in nearby Round top. Recent excavations show the two mounds were enclosed by a low platform, supporting the idea that they functioned as a unit. Around the ceremonial district was a wooden stockade or palisade, possibly plastered with a mixture of clay and prairie grass. The stockade ran for nearly two miles, evenly spaced bastions or guard towers ran along the wall." He paused, scratching his beard. "What was the stockade for? We don't really know. Most think it was for defense. However, we have no definitive evidence they were ever attacked. Perhaps it was a social barrier, separating the central ceremonial district from the surrounding residential areas." He laughed, "Perhaps separating the elite from the great unwashed."

Pointing outward again, he continued. "Beyond the wall were city dwellings, which housed approximately 20,000 of the common people. I want you to examine the thatched hut replicas in the Visitor's Center; they are rather ingenious in design. At the time of Cahokia's heyday, it was bigger than Paris or London."

"Now, look off to the left. A great circle of large upright poles was used as a solar calendar to mark the changing of the seasons, which was important in rituals concerning the life cycle and planting. And finally, beyond the city were endless fields of corn, sunflowers, and squash. This area is known as the American Bottoms. Due to years of flooding, the soil is dark, rich and fertile. Imagine the pride Sun Born must have felt climbing to the top of this mound. No other people in the area were as well organized, well traveled, wealthy, or powerful. If you were standing here in 1200 CE, you would have witnessed the very pinnacle of Cahokia power and prestige."

The contours of Monk's Mound were now clearly visible in the morning sunlight. "We are standing on the largest prehistoric earthworks in the Americas. The base occupies about fourteen acres, the mound rises to about 100 feet, and the volume of earth is about 22 million cubic feet. If you will stand up, you will find that you've been sitting on sandbags filled to about fifty-five pounds. I want you to pick them up and balance them on your head or shoulder." He waited until each student picked up a bag. "The early people didn't have sandbags, but they did have baskets which held about fifty-five pounds, approximately the same weight you now hold. When you carry your bag back to the bus, consider that it took them only about fourteen million basket loads of soil to bring the necessary 22 million cubic feet to build this place." He smiled, noting several students shifting the weight uncomfortably. "Now if you'll follow me." Some students groaned. "It's so unseemly to whine," he laughed. "And, as a reward, we'll go back to the Visitor's Center and finish the seminar there, where there are soft seats, and hot coffee.

After helping themselves to coffee or soda, the students sat around the seminar table. Samantha Johnson, a transfer student from Louisiana Tech. at Ruston, raised her hand. Her blue eyes, small stature, and southern charm gave the impression of softness and weakness, but behind the dimples, Eldrege knew there was a smart, ambitious young woman. He smiled, thinking of President Bush's crafting of the English language. *This was a young woman easily 'misunderestimated.'* "Samantha?"

"Well Professor, I guess the main question is, why here?"

Eldrege thought for a moment. "You have to consider the role of the two great river systems that come together here. Certainly, the fertility of the floodplain soil was important." He looked up at the ceiling, prioritizing his thoughts. "Maybe the most important element was the early introduction of corn, which allowed the natives to produce an abundance of food and support a large population. The success of agriculture created time for nonsubsistence activities, a luxury unknown to other societies north of Mexico. With the arrival of corn came the development of elaborate religious belief systems, and increased use of specialists, such as astronomers, priests, merchants, and craftspeople. Corn allowed them to quickly develop most of the trappings of a full blown civilization."

Josh Green interjected, "Professor, are you using the term civilization loosely?"

"How so, Josh?" Eldrege asked.

"Well, they had no writing. Isn't that required?"

"You're right. The technical definition of civilization includes advanced cities, specialized workers, social classes, organized government, complex institutions, and as you point out, methods for keeping records." He looked at the class. "Josh brings up a good point. As far as we know, they did not have writing." He paused, thinking. "Yet I remember when I was a graduate student studying the early hominid Homo erectus. Our professor told us they had a spoken language. When I asked how he could know, given that the human voice apparatus is not part of skeletal remains, he said because of the things they did. According to him, the way Homo erectus hunted required pre-planning and assignment of tasks, which he thought required language. Think about it. Try to imagine a Native American buffalo jump, without attributing human language to the natives. How would they know who was to lead the herd to the cliff, and who was to chase? So I will leave it at that. As far as we know Cahokia had no written language or record keeping system, yet some of the things they did make me think perhaps we just haven't found the evidence yet."

Samantha followed up with a second question. "Did they get the corn and mound culture from Mexico? Is that how they became advanced so quickly?"

Eldrege shook his head. "That makes sense, but we have no evidence to support cultural or technological infusion from Mexico. The mound building similarity to the Mexican cultures began much earlier than the introduction of corn. However, it's the arrival of corn that's associated with an abundant food supply and rapid cultural development. Paradoxically, we also know the corn was a mixed blessing. The long term effects of corn cultivation undermined them sociologically and medically. Grinding stones used to create cornmeal left bits of grit in their food, wearing down the teeth prematurely. The enormous population growth led to a depletion of other foods beyond corn, giving them a nutritionally unbalanced diet, high in carbohydrates, and low in protein. Consequently, they suffered a higher rate of infant mortality and chronic illness than did their wilder, less civilized nomadic neighbors. Other questions?"

Another student asked why Eldrege used the term 'Sun Born' during his presentation?

"Well, there's evidence that Cahokia developed a theocratic chieftainship. Their leader Great Sun, was similar to Japan's imperial family and was thought to have divine powers gained by his direct relationship with the sun itself. In fact, he was considered the sun's brother. The dominant chief of Cahokia, his family and allies, sat atop a well-defined social order.

Josh raised his hand. "Professor, if the culture collapsed prior to the Spanish arriving, and given no written language, how do we know about the Sun Born?"

"Josh brings up another important point. The city of Cahokia collapsed by about fourteen hundred, so it was gone by the time the Spanish arrived. However, along the great rivers, some hereditary chieftainships, and cultural remnants similar to that of Cahokia survived. At least that's what we assume, and of course, you all know the problem with the word assume."

Another hand went up and Eldrege called on the student. "Professor, we were on Monk's Mound. Is it called that because of the religious ceremonies that took place? Were the religious leaders thought of as monks?"

Eldrege smiled. "Another good question. What you say makes sense. However, like many things that make sense, it is not true. Monks Mound is named after some French Trappist Monks who lived nearby and gardened on the mound in the early eighteen hundreds."

The door opened. "Dr. Eldrege? I'm sorry to bother you, sir, but you have a phone call."

Eldrege frowned. He hated being interrupted in class. "Take a message. I'll get back to them later."

"I'm sorry. Its Dr. French, she says it's important. Something strange was found at the dig site."

"Okay, class. This will only take a moment. While I'm gone, get ready for your seminar presentations. I'll hear Josh's first on the Cahokia burial sites. Be sure to cover the Mound 72 burials of the four men found with their arms interlocked and hands and heads removed. Following Josh, let's hear from Samantha on the

Woodhenge findings. Remember the two rules, First, you may not read to me. I know how to read already. Second, never bore yourself with your presentation. I'll be right back."

Eldrege returned several minutes later. From his demeanor, the students could tell he was unhappy. "I'm needed out at the site, so we'll continue this later."

Josh and Jenn left the seminar room together. "What do you suppose put a bug up Eldrege's butt," she asked.

Josh laughed and they knuckle bumped. "I can't imagine. You suppose the Beringer Cell has struck?"

Chapter 25 ~ A Duty Passed

Standing in the morning sun, Snow Pine looked at her reflection in the still pool. *How I have changed* she thought. She was no longer the rounded young figure Sun Kai loved, the figure reflecting back was hewn from the new land. The seasons had burned off excess flesh. She was hard, long, and lean, a woman in autumn facing winter, a woman who had borne loads from a thousand harvests. Although her breasts were firm, they no longer jutted outward but rode closer to her body. She was lean, yet the skin on her arms hung loose, and she still carried a soft small pouch at her stomach, which would never quite return to firmness. *The price one pays for bearing and feeding young ones,* she thought. Lifting her chin, Snow Pine noted how brown she had become, as if washed by berry juice in broad sweeps that left uneven patches of light and dark. She stretched, watching her muscles pull into cordlike lines beneath her skin. *How like the old oak I have become, weathered, worn, but made strong by the elements. Sun Kai would approve, she thought, this woman of autumn would please him.*

Across the steaming pool an ancient buffalo wallowed in dust. On earlier occasions the massive bull stood on the hillside, but of late he responded to the chill by lying in the heated mists given off by the water. Stepping back, she raised her arms to embrace the sun. *I have become the great oak, she thought, sturdy and well lived, providing nurture for countless creatures. But like the ancient tree, I too have my time. Just as old growth falls in the forest, I will not be here for many more seasons. It is time to plan for the time without me.* She turned, picked up her clothes, and walked back to the camp she shared with Little Sun. "My son," he stood at the sound of his mother's voice. "It is time for us to return to the valley. Our work here is done. I wish to be buried near Sun Kai, and it is time for you to choose a mate."

Little Sun broke camp and packed for the trip. The color in the trees that dotted the hillside had changed. *Mother is right,* he thought, *it is time to leave. In the valley of the heated pools and gushing waters, winter never comes, but soon the high mountain passes will close. It is time to leave.*

The journey from the high mountains, across the plains to the great river, took several moon cycles. As they traveled, Snow Pine thought of her problem. *If Sun Kai's people do not come in my lifetime, who will wait, watch and remember?*

Approaching the great river Snow Pine's heart beat faster. Across the water on the cliff side, the winged beast marking the position of the valley stared across at them. "It will be good to see Ming," she said. "We have been away too long."

Little Sun nodded agreement. He stooped and scratched the wolf, who'd been their constant companion. "Even wolf's steps grow lighter; Ming was always his favorite."

When they came to the last turn in the path overlooking the camp, Snow Pine paused. *It has been so long,* she thought. *So many things could have happened.* Looking down, the camp appeared empty, but then a small child came into view followed by a wobbly-legged wolf puppy. Snow Pine smiled; the peace of the valley remained. She quickened her stride, happy to be home.

The child looked up when they came into camp. Snow Pine's heart wrenched. The girl was a miniature image of Ming. "Where's your mother, Little One?"

The girl pointed toward the small glen that held Buffalo

Woman's grave. "In the garden," she said. "Is that your wolf?" The girl pointed to the puppy at her heels, "He's mine. His name is Howl of Victory."

Laughing, Snow Pine said, "Such a grand name for such a little wolf." She patted Wolf, who was standing by her side. "Wolf belongs to himself, but he stays with us." Snow Pine reached down and picked up the child. "And what is your name"?

"Cassie. I'm named after my grandmother, who was named after a great queen."

"Cassie is a wonderful name; your mother has a good memory." Snow Pine smiled, remembering when she told Ming about her Praxen name, which changed to Snow Pine after her capture by the Chin'in. As Snow Pine carried Cassie toward the glen, she heard voices laughing and talking. Coming to the edge of the meadow, she saw Ming, Young Wolf, and Fawn Heart harvesting herbs from a large garden. She stopped to watch, wanting the moment to last; Cassie was warm in her arms, and the four people she loved most were together. Seeing Ming, the wolf whined in delight and ran forward, drawing the attention of the group.

"Mother," Ming cried, rushing toward her.

Snow Pine put Cassie to the ground and held Ming at arms length looking at her. "How beautiful you are," she said. "I am proud of you." She reached down, stroking Cassie's hair, "And this one, what a treasure." They spent the day by the campfire, laughing and telling stories.

After the evening meal, Snow Pine sat near the fire with Cassie in her lap. "Were you really called Cassie when you were young?" her granddaughter asked.

"Yes, but that was long ago, in a far-away land, even before I met Sun Kai. His people renamed me Snow Pine. Before my people came to Chin'in, they lived in a wonderful golden city next to a warm sea. They were ruled by kings and queens; the sister of the last great king was called Cassandra. She was a woman of great power, for the Gods granted her the gift of foreknowing the future. However, to keep her from becoming too prideful, they cursed her with the inability to convince others of her foretellings. When I was born, I was called Cassie, after Queen Cassandra." Snow Pine placed her finger on the girl's nose. "Just like you. One needs to be very careful in accepting gifts from the gods. And you Little One," she squeezed Cassie, "must always remember Cassandra. Like her, you will grow to be smart, and beautiful. But remember the story, and try not to be too prideful."

Later, after the others went to bed, Snow Pine and Ming talked by the fire. "Daughter, there are things that must be discussed," Snow Pine said. She undid her coin necklace and handed it to Ming. "This necklace is a symbol of the sacred promise I made to Sun Kai that I would wait, watch, and remember, until his people came again." She shook her head, at a loss for words. "I have waited, but they have not come." Snow Pine thought of the aging buffalo resting beside the heated pool. "Of late, I have felt a chill in the mornings that the sun does not relieve. I can not wait for them much longer."

"Mother," Ming began, but Snow Pine stopped her.

"I must ask you to take my place. It is important that someone be here when they come. We must honor the promise." Snow Pine placed the necklace around Ming's neck. "You must become, 'she who remembers.' I promise you they will return, and you must be here to give them Sun Kai's record. He should not be lost to his people." She reached into her medicine bundle, bringing out Sun Kai's journal sealed in bee's wax. "This is a sacred promise and duty. Keep this until they come."

Snow Pine paused. "I have a story I must tell you. It is Sun Kai's, and mine. Every year, when the sisters gather, I want you to tell how we came to this place so long ago. I want you to train them to become the watchers, they who bring the news of the arrival of strangers. When his people come, someone must be here to tell our story."

Again, Ming protested. "But what if they do not come?"

Snow Pine smiled sadly. "They will come. I do not know when, but they will."

"But what if they don't?"

"Then someday, you must have this conversation with Cassie. Daughter, I grow tired now, I must rest." Snow Pine picked up her sleeping furs and walked away.

Ming stared into the fire. *Am I ready?*, she thought. *Can I do this?* She felt the cold metal coin against her chest. *There is so much to learn.* The night air was clear and crisp, the moon full. Ming placed a log on the fire and pulled the buffalo robe about her shoulders, warding off the cold. The warmth of the fire and robe lulled her and her eyes closed. A moment later she felt a shadow pass across the moon, and was startled by the sound of great wings. She was at first frightened, and then smiled. *The wind* she thought. *It is the wind across the rocks.* Gathering up her robe, she joined her sleeping husband and daughter.

That night Ming dreamed of the great winged beast. It took her onto its back and flew over the plains to the high mountains, to a place of hot pools, roaring fissures, and gushing waters. *The place that Mother spoke of,* she thought, *the place where winter never comes.* The great winged beast turned then, and the land below became a flat ocean of grass. Ming saw two women in white and a warrior near the great sentinel rocks that marked the plains. They waved as she flew over, but when she looked back, they were no longer there, but replaced by three white buffalo.

At first light Ming awoke. Moving slowly from the sleeping furs, wishing not to awaken Young Wolf or Cassie, she dressed and went to tend the morning fire. Once a fire was in place, Ming wanted to waken Snow Pine, so they could continue their conversation. She wanted to tell her mother to take the necklace back, tell her she needed more time. She was not ready. She went to awaken her, but Snow Pine's bed was empty. *Where could she be this early?* she wondered. Hearing the wind blow through the rocks along the cliffs, she shivered. *The winged beast stirs*, she thought. *Perhaps Mother is in the cave.*

Entering, Ming found Snow Pine lying next to Sun Kai's wall. She seemed to be sleeping, her body wrapped in furs, her head resting against the wall. "Mother," she called. Snow Pine did not stir. Ming shook her and found her skin cold to the touch. "Oh Mother." She fell to her knees, her tears washing Snow Pine's face. She gathered her mother into her arms and sat stroking her hair and face. Finally, she whispered, "Yes, Mother. I will do as you ask. I am she who remembers."

That afternoon they gathered at the burial site. Dressed in the white robe of the Sisterhood, Snow Pine was buried next to Buffalo Woman. Fawn Heart, oldest of the Sisterhood present, presided and gave the blessing. Each took a handful of soil and sprinkled it over the body. As the soil fell from her fingers, Ming prayed, "May this be a blanket that shields you from cold and protects you." She reached into her robe and found the small carved green stone cicada Snow Pine had given her so long ago, and placed the carving in her mother's mouth. "May this help Sun Kai find you, Mother." Unable to contain her sorrow, Ming collapsed. Fawn Heart enfolded her in her arms. She nodded for Young Wolf and Little Sun to complete the burial, and holding Ming's hand, helped her back to the camp.

When the men returned, Fawn Heart and Ming were sitting by the fire talking, the great buffalo hide draped over their laps. On the skin next to the small figure that represented Buffalo Woman, was a second woman in a white dress.

Chapter 26 ~ The Continuation

Sitting in the darkness, Ming felt the presence of those around her. As each woman arrived she gave them a small dish of shavings drenched in pitch and a flint to ignite the tender. They sat in a circle before the large pile of wood that would soon be the ceremonial fire. Being the last night of the sun-stand-still conference, the days after would grow longer and Earth Mother would be renewed. Ming spoke quietly to herself, "Mother, be with me tonight and guide this conference."

She struck the flint, and the tinder in her bowl burst into flame. "Sisters," she called, "the blessing I feel most appreciative of, is you. Following the death of Mother, my heart was cold, but you have held me up. I ask you in turn to light your bowls and express what the Sisterhood means to you.

One by one the bowls were lit, and a great circle of light grew. Women told how the herbs in the medicine bundles had restored health in their families. Some thanked the Sisterhood for making them better mothers and wives. Others recalled how the predictions of animal migrations led their clans to successful hunts. Some spoke of small kindnesses, such as food brought to families in need. Many spoke of their joy now that the long madness of war, like a prairie fire, had burned out, and how their husbands and sons no longer lusted after killing.

As the last voice died, Ming stood. "The Sisterhood is a great blessing to us all. Our unity gives us strength." She threw her burning vessel to the top of the stack of wood. "Join me in creating a common fire of Sisterhood." Each woman added her light to the central fire until all were illuminated and warmed by its flames.

"We are now joined in Sisterhood. We are no longer Osage or Trading People, but Sisters. Our numbers have grown to fifty companionships. We are appreciative for all you do and for the Protectors who travel with you. Ming reached down and picked up a medicine bundle. "At your side is a new medicine bundle. Sisters, you must review with each other the use of all the medicines. Do not touch those found under the sign of the two insects in a bowl."

One of the women broke in. "But for what purpose are the medicines found in the shafts of the eagle feathers? Why can't we use them?"

"Mother told me that in her homeland they are known as ku and contain great power, but she warned it is unwise for you to be taught their use at this time."

The woman broke in again. "But why?"

Ming shook her head. "Some things are best left unknown. Perhaps, it is a test of our faith that we carry them without knowledge. But, I promise you this, when the time comes for their use, you will be told."

"Well, I want to know!" the woman protested. "I am not a child!" Several other sisters hushed the woman.

Ming raised her hand silencing them. "I understand your concerns, but here, we are all daughters of White Buffalo Calf Woman. We are all her children, and she taught us to follow our leadership. Do not break the unity."

The woman sat. She muttered something inaudible, but held her peace. The sisters around her began to review the herbs within their medicine bundles, and shortly she joined her companions in study.

Ming reviewed the medicines in her bundle with Fawn Heart. She questioned her as to the identity of the questioning woman. Fawn Heart answered, "She is of the Trading People. Her name is Precious Woman and she comes from the family of Eagle Feather. Many in that family still feel that Snow Pine was a witch. They blame his death on her." Ming started to defend Snow Pine, but Fawn Heart shook her head. "I loved your mother, but even I feared her use of ku. Who is to say what is right in this matter? Some of the sisterhood see you only as the daughter of Snow Pine and oppose your leadership."

As the early morning light broke across the low hills, the women finished their studies and broke their fast, feasting and giving thanks for the earth's renewal, and for the Sisterhood that sustained them. While Young Wolf and Little Sun held up the buffalo skin, Ming retold its history, pointing at marks and symbols painted on the leather. "Many have reported animal movement here," she said, pointing to the moon signs and animal figures which dotted the map. "In the next season of renewal, you should be able to advise your hunters to seek the animals, here, here, and here. May you bless your clans with this knowledge." She pointed to other marks on the skin. "Here is where the men invaded our valley, and the great winged beast, our protector, killed them."

Precious Woman stood angrily, "No! It was not the winged beast that killed Eagle Feather, it was Snow Pine. She killed Buffalo Woman too. We all know the truth."

Fawn Heart rose next to Ming. "Precious Woman, you speak the gossip of the village. I was there; Eagle Feather was punished by the great winged beast for attacking innocent sisters. He died, screaming about being eaten alive. As for Buffalo Woman, no one loved her more than Snow Pine. Be still.""

Precious Woman tried to continue her protest, but the sisters sitting around her echoed Fawn Heart's admonition. "Be still!"

Ming continued the telling from the history skin. Pointing to a scene showing the arrival of Snow Pine and Sun Kai, she explained how they had been attacked along the coast and fled to this place. "Here, see the burial mound that indicates the village of the Trading People who took Snow Pine in and saved her life. Sun Kai died in the cave above this camp. There, he rides the great winged beast protecting us." Ming paused. "Before Sun Kai died, Snow Pine made a promise to watch, wait and remember so that when Sun Kai's people returned they could learn of his history. That is why we ask you to record your travels, being especially careful to watch for animals and strangers." She pointed to the stick figure marks and the arrow pointing to the river. "This is the sign for strangers. We must know if they come." Ming pointed to the two small figures of women in white. "Buffalo Woman and Snow Pine lay side-by-side." She pointed to the small meadow where the herbs were grown. "Like you, they are under the protection of the great winged beast that guards this valley."

Ming laid the great history skin aside, "It is time for us to refresh the great beast that protects our valley." She led the women through the cave to the opening in the cliff overlooking the river. "This will be our last duty at every conference of the Daughters of White Buffalo Calf Woman. We must re-paint the creature and honor him."

That afternoon after the last of the sisters left the valley, Ming noticed that Young Wolf avoided her gaze. "What bothers you, my husband?"

"Is it true? Did your mother kill mine?"

Fawn Heart, who was sitting by the fire, came to stand between

Ming and Young Wolf. "She does not know, she was not there."

Angrily, he turned toward her. "But you were. Did Snow Pine kill my mother?"

Fawn Heart put out her hand and pushed him away. "The answer is not an easy one. I will tell you that your mother pleaded with Snow Pine to rescue her. In her own way, Snow Pine honored her request. There are worse things than dying that can happen to a woman."

Before the conversation could continue, the protector of Precious Woman rushed into camp. "Precious Woman has collapsed. I fear she is dying."

Ming looked at Young Wolf. "Stay here and protect Cassie. Fawn Heart and I will go." Grabbing their medicine bundles, the two women ran toward the valley entrance. As they ran, Fawn Heart reached over and touched Ming's arm. "Have you embraced the ku?"

Chapter 27 ~ A Suspicious Find

Daniel looked up as a black Dodge Ram pickup with the department logo pulled off the highway and crossed the field. *Good. Fred's here*, he thought. After finding the artifact, Lauren sent the rest of the crew home for the day. They wanted to speak to Fred alone. *The 'Old Man' is going to go nuts when he sees this*, he thought.

The truck sprayed gravel as it came to a stop. Eldrege opened the door, and stood waiting for them. Because they had interrupted a seminar and taken him out of class, he was in a foul mood.

Lauren reached him first. "Hi, Fred. Thanks for coming. Sorry to drag you out of class, but we found something strange. We wanted to think through this before saying anything."

Daniel came to her side. "Let's go into the tent," he said, "We have a table set up in the screened room. We put the artifact and a few other pieces there. Maybe we can sit and talk. Want some coffee?"

"Yeah, thanks," Eldrege grumbled.

The three walked over to the screened room. Daniel poured the coffee. "Cream, or, anything?"

"Black." Without preamble, Eldrege leaned over the table and picked up the buffalo skin. "Looks to be a Mandan skin," he said. "Haven't seen one of these in years."

Lauren took a sip of her coffee to brace herself. "Fred, it doesn't make any sense, but we found it in an old box while we were working at the site this morning. It was in an area badly disturbed by the construction that was going on when we found the first skeleton. The dirt had been pushed aside by a backhoe when they were making a trench. The process crunched the box pretty badly. It's hard to say where the box was originally, given all the earth removal."

Eldrege examined the artifact in the light. "Well, at first glance, it appears authentic." He paused, "But, and this is a big but, it sure the hell doesn't belong here." He dropped the skin on the table, laced his fingers behind his head and leaned back. "Any ideas?"

When neither Lauren nor Daniel spoke, Eldrege continued: "For generations, Plains Indians drew pictures on skins to document their experiences." He took a sip of the coffee, relishing its warmth. "The pictures on the Lakota winter count skins were created to serve as mnemonic devices. The count skins are much simpler than ones they drew for other purposes. When we Europeans showed up, they shifted to muslin and paper. However, when they saw that we valued the skins as art, they shifted back to painting on hides, satisfying the expectations of the curio trade. This appears to be one of the earlier skins."

For a time they sat in silence, each thinking about where to take the conversation. Finally, Eldrege began. "A few years ago I wrote an article and prepared a seminar on Native American art and the symbols of buffalo skin painting. Let's see what we have here." He put on his glasses and leaned over the skin. "Okay, see the nine small white buffalo skins forming a circle near the center? That's a symbol for herd abundance. Over here," he tapped two small buffalo masks, "we have a Mandan skin. Mandan Buffalo Dancers Society members wear masks like these during the society's ceremonies.

The society was the guardian of the village and people." Pointing to four more masks, he said, "And here, these protect the earth lodge and the people." He pointed to a series of small rectangular symbols at the bottom of the skin. "Here we have the symbols used by Indian women; these represent a desire for many children, abundant food, and other gifts from the earth. See, over here the hunters are not on horseback, which would indicate a pre-Spanish contact skin."

He straightened. "This appears to be the real thing, and if it is, it has real value." He shook his head. "But why is it here? Maybe it's been stolen from a local museum and hidden. Maybe some earlier settler family owned it and for some reason buried it. I doubt it has anything to do with the skeletons you're working on. You know what's really strange? I think I've seen it before. I can't remember where, but the arrangement of the symbols seems so familiar. As I was explaining them to you, I had déjà vu." He laughed at himself. "But, it's more likely just a senior moment. We can at least check out the local museums to see if they've lost a skin." Eldrege frowned. "Suppose this has anything to do with the CAS?"

Lauren laughed. "I can't imagine. This is a small construction project near a small town. We're pretty small potatoes. Why would anybody care?"

Eldrege took another sip of coffee. "Crazy bastards. Who knows why anybody does anything these days, but you're probably right. Why would they bother us? What else do you have to show me?"

Daniel hesitated, then handed him the small cicada piece. "We found a jade mouth amulet associated with the second skeleton."

Eldrege took the piece, turning it in his hand. "Now, let me guess," he growled, "you want to tie this to the cockamamie story of the Piasa Bird you drove me nuts with when you were my grad students? Maybe even claim that this proves the skeleton was Snow Pea, or Snow Pine, or whatever the hell her name was?" He turned red remembering heated conversations they had when he was their major professor. The time when Lauren and Daniel were obsessed with the crazy notion that China discovered America. "Christ, Daniel! You know that all men with hammers see a nail in every problem. I don't care that you wrote the novel _Flight of the Piasa_. Just remember, its fiction! This idea of yours is nuts." He glared at Lauren. "And you, you should not be supporting him in this."

Daniel took back the small jade piece. "Look, we know you don't agree, but this could well be a mouth amulet like those associated with early grave sites in China. A cicada is a symbol of rebirth or hope for renewal."

Eldrege leaned forward, supporting his head with his hand. "Daniel, you are connecting too many dots. Where's the evidence?"

"Well how about the seven voyages of Zheng He during the Ming Dynasty. In the book _1421 The Year China Discovered America_, Gavin Menzies makes a good case for one of his admirals, Zhu Wen, reaching the new world. They've even found an iron pot and stern post from a teak sailing vessel in the area where Columbus's crew was attacked by the Carribs. The Chinese had the technology. They coulda made it here."

Eldrege let out a long sigh. "Woulda, shoulda, coulda. Gavin Menzies is probably a good naval man, but remember, writers should write about what they know. As an archeologist he's a bust. They ought to have charged his publishing company with false advertisement when they published his book as non-fiction. Hell, it's just an idea. No real evidence. Come on, Daniel. Let's get real."

Lauren saw that Daniel was not going to win. Eldrege was a good, but stubborn man; once he made up his mind he rarely changed. "Okay, guys" she said, "let's not rehash the old argument." Both men leaned back, happy to change the subject.

"Fred, what do you think of the burials?" Lauren continued. "So far we've found about two dozen skeletons, all female, not much by way of associated grave goods. We found an obsidian knife, perhaps associated with the first skeleton, and this small jade piece with the second." Lauren's look told Daniel that she did not want the amulet argument restarted. "Fred, what do you think these burials were about?'

Eldrege took a deep breath. "You're right. They do seem strange. I can't think of another case like it among Native American grave sites. I suppose it could be some sort of female cult burying their dead. The Daughters of Diana or Vestal Virgins of Rome are similar, but nothing like it in the new world. There was that nasty bit of business in early China's female cult of ku. I don't really remember anything in America, although there are stories of a women's service group associated with White Buffalo Calf Woman. I always liked her, the woman who taught the people how to be Indians."

Daniel was glad to be on to a new subject. "What's the cult of ku? Never heard of it."

Eldrege shrugged. "According to tradition, T'ung women on the fifth day of the fifth month, went to a mountain stream where they laid out their finest clothes alongside a bowl of water. The women sang and danced naked around a great fire, inviting the spirits to assist them. During the ceremony, poisonous snakes, lizards, and insects would come to bathe in the bowl. The next morning the women took the bowl of water and poured the poison on the ground in a shadowy damp place. According to the story, poisonous fungus would grow at the site, which the women later ground into a paste. They hid the poison in shafts of goose feathers, and wove them into their hair. Apparently their killings were motivated by greed, since they poisoned mostly landholders, and assumed control of the land. If the stories are to be believed, some became addicted to the process and just poisoned for the thrill of it."

Lauren shuddered. "God, it sounds like an early version of the Japanese Aum Shinrikyo death cult. Let's hope it's just a myth."

Eldrege nodded agreement. "So we have no clue why the women are buried here. If they died violently, we may find evidence in bone fractures. The lack of grave goods is interesting, but I'm not sure what that tells us. Whatever they were doing was important enough to keep at it for a long period of time."

Eldrege stood. "Look, I've got to get back to the department. Let's continue the conversation later. I don't think the box with the buffalo skin is really associated with the burials, but let's think about it for a while. No leaking any of this out to the public. Okay? And Daniel, remember, *Flight of the Piasa* is fiction."

Lauren and Daniel watched as the black pickup made its way toward the road. Daniel shook his head. "I didn't think he was going to buy my mouth amulet theory. But, as my mother always said, 'everyone has to be somewhere.' This really could be Snow Pine's burial site."

Lauren giggled. "You heard him tell me to keep you in hand and not support your crazy ideas. Let's see …where did I hide those goose feather shafts? Cult of Ku? Where do you suppose he comes up with those stories? Really, Daniel. He's worse than you."

Chapter 28 ~ Cassie

Cassie sat in the early morning chill. Last evening's embers burnt low and gave little warmth. She pulled her furs tighter about her shoulders. *I grow old*, she thought. *It is harder to get the chill to leave my body.* She added a new log and poked the ashes into flame. Her husband Lame Deer and their children still slept in the cave. As the seasons changed and the air grew colder, the family always moved to the cave for shelter.

She reached down, pulled the buffalo skin to her lap, and unrolled it. Her hands played across the three figures in white along the top. *This one is Buffalo Woman*, she thought, *she who helped form the Sisterhood and brought the Osage women to the first conferences.* She touched the second figure. *Snow Pine, the great one, wife of Sun Kai who sleeps in the cave, mother of Ming. Snow Pine, the foreign woman with the strange eyes, the healer, the poisoner. Snow Pine, the first of the rememberers.* Cassie smiled as she touched the third figure. *Ming, my mother, one who embraced the ku, not in madness, but in love.* Cassie remembered her gentle mother, a woman of great kindness, who in the end could not withstand the persuasive power of ku. Shaking her head in sadness, she remembered how her Mother became like one who tends a garden, pulling out weeds, pruning trees, and felling those that blocked the sun from others. She remembered her father, Young Wolf, protecting Ming and her sister companions in their travels.

Young Wolf, greatest leader of the Protectors, men who wore the stone necklace inscribed with the man in the feathered cloak. As the heat from the fire finally warmed her, Cassie's eyes closed. In her mind's eye she saw her mother and father's faces. How strong they were. How secure she felt in their presence. Leaning forward she could hear her mother's voice.

"Cassie, remember the uses of all the herbs, and teach the sisters."

"Cassie, avoid the herbs stored under the bowl with the two insects, for they are ku, and will call out to you."

"Cassie, if a people master the five relationships, they will prosper."

"Cassie, I grow old. You must take the gold coin necklace."

"Cassie, wait, watch, and remember, for they will come."

The faces faded. "They never came," she shouted. "I waited, watched, and remembered, but they never came." The sound of her own voice startled her awake and Cassie cried. "They have not come!"

Suddenly birds in the area took flight. Now alert, Cassie wondered *what frightened them?* She started to call out to Lame Deer. It was then the earth moved, followed by a great sound of thunder, right over her. Strong winds filled with a heavy dankness made it difficult to breathe. Cassie choked, her lungs desperately starved for air. "Ancestors, please help," she rasped, as she tried to make her way toward the cave. The earth moved again, and she fell. Off to her left, she saw a gaping hole form in the earth, from which sand burst forth in a great geyser. The air grew dark; the day turned night. Unable to regain her footing, Cassie reached out and pulled the buffalo skin over her. She moaned while the earth beneath her shivered like a freshly skinned carcass.

She did not know how long she remained huddled and terrified beneath the skin. It was still dark and hard to breathe. Sometimes the earth grew calm, and she thought to leave the skin and find her husband and children, but then the shaking would return. From beyond her hiding place she could hear trees cracking, the cries of frightened animals, and falling rocks. After what seemed a lifetime, sleep overtook her, and when she awoke, it was day.

Crawling free from the buffalo skin, she looked out on a changed valley. Tree trunks littered the ground. A great crack ran the length of the valley. The small creek flowed in a new bed. Ducks and geese flew about aimlessly, and small birds came to light upon her, as if seeking the comfort of another creature.

Cassie turned to look at the cave where her family slept, the mouth had collapsed. She rushed to the entrance and found it sealed with large stones. Cassie fell to her knees, her hands tearing at the stones, but finally helpless and hopeless she collapsed. And then the shaking began again.

Later that afternoon, Raven, great granddaughter of Fawn Heart and member of the White Buffalo Calf Women, came to find her. The earth shaking destroyed the Trading People village, and many were hurt, dead or missing. For a period of time, a large island formed downstream, causing the river to run backward and flood the village. Only those who sought shelter on the great mound were saved. As the earth again sank, the island disappeared; the river again reverted to its normal course.

As the waters receded, bodies were seen floating in the river. In desperation, the remaining members of the Council of Elders sent Raven to the valley of the winged creature to seek the aid of the healing woman. She found Cassie collapsed at the blocked entrance to the cave, her face and hands cut and torn from attempts to move the stones.

"Mother," Raven called as she touched Cassie, "we need you."

Cassie stirred, "Need Mother?" She repeated the words, and then stood, a blank look on her face. "Need Mother?" Glancing down, Cassie gathered her medicine bundle and buffalo hide. She thrust the buffalo hide at Raven. "Carry! Need Mother? Need Mother?" In a shuffling run, she led Raven from the valley toward the village.

"Need Mother," Cassie mumbled. "Village need Mother." She paused, Mound City coming into sight. Before her was a distorted nightmare world that was to disturb her dreams for the remainder of her life. She grabbed Raven's hand, seeking stability as the land again moved under their feet. The river roared like a wounded beast, banks collapsing, trees, canoes, parts of houses and bodies twisting in the rushing waters. Great geysers broke through the earth, spewing sand upward to the height of the tallest trees, creating cone shaped mounds.

The people huddled together mutely silent, as if their cries of anguish had emptied into the night, leaving them voiceless in the light of day. Their faces and eyes were blank; the night's terror and morning's desolation pushing them beyond feeling. They sat in small groups on top of the burial mound. Even the council house of the elders now lay in ruins about them. Several of the elders could be seen ministering to the families, but most stood staring at the water, or moving aimlessly about, picking up small pieces of debris.

The suffering brought purpose to Cassie, and she began to walk among them, touching, healing, and praying. She blessed the living with the courage to continue, calling upon First Man and Woman to come and restore harmony. She called upon the spirit of White Buffalo Calf Woman and the Great Winged Beast to raise the souls of the dead and lead them to the spirit trail, pathway to the ancestors.

As Raven stood watching Cassie minister to the village, she heard her talking to Lame Deer and White Buffalo Calf Woman. It was as if the veil between the two worlds had split, and now Cassie lived in both. Raven felt power prickle over her chest and arms. *It is the medicine bundle*, she thought, as she watched Cassie put the bag to the lips of a young man and saw his face cease to grimace and become calm.

Blessing eagle feathers, Cassie tied them to the hair and shelters of those needing comfort. "The Great Winged Beast protects you," she promised. "Do not fear. You are not forgotten by First Man and Woman." Women in white from nearby clans and tribes arrived to give aid, saying they had heard Cassie call to them.

Slowly, under their ministrations, the village began to heal. When word spread that the mere touch of a medicine bundle restored health and calmed minds, the bundles grew in power. That time was remembered and tales told around the night fires for many generations. Some said that Cassie, standing on the great mound, held her bundle above her head, and commanded the roaring river to be stilled. Others remembered the Sisters in White jointly placing their hands on a dead child, whose soul already journeyed on the spirit path. The women called upon White Buffalo Calf Woman to find the lost child and return her to the grieving mother. Under their hands, the girl breathed, stirred, and cried.

Chapter 29 ~ Call to the Southwest

Cassie and Raven returned to live and tend the herbal gardens in the valley. The cave entrance was gone, but the opening where the winged beast looked down upon the river remained. They built rope ladders down to the opening and found they could still enter the cave's river entrance and reach Sun Kai's wall, but rocks blocked the path to where the bodies of Cassie's family lay. The women in white continued to come during sun-be-still for conferences, where they received instructions on the duties of womanhood, and each year, restored the great winged beast's colors. Peace had come to the Osage and Trading People. Osage trappers brought furs from the far north and western mountains, while the Trading People extended their routes to the Eastern, and Southern Oceans. The Sisterhood's great buffalo skin map now outlined a vast land.

Often Cassie sat staring at the blank cliff face, waiting for the rocks to open and return her family. On these occasions, when Raven spoke to her, Cassie did not answer and remained mindless to events around her. On other days, clarity returned. She then resumed teaching Raven the power of herbs, the story of Snow Pine and Sun Kai, the tale of White Buffalo Calf Woman, the duty to wait, watch and remember, and the meanings of symbols drawn on wood or leather that carried messages.

One day as Cassie drew the stick figures and arrow pointing to the river, she began to weep. "They never come," she said, "I wait, watch, and remember as I was told, but they never come."

The next morning Raven found Cassie sitting by the fire. Without salutation, Cassie spoke. "Each night the winged beast takes me upon his back and flies me across the land." Tears swelled in her eyes. "It is wonderful. I have seen and spoken to the others who have gone before. I held Lame Deer and my children again. I cried and asked them to allow me to stay, but they had a message. They said there are things we must do."

Cassie stopped speaking, and Raven's heart was filled with the anguish of the other woman who wished to leave and join her family. "What do they want?" Raven asked.

"We must prepare for a great journey; you must take two other sisters and six protectors with you. Go to the far southwest, where the land is dry and hostile. You will be afraid; you will thirst, but do not turn back. There you will find the City of the Gods. It is an empty city. The Gods have abandoned it and returned to their homes in the earth. But it is still a place of great power; there the Gods fought to bring harmony to the world. Before the great battle, darkness ruled."

Raven looked at her. "But, Mother, how will we recognize the place?"

"Have no doubts. You will know it by its size. Only gods could build such a place. There are many temples, some so high they bring Earth Mother into the arms of her husband, Father Sun. You will know it. You do not seek those who built the city, or its hidden wealth. You seek the gold held by those who work the fields. Seek baskets of golden kernels. Before they left, the God's gave the people this great gift." Cassie ceased to speak; her lips moved soundlessly. Her eyes peered inward. She tilted back her head, opened her eyes, and said, "Bring only the baskets of kernels, no humans are to be brought. They are evil; they will bring as large a measure of harm as the golden kernels bring good. The humans have the smell of ku about them." She ceased speaking, her eyes went blank, and her head fell to the side. "Mother, don't leave me," Raven cried, holding the old woman's limp body to hers.

She buried Cassie in the valley next to the others who went before. She sprinkled a handful of dirt over the body. "This shall form a blanket for you; it will shield you from the cold of winter and heat of summer. Go now, follow the great beast. Your family waits." Raven pushed the remaining soil over the body, and placed stones across the top to discourage animals from disturbing it. Returning to camp, she opened the great buffalo skin and with her marking stick, added another small woman in white along the top. "Mother, I am afraid. I cannot do this." In the afternoon breeze, she heard rustling wings, as though the great beast overlooking the river stirred.

That night the great beast flew Raven to the sentinel rock that marked the grass lands. Waving to her from below was Cassie and her family. The beast flew onward to the southwest, where Raven beheld the City of the Gods. Rising the next morning with new resolve, she said. "I will go and do as you ask."

Raven stood by the central fire looking at the women who had answered her call. Before her were twenty of the most devout of the Sisterhood drawn from Osage and Trading People clans. "Before she went to join her family, Mother told me of a request that has come from beyond the veil. We are to send three sisters and six protectors to the Southwest. It will be a journey of great hardship, but the Gods have prepared a great gift for us to bring back. A gift so powerful that it will transform and make us new."

Several women began talking at the same time, asking about the journey and gift. Raven held up her hand stilling the conversation. "We must choose three women and six protectors. Come with me and sit below the great winged beast that protects us. There we will remain for a day, refraining from all food or drink. Let no woman speak, but ponder these matters in their hearts, calling upon the ancestors to tell us who is worthy to make the journey."

The next morning the women returned to the valley to pray before breaking the fast. "Who has been told the answer?" Raven asked. "Who knows who is to go?" All hands rose. During the night, White Buffalo Calf woman had visited each and revealed the names. "So, as Mother foretold, I shall go, accompanied by Calm Water of the Trading People Clan, and Moon Blossom of the Osage. Six protectors are to be drawn equally from the Osage and Trading People Clans." All nodded, confirming they too had received this message.

One Sister asked, "Who will stay to tend the valley and honor the winged beast in your absence?"

Raven replied. "The mother whose child was restored has been renamed Happy Woman, and has joined the Sisterhood. Her husband, Coyote Howl, has agreed to move his family here to tend the herbal gardens for the Sisterhood. The restored girl child, Locust, exhibits great power. Perhaps, she also sees through the veil."

Chapter 30 ~ The Buffalo Skin

Fred Eldrege sat back in his leather chair, his feet propped up on an ottoman, Mahler's 7th symphony playing softly in the background. *Such a great composer*, he thought. Around him the shelves and desk of his home office were crammed with books, papers, awards, all artifacts of a long academic life. He sipped his wine, thinking about the bottle's label and smiled to himself. It was *Piasa Red*, a gift from Daniel and Lauren. *They never give up*, he thought.

Of late, he often thought about retirement. Each day the aches and pains and physical limitations reminded him it was almost time to give it up. He could still write, his memory was good, but the field work was getting to be a bit much. Somewhere along the way, the allure of sleeping on the ground in the great outdoors had lost its charm, a thing to be avoided, not looked forward to. Or maybe it was the constant reminders he received from working with students. *God, they're so young*, he thought, *most can't remember a president before Reagan.* He thought of an interaction he had with a young female student named Charity. He told her that when he was young, many women were named after virtues, such as faith, hope and charity. Smiling, she'd told him she didn't think that's what was on her parent's minds. She was named after a song by the band *'Guns and Roses'*.

"I grow old, I grow old, I shall wear the bottoms of my trousers rolled." He remembered hearing T. S. Eliot do a reading of *'The Love Song of J. Alfred Prufrock'* at Kensington Gardens in London when he spent a summer there as a young student. *God, how old and frail Eliot looked,* he thought. *Just a few years after, he died from emphysema.*

Suddenly, Eldrege sat up, his mind racing. *That's it,* he thought. *That's it. I saw the buffalo skin in England.* As a grad student, he wrote an article titled *The Symbolism of Native American Art as Recorded on Animal Skins,* and Sir Thomas Beechley, a curator at Oxford, read it and invited him to come to the university to examine a buffalo skin in their collection.

"Marge," he called, "What time is it in London?"

"Let's see, I think they're about six hours ahead of us. That would make it about four in the morning."

Emptying his glass, Eldrege wondered if Sir Thomas was still alive. One of the good things about getting old was all the great memories. Sometimes it was hard bringing them to the surface, but dammit they were all still there.

"Marge, I'm off to bed. Got a telephone call to make to an old friend of ours in the morning."

"Who?"

"Thomas Beecham, you remember him. We visited him at Oxford, a lifetime ago."

"Oh, yes. Sir Thomas. When you talk to him, give him my love and ask about Paula. I always liked them. Goodnight, dear."

At four-thirty the next morning, Eldrege was up, drinking coffee. Surely, Sir Thomas would be up by now. He picked up the phone and dialed the international number. The voice at the other end of the line was female, with a clear crisp English accent. "Sir Thomas Beecham's office. How may I help you?"

"Yes, Is Sir Thomas about? This is Dr. Frederick Eldrege from

America, an old friend."

He heard sounds at the other end of the line, followed by Sir Thomas's rich deep voice. "Fred, so nice of you to call. What can I do for you, old man?"

"Sir Thomas, nice to hear your voice. Marsha sends her love and asks about Paula."

"Paula's fine. She always says we need to cross the pond one of these days and visit you and Marsha. I hope you're calling to tell me you and Marsha are stopping by?"

"Well, no, not this time. Say, do you remember when I was there and we examined a buffalo skin from the Mandan people? Do you still have it?"

"Up until two years ago we had it, but, unfortunately, it was stolen from our collection. Why do you ask?"

"Because I think I saw it yesterday morning at one of our dig sites. Any idea who might have taken it?"

"Nothing we can prove. A young yank from the University of Chicago was here at the time, a guy named Aaron Smirl. Some of the staff suspected him, but without evidence or proof, we didn't pursue it."

"What was he doing there?"

"Oh, just summer study. He was a bit strange, but until we lost the skin, no one thought he was a problem."

"If the skin I saw this morning was the same one and this kid came from Illinois that at least puts it in the right state. I'll call the Dean at the University of Chicago in a few hours and see if she knows the guy. I know her pretty well; I'm sure she'll be helpful if she can. Either way, if I find anything out about it, I'll get back to you. If it's the same one, maybe it will give Marge and I an excuse to come visit, and repatriate it to its rightful collection. Thanks for the help, Sir. Henry."

"My pleasure, Fred. Keep me advised will you, and give our love to Marge." Eldrege hung up, He shook his head, *'repatriate' was a funny word. How would a claim from the Brits stand up to a claim for 'repatriation' from the Mandan people? Well, what they don't know won't hurt them.*

At 7:45 Eldrege entered the department and smiled at Betty, who was pouring him a cup of freshly brewed coffee. "Betty, you do spoil me. But keep it up." He opened his office, took off his jacket, and reviewed the day's schedule. "Betty," Eldrege called, "at some decent hour before 9:00, try to get Dr. Carol Manley on the line for me.

"Sure, Dr. Eldrege. Anything else?"

"Let's go over the morning schedule. I need to reserve the conference room for a small staff meeting." After reviewing the day's calendar, Betty rose to leave. "If you don't mind, I could use another cup." He handed her his cup and watched as she went out. *God, what would I do without Betty,* he thought. *It's almost as if she reads my mind.*

At 8:30 Betty rang into the office. "Dr. Manley on the line for you, sir."

"Carol, how are you? If you have a minute, I have a few questions. Do you remember a student or junior faculty named Aaron Smirl?"

There was an abnormally long pause at the other end of the line. "Ah, yes. I do know Aaron. Why do you ask?"

"Oh, his name came up in a conversation I was having with Sir Thomas Beecham. I think you know him, the curator at Oxford."

"Sure, I know Sir Thomas. We archaeologists live in a pretty small world. What was the conversation about?"

"Had to do with a missing artifact from his collection." Eldrege could sense Carol carefully selecting her next words.

"Carol is there a problem?"

"Well, Aaron is one of our graduate assistants. Very smart, very able, perhaps a bit intense in regard to environmental issues. Up until last week, I would have said he was a real prize. Now I don't know. One of our faculty accused him of stealing artifacts and when he was called into the office, he denied the accusations. Since then, we haven't been able to get back in touch with him. He just disappeared."

Eldrege looked at the ceiling. "No way to contact him?"

"He was living in one of the dorm rooms, but when I called the housing director, I found out his room had been vacated. I checked his file and my secretary made some calls, but no one seems to know where he went. Honestly, we don't know what to think or do; the faculty is not absolutely sure he stole the artifacts, so we feel uncomfortable calling the police."

"If you find him, let me know, will you? I've got a few questions I want to ask. And thanks, Carol. I'm like you, not sure what to do at this moment." He disconnected and for a second sat listening to the dial tone, his mind elsewhere.

Across town the phone rang. "Josh here."

"Josh, this is Aaron. Man, the shit just hit the fan. They are all over my ass. Just wanted to give you a heads up. I'm outta here."

"What? Aaron, what do they know? Where are you going?"

"Better you don't know. Anyway, just giving you a heads up. Keep outta sight. Lay off any CAS tricks for a while."

The line went dead. Josh could feel his heart racing. "Shit! Shit! Shit" *Get a grip,* he thought. *They have Aaron, but nothing ties him to me. We're okay.* He smiled, grabbed his favorite T-Shirt, feeling the need to make an impression today. The shirt showed a picture of an Indian under the caption, *'I'm half White but I can't prove it.'*

When the department line rang, Betty answered. "Oh, sure. Dr.

Manley; he's still here." She connected the line to Eldrege. "Carol Manley on the line for you, sir."

"Fred, this is Carol. After your call, the campus police called and said they searched his room. The place was cleaned out, but in the back of one drawer they found a telephone bill. Not sure this will help, but there are several calls made to your area code, all to the same number."

He took down the number, "Thanks, Carol, I'll give this number a call and see what we have. Thanks for thinking of me." He pushed the button, ending the call, and dialed.

"Josh here. Can I help you?" Josh looked at the caller ID. "Oh, Dr. Eldrege, how can I help you sir?"

"Josh, do you know a student named Aaron Smirl from Chicago?"

"Aaron Smirl? Doesn't sound familiar. You know you meet a lot of people, hard to remember em all."

"He was someone that came up in conversation. Thought you might know him. I wonder if you could make an appointment with me early next week? Maybe you can help me answer a few questions?"

"Oh sure, Dr. Eldrege, anything I can do." Josh hung up the phone and banged it against the wall. As Jenn came out of the shower, she heard the noise. One look at Josh's face told her they had a problem. He folded up on the bed, his head, in his hands. "Oh shit, oh damn, we're screwed. Dr. Davidson saw me delivering the package to the site. I told him I was picking up a soil sample."

Jenn curled up beside him and held him in her arms, trying to give comfort. "It'll be all right, baby. It'll be all right. Anything I can do?"

Josh sat up. "We need a fricken distraction, something that'll tie em in knots, get em thinking about something else."

Jenn kissed his neck and face. "Anything for you, baby. You know that. Anything."

Chapter 31 ~ The Golden Kernels

Wildcat looked out over the land and back toward the three women and five men who were making their way toward him. During the trip he'd become the lead Protector, responsible for scouting the way. As the group got closer, he could see Raven in the lead, her long black hair swinging with each step, followed closely by two other women in white. The five other Protectors were fanned out to the sides and rear as a shield from attack. Wildcat licked his lips and cleared his throat, unable to create spit. *We need water*, he thought. *We can't go another day without water*. His face wrinkled in disgust at the scene about him. *How dry the land is, how poor the soil*. The only living things he'd seen that day were vultures, beetles, and scorpions. He hated this land; the spines of cactus fell to the earth, and lay hidden in the sand, waiting to puncture your feet. This godforsaken land burned by day and froze by night; even shady places which promised a refuge from the sun, treacherously hid snakes and poisonous lizards. Grunting to himself, he wondered for perhaps the thousandth time, why they were there. But he knew the answer, it was Raven. He looked back along the trail, they were closer now, and he could make out their faces in the distance. Raven led the way, her strides strong and sure. He shook his head in annoyance. *She will not turn back*, he thought. *We need water, but she will not turn back*. He thought of their home in the land of the

Mother rivers, a land of abundance, with plants, and animals, a land of water, a land that nurtured life. He wanted to scream, *why have we come!* "Women should walk behind men," he said to himself. "It is our way."

Later in camp they ate dried cakes but conserved their water. Raven went among them, giving each an herb to place under the tongue. Their mouths soon gave off liquid which eased their sense of thirst. Because it was unwise to make their presence known in such a hostile land, they slept without fire.

The next morning after breaking camp, the Protectors came and stood before Raven. Wildcat shifted his weight uncomfortably as he confronted the woman. "This is a fool's errand," he said. "We," indicating the men, "are taking you home."

Raven smiled. "Brother, you are one of the Protectors, a man dedicated to the service of the Sisterhood. You know all sisters love and appreciate you for your service, but you do not decide these matters." She gestured, and the two other Sisters rose to stand behind her. "Last night I flew on the wings of the great beast that overlooks the river." She pointed toward the distant hills. "Beyond that lies a river, which marks the land we seek. We are not far, and we shall go forward." Without further comment the Sisters began walking toward the trail, but Wildcat blocked their way.

"We go back," he insisted.

Raven straightened her back and stared at him directly, knowing this would cause him discomfort. She raised her medicine bundle over her head; the inscribed symbols glowed in the morning light. She cocked her head to the side and said, "The power bundle speaks to me. Hear this—stand aside or die."

Terror filled Wildcat's heart. He stepped aside. "Forgive me, Mother."

Raven looked straight ahead, avoiding his eyes. "Today, take a position in the rear. I wish the Protector Young Jewel to lead the way." Without looking back she and the sisters walked toward the distant hills.

Moon Blossom, walking by her side, asked, "Was it necessary to embarrass him? Wildcat is a good and brave man. He would die for you. He doesn't understand."

"I know, but we are so close now," Raven said. "Three days beyond the river and we will reach the city." Conflicted, she shook her head. "You are right, Wildcat did not deserve to be embarrassed. At times, he makes me so angry." Shortly they came to the river where they filled their vessels and slaked their thirst. Raven sought out Wildcat to apologize, but he moved away.

Three days later, they crossed the final ridge. A great city lay stretched out before them with hundreds of tiered pyramids, vast temples, great walkways, wide plazas, and sparkling pools of clear water. They were stunned. For a time they stood and stared in awe. Then Calm Water spoke, "It is beyond any dream or vision. Only the gods could have done this." The city glistened in the sun, but there were no signs of life: no sounds, no smoke from fires, no movement of people.

They felt drawn to the city, but as they approached, they were again struck by its emptiness. The multi-tiered stone pyramids towered above them. In the temples' shadows the air felt frigid, and the blowing wind gave off a soft moan. The group huddled together tightly and walked in the center of the streets, avoiding the shadows, seeking the warmth of the sun. Moving to Raven's side, Wildcat said, "This is a place for the dead. We must leave."

Raven started to remind him of who made the decisions, but then nodded her acceptance. "You are right. Only the dead live here now. This is not the place we seek. There is nothing here for us." She turned and led the group out of the city toward the east.

Late that afternoon they arrived at a small village. Thatched huts were circled by fields of tall green plants. Seeing the group of strangers, the people working the fields gathered about them, gesturing and talking in their own language. Wildcat formed the Protectors around the three women in white, but it was soon apparent the villagers were merely curious, not hostile. An elderly white haired man with elaborate tattoos came from the village and through sign language, welcomed them and led them toward a central hut. When they were seated, a younger man came to sit by the side of the elder. After several moments of conversation between the two, the younger man turned to the group, and said, "I am known as the Trader. Once when I was very young, I traveled to your land along the great river. That is where I learned your language. My father," he indicated the elderly man, "has asked me to welcome you. We are known as the Crafts People. He apologizes for not knowing your language."

Wildcat started to speak, but Raven's hand stopped him . "Tell your Father," she said, "that we thank him for his kindness. We have much to learn from your people. It is for this reason we have come."

Trader translated the message to his father, who nodded and grunted his satisfaction. "My father is the wisest of our people," he continued. "He remembers our past and sees our future. He dreamt of your coming. You seek the golden kernels. We are people of the golden kernels; it is a great gift from our god. We have little here, but of that little we give freely." He clapped his hands, and women appeared with heated wet cloths to wash away dirt from the traveler's hands and faces. Once refreshed, the man rose and again addressed them. "Stay and feast with us tonight. Tomorrow, we will talk of the golden kernels." He clapped his hands again, and food was placed before them.

While eating, Trader said, "My father wishes you to know us. We are known as the Crafts People, the first people of the fifth world. We are the clever ones." He laughed, "I will tell you how we came to be."

"Before this world there were four other suns. These were the suns of earth, fire, air, and water. The people of the first world's sun were destroyed because they acted wrongly; their bodies were consumed by ocelots. Their sun died with them. The second sun was known as the pure. The people of that earth were turned into monkeys for their lack of wisdom. Next came the sun of fire. The people of this world grew impious, refusing to sacrifice to the gods. That world was destroyed by earthquakes, volcanic eruptions, and flames. The fourth world perished in a great flood, which also drowned its sun."

"Before the birth of our world, the fifth, the gods assembled in the darkness on the highest pyramid of the city, the one you passed through. They needed a hero, one who could light up the fifth world. One named Teccizecatl volunteered, hoping to gain the praise of the gods. He was arrogant and proud, and dressed in iridescent hummingbird feathers, jewels, gold, and turquoise."

"A great fire was built and Teccizecatl was called upon to jump into the flames. Four times he tried, and four times the heat and flames, along with his fear, drove him back."

"Then the lowliest of all the gods, Quetzelcoatl, dressed in humble garments of woven reeds came forward offering himself. He disguised himself as a misshapen being, ugly, and covered by scabs. None of the other gods paid him the slightest attention."

"They joined in one voice, *Oh Scabby One, be thou he who relights the sun.*"

"Without hesitation, Quetzelcoatl hurled himself into the fire and burned with a great crackling sound; his reed garments burst into flame and pushed back the darkness. It was the despised Scabby One who gave the fifth world life and lit the sun. Ashamed of his cowardice, Tecciztecatl followed Quetzalcoatl's example, and jumped into the fire."

Trader paused and looked at his guests. "There are those, the Wild One's, who lack skills and dwell in the nearby deserts. They believe Tecciztecatl restored the sun, but we know Quetzalcoatl gave us life. It was he who shaped us from the golden kernels. He is the god of wisdom and light. We, the Crafts People, are his children."

"Where is he now?" Raven asked. "Where does Quetzalcoatl reside?"

The man shook his head in sadness and pressed his hand to his breast. "He resides in our hearts," he said. "Quetzalcoatl was betrayed by Tecciztecatl, who became a fierce and uncivilized god of war and fire. Forced to flee to the coast, Quetzalcoatl built a great raft of serpents and floated away, promising someday to return. We await his return, and remember him as the plumed serpent." Pulling back his tunic, the man showed a tattoo of a feathered snake. After dinner Trader addressed the group. "My father says you have come far and need rest. We prepared a shelter for your needs. We can talk of the golden kernels in the morning."

The next morning the group was again led to the village chief, where they were offered a breakfast of bread and drink. The translator held up golden kernels and poured them from one hand to another. "This is our life," he said. "The drink you take is tea made from the plant's corn silk. It restores the heart." Holding up a piece of bread, he continued. "This is made from ground kernels." He pointed to the cooking area. "See the women with the stones?" He then handed each woman in white a small doll made from the corn shucks. "We make these for our children, but the stalks and leaves also feed our animals and are used in building our homes. Mahiz is what we call this plant. It is a true gift. It heals us, feeds us, and shelters us. We are its people." He paused and pointed to the chief. "My father dreamed you here. He has prepared bags of kernels for you to take to your land. He promises this gift will bless your people."

Later that morning as they prepared for their return to their homeland, Trader came to them. "My father has ordered that I go with you to the borders of our land. We will pass through the deserts of the Wild Ones. They are followers of Tecciztecatl, and like him, they are uncivilized and cowardly. It is best to be careful in their presence."

On the third day of their travel they crossed the river. Reaching the other side, they saw a small camp of natives. The leader of the group was a thin filthy man dressed in a single loincloth, and covered in tattoos. He came forward, his arms open in greetings.

Trader whispered, "Wild Ones, we should not stop."

Wildcat looked at Raven and shrugged his shoulders. "Two women, three men. We have nothing to fear here. Do what you wish. We will protect you."

Raven turned to the Trader. "Tell them we're thankful for their welcome. We will stop and share a meal. Perhaps there is something to learn here."

Trader frowned but did as he was told. Giggling, the old man ordered his woman to prepare for guests. The woman spread blankets before the fire and an ornate drinking vessel with a face on each side was brought forward. Raven took the vessel and brought it to her lips, the liquid was sweet to the taste. Passing the vessel along, she asked, "Who are the beings on the sides?"

The young man translated the question. The old man pointed to the side with the woman. "This is Chicomecoatle," he said, "goddess of mahiz. The other is Tlacoc, god of water." He laughed, pointing at Chicomecoatle's face. "It is said that no man may embrace or mount her without dying. Each year, the most beautiful of women is selected to act in her place."

Wildcat smiled to himself. *This Goddess is much like Raven,* he thought. *What man would dare embrace her? Why can't that woman ever obey?* The old man clapped his hands, and the women handed out small cakes, nuts and berries.

When the vessel came back, Raven thought it was alive. The figures on the sides moved and changed shapes. The air about the vessel filled with color, and gave off a sweet-sickly aroma. She shook her head to clear her mind, and attempted to speak, but no words came; her eyes closed and her mind filled with darkness.

The next morning Wildcat awoke, his temples painfully throbbing. The sun was high in the sky and painful to his eyes. He looked around and saw his companions asleep on the ground. The natives who previously welcomed them were gone.

Damned thieves, he thought. *They probably took everything.* Shaking his head to clear his thoughts, he moved around his sleeping companions to awaken them. As each came awake they complained of thirst and head pain. Suddenly, he stopped. *Where is Raven?* Her absence brought dread and cleared his mind. Both she and Trader were missing. He spotted their bodies under a nearby tree. Rushing to them, he recoiled in horror.

Trader lay with a knife sticking from his chest. His man parts were cut from his body and shoved into his mouth, but it was Raven's body that brought the greatest horror. She'd been decapitated and her skin flayed from her body. Wildcat fell to his knees. "Why did you listen to me?" he sobbed. He lifted her body into his arms. "After so many times, why did you listen to me?"

When he regained his composure, a cold purpose filled his

mind. He covered Raven's body with a robe, then ordered Young Jewel to make camp for the sisters. "Protect the sisters with your life," he said. "I will take the others. Those who have done this will pay." He set out with the four other Protectors to track and punish the Wild Ones.

Late that evening, the Protectors found the encampment. The wild ones danced around a large central fire. The elderly man who had welcomed them the day before, stood nude before an alter, drinking from the vessel with the two faces, his tattoos seeming to writhe in the flickering light. He lifted the cup to his mouth, blood splashing from its sides, running down his chest and arms. He reached atop the alter, gathered the skin taken from Raven, and fitted it to himself as if it were a second flesh, then joined the dance.

Watching the dancing figure mimicking Raven's body, Wildcat's anger rose in him, and he sprang forward toward the obscenity. His mace slammed into the back of the man's head dropping him to the ground. The other Protectors followed and within seconds, the Wild Ones, both men and women, lay dead. Wildcat continued to pound the man's head with his mace until nothing remained of the skull. Finally, he stood, "It is not enough," he screamed. "It is not enough."

The Protectors moved around the camp, gathering up the bodies and throwing them into the central fire. As they searched the tents they found two nude children, a boy and a girl, enclosed in a cage. These they brought to Wildcat. The two stood before him, nude and afraid. *Enough have died,* he thought. *Probably prisoners, meant for sacrifice.* "Bring them" he said, gathering up Raven's skin.

They returned to camp and prepared to make the journey home. Calm Water spoke to Wildcat about the children, reminding him that nothing other than the kernels was to be brought back, but he seemed lost in thought, unable to listen. Suddenly, coming to a decision, Wildcat called to Young Jewel. "I will make a travois and bring Raven home. Take the group ahead, we will travel more slowly."

As he watched them leave, he prepared a handled litter. He laid her body on his blanket and slowly dismembered it. Then building a slow smoky fire of mesquite brush, he laid the pieces of her body near it to dry so they could be transported home. For the next three days he sat, eating nothing, tending the fire, talking to her. When sufficiently dry, he wrapped each piece in a tight small bundle made from small patches cut from two buffalo hides, and placed them on the travois. Grabbing the handles, he began dragging the travois. "Women should follow men," he shouted. "It is our way." He fell to his knees, overwhelmed by grief. "Why did I brag that I could protect you? Why did you trust me?"

Chapter 32 ~ Woodhenge

Eldrege looked around the conference table. He didn't want to bring the whole department into the problem, so he restricted the meeting to Daniel, Lauren, and Jared. "We seem to have a problem at the burial site dig," he said. "Lauren and Daniel showed me a buffalo skin they discovered yesterday." He unfolded the buffalo skin and laid it across the table. "When I saw it, I felt I'd seen it before, then last night it came to me. "I saw this very skin in England several decades ago. When I called a colleague of mine at Oxford and asked if they still possessed the artifact, he said it had been recently stolen. He also told me they suspected a student from the University of Chicago who was doing a summer term at the time. Lacking evidence, they didn't prosecute. He paused, sipping his coffee. "I called Dean Manley." He looked around the table. "I think you all know Carol. She said this guy was suspected of stealing artifacts from them, but before they could prove it, he skipped school and disappeared. Anyway, if he took the skin, that explains how it got to Illinois. She also told me this fellow had contact with one of our students, Josh Green"

The group sat in stunned silence. Finally, Lauren spoke. "Fred, I can't believe Josh would be involved. He's doing yeoman service at the dig site. I've put him on flotation duty, and he's come up with some really interesting findings. From the seed pods he's collected, we've determined that part of the area was used for an herbal garden for an extended period of time. The plant patterns are really interesting. Maybe a pharmaceutical garden." She paused looking around at the group. "Really, he's doing first class work. Besides, why would he do such a thing?"

Eldrege put up his hand. "Lauren, I only said that the student at the University of Chicago had contact with Josh. When I asked Josh about it, he denied even knowing the guy. I asked him to come in for a talk sometime next week. Maybe, I'll know more after that."

Jared turned to Daniel. "Did you say you found the skin yesterday?"

Daniel nodded. "Yeah, that's why we closed up early. It didn't feel right, and we wanted to talk to Fred before saying anything."

"This is kinda strange," Jared said, "artifacts are missing from the department and Josh is caught on camera. We find an artifact at the site that doesn't appear like it belongs, and I saw Josh at the site after dark the night before you found the skin. When I spoke to him, he said he'd left a soil sample and needed to take it to the lab. At the time I didn't think much about it. Do you suppose?"

Lauren shook her head no. "I still don't believe it. He showed up on the camera because he was working for me. And, why shouldn't he visit the site? He's doing valuable work there. This is pretty circumstantial. We may be selling him down the stream for being conscientious."

"Look Lauren," Eldrege said, "no one is being accused of anything. Josh will make an appointment and I'll talk to him about it. We're not rushing to judgment here. However, I would like you to keep this under your hats until we get things sorted out. For now, let's stop work at the site. We're getting to the end of the season anyway, so we need to close up until warm weather returns. Let's put a fence around it and drape it with tarps to keep out the rain.

The remaining skeletons have been there a long time. They can wait a little longer." He looked around the table, seeing in their faces that stopping was not what they had in mind. But, it was his call, his decision to make. "Rushing makes for bad science," he said. "Besides, we've been lucky with the weather. This Sunday is Winter Solstice, and we're facing Winter Break. You guys can spend the time working in the lab on what you've already collected, and be ready when we open up again."

Looking at Daniel, Jared said, "Oh, that's right. You still planning to car-pool with me this Sunday for the Solstice at Cahokia? I'm told Dr. Eldrege does an incredible job of explaining Woodhenge. Really looking forward to it."

"Sure, never miss it. But we'll need to take two cars. Little Cassie is sick, so Lauren can't make it. She wants me to do some errands on the way home. What time does it start this year?"

Jared looked at his calendar. "Seven. I'll meet you there at six thirty."

In their apartment across town, Jenn sat looking at Josh. He slowly calmed down. The panic look was gone from his eyes, replaced now with something steely, even a little frightening. "Look," he said, "we need to give em something else to worry about. I need you to do this for me."

"But…"she protested.

He took her in his arms, kissing her, sealing off the argument. "It's just you and me, baby. Do this for me."

"But Dr. Davidson is so nice. I even met his wife and kids. He's a really nice guy."

"Nice guys finish last. Look, it's him or me. Screw Davidson." He pulled her close, kissing her neck, his hands unbuttoning her blouse. "Do this for me, baby."

On Sunday morning, Daniel pulled his Nissan into the Cahokia

Visitor's Center back lot. Only one light was visible; the parking lot, with the exception of a large black Dodge pickup was empty. *Still pretty early*, he thought, *bet that's Fred prepping for the presentation.* The 'Old Man' was never late. *Wonder how long he's been here?* Daniel looked at the sky. *This is going to be a great Solstice*, he thought, shivering in the cold air. The night was clear; and the stars shimmered in the darkness. He knocked, and the security guard opened at the back door. "Hi, Joe. Is Eldrege about?"

"Sure Doc. He came in almost an hour ago. He's up in the conference room."

Daniel found Eldrege sitting alone in the room, cup of coffee in hand. "Morning Fred. How's it going?"

Eldrege pointed to the coffee pot. "Glad you're here. Grab some coffee. There's pastries too" Eldrege looked tired. "What do you think of this Josh Green thing?"

Daniel poured himself coffee, grabbed a donut, and sat. "Actually, I don't know. Lauren is high on the guy, and her instincts are usually pretty good. Have you talked with Dr. Davidson about it?"

Eldrege laughed. "Not really. Jared is as straight as a string. He came to us from Brigham Young University. Really smart guy, a few crazy ideas about Indians being part of the Lost Tribes of Israel, but it could be worse; he could believe that the Chinese discovered America.

Now it was Daniel's turn to laugh. "Coulda happened, Fred, coulda happened. Never bet against the Chinese. The Piasa Bird resembles the Qin Dynastic battle flag. You're right, though. Jared is a real straight arrow. Those Mormons are really into the 'Thou Shalt Not Judge, Lest Ye Be Judged' thing. Bet he hates to do grades. Probably comes from their persecution history. If I had to guess, I imagine he would agree with Lauren and come down on Josh's side. I'm going to see him at the Solstice presentation, you want me to ask then?"

"Nah, I'll ask him myself. Now, if you would excuse me, I've got some reviewing to do."

Daniel looked at his watch. "Sure, I still have time to go to the top of Monk's Mound before your presentation." He paused. "You know, I still remember you taking us there when we were just starting out. It was cold as hell that morning. Now it's one of my favorite things to do." He smiled, "never told you before, but thanks." He stood and left the room.

Standing on the Mound in the early morning light, Daniel saw Jared's car drive up. *Looks like he gave Jenn Rausch a ride,* he thought as he saw her open the passenger side. *Cute kid, she looks like a snow angel with her white fur-lined jacket. Guess it's time to go join them.*

Daniel went down to the Woodhenge area, where several dozen people waited for Eldrege. He joined Jared and Jenn. Jared poured him a mug of hot chocolate and sprinkled marshmallows on top. "Maria sent it," he explained. "She's worried we'll get cold." Daniel liked Maria. Jared told him they'd met when he was on a church mission to Chile; he converted her, baptized her, and after release from his mission, went back to Chile and married her.

Daniel sipped the chocolate. "You tell Maria thanks for me. Tell her it saved my life. It's brisk this morning."

Eldrege walked to the center post, and looked around, acknowledging a few faces. "Good morning. When the sun begins to rise, I want you to come to the center of the circle, since that's where the viewing is done. However, for now, let's just talk about what we know of this site." He cleared his throat. "In the early 1960s, a team of archaeologists under the direction of Dr. Warren Wittry were working desperately to save archaeological information about to be destroyed by interstate highway construction." Eldrege gave a self-deprecating laugh. "As for me, I was here as an unpaid student volunteer, a beast of burden. Anyway, as the summer was coming to an end, Dr. Wittry noted on excavation maps a series of large oval-shaped pits, which were arranged in arcs and circles." Eldrege paused. "Now comes the amazing part, that spark of insight that separates the truly great from mere practitioners. Wittry theorized that if you placed posts in these pits at certain times of the year, they would line up with the rising sun and create a solar calendar. He gave this site the name by which we know it today, Woodhenge, after the United Kingdom site.

A female voice spoke from the darkness. "Dr. Eldrege, in a book I'm reading, *Cahokian Illusion,* Dr. Jenson makes the argument that all of this is supposition, and that Native Americans north of Mexico were not up to the task of creating a solar calendar."

Eldrege snorted. "Young woman, this is an example of why one need be careful in selecting what one reads. Not to disparage a valued colleague, but Jenson is an ethnocentric idiot and his ideas are frankly racist." Some in the group laughed at the 'Old Man' comments. He could be tough. When no one else spoke, Eldrege continued. "After further excavations, Wittry accurately predicted where further oval-shaped pits would be found, based on his calendar theory. He thought they'd been built during a hundred year period around 1000 CE. Recent carbon dating and ceramic studies put the dates between 1100 and 1200 CE."

Again, the same voice asked a question. "Professor, what tribe built the mounds and solar calendar?"

"The people who were here when the early Europeans arrived were the Illini Confederacy, and members of the Tamaroa, and Osage Tribes. When asked about the mounds, they said they didn't build them. The word Cahokia comes from one of their tribal languages and means wild geese." Eldrege laughed. "I have just revealed to you an important fact about all university professors; when we don't know, we don't admit it, we just ramble on about something else, hoping you won't notice."

Another voice called from the darkness. "Is it true that there was more than one Woodhenge built at this site? And, if the answer is yes, do we know why?"

Eldrege nodded. "Well, the answer is yes. At least five calendars were built here. The first circle consisted of 24 posts, the second, 35, the third 48, and the fourth 60. The final Woodhenge had only 12 or 13 posts located on the eastern sunrise arc. If completed, it would have had 72 posts. As to your second question, we don't know why they shifted locations and sizes. Perhaps, the changes were to include more festival days, or used as alignments for other structures within the community. We know that Monk's Mound was a work in progress, maybe Woodhenge changed to accommodate the increased size of the mound. The truth is, only a few are crucial as seasonal markers—those that mark Winter and Summer Solstice, and those half way between—marking the days of the Spring and Fall equinoxes. You really should come here during the equinoxes when the sun rises due east. It's almost like Monk's mound gives birth to the sun."

He looked up, gauging the light beginning to show on the horizon. "Okay, let's stop here. If you will come to the center post, you can line up the posts and see how effective the calendar predicts Winter Solstice. Once you finish, join me at the Visitor's Center for coffee and pastries. There, I'll show you a beaker fragment found by Dr. Wittry near this very spot. He believed the fragment incorporated the two great world symbols of the cross and circle, representing the earth and its four directions."

"That was wonderful," Jenn said. "Some students don't like Dr. Eldrege, but he sure knows his stuff."

Daniel laughed. "He can be a bear at times, and a bit intimidating, but he's a good guy. You're right…he knows his stuff." Daniel walked with them over to the parking lot, where Jared opened the door for Jenn. "See you Monday, Jared. Don't forget to tell Maria hi, and thank her for the chocolate. She's a life saver." He watched as they drove off. *Need to invite the Davidson's over for dinner*, he thought.

"I admire you and Dr. French so much," Jenn said, moving closer to Jared on the seat.

Jared smiled. "You're right. Daniel and Lauren are first class archaeologists. Top notch people. I'm lucky to be associated with them."

"No, you're wonderful too. She leaned against him, and he felt her hand stroking his leg.

Jared didn't move, nor reply. *My God*, he thought, *this can't be happening*. He felt his pulse and breathing quicken. She was leaning against him; he could feel her warmth and smell her perfume. Suddenly she was fumbling at his zipper. He felt cool air; then her soft hand against his skin. *No*, he thought. He reached down to pull her hand away.

"Oh, please let me," she said. "I admire you so much."

Chapter 33 ~ The Sun Born

When Moon Blossom and Calm Water returned from the Southwest, the boy and girl found in the cage were sent to the village to be cared for. Mala and her brother, Blood Jaguar, adapted well to village life where they helped plant the first fields of mahiz. Since the Trading People had no understanding of the term Jaguar, they quickly renamed the boy He Looks Up, due to his practice of welcoming the sun each morning from atop the Great Mound. The youngsters soon became village favorites, always willing to help and assist those in need. When asked why they were so kind, they answered, it was expected of Sun Born.

Upon her return, Calm Water moved to the valley and became She Who Remembers, Witch of the valley of the winged beast, keeper of the record, and leader of the Sisterhood of White Buffalo Calf Woman. Women in white from the various clans came to the valley, exchanging small pieces of leather for new medicine bundles. The marks on each small piece of skin held secrets of clan travel, successful hunts, and strangers encountered. As had all the other She Who Remembers before her, Calm Water updated the great buffalo skin of memories, looking for the small stick figures with an arrow pointing toward the great river. But each time she examined the leather pieces she received, she found none. They for whom the women promised to wait, had not been seen.

Both brother and sister lived in the village when the first of the small mahiz plants broke through the dark soil and grew strong and green. Although most adults in the village were amused by the young ones' religious practices, they appreciated their knowledge in regard to the new crop. When anyone would listen, He Looks Up would tell of the Great Sun God, who was known as the iridescent humming bird. He taught of Chicomecoatl, Goddess of mahiz, the Corn Woman.

When the first plants showed kernels, He Looks Up and Mala went to the field and selected the most beautiful and fruitful plant. This they pulled from the ground, wrapped in cloth, and buried on top of the Great Mound. When asked why, they explained the Sun God required sacrifices of the most pure, so as to continue to bless the people with his light and warmth. "In the beginning," they explained, "the world was dark. Our god went to the tallest temple and built a fire to push against the darkness. In desperation, he threw himself into the fire, bursting into a bright flame that increased until it became the sun which lights our world. In order for darkness not to return, we too must sacrifice the most pure and beautiful among us."

Most people smiled in regard to these teachings. The children were loved, and their practices seemed harmless. However, a few of the young did not smile or mock. They listened. Some began to mimic the morning rituals of He Who Looks Up, meeting with him in secret to learn his ways. Followers of this new way took upon themselves the name, Sun Born.

With the first crop established, Mala joined Calm Water in the valley of the winged beast to learn from her the secrets of the medicine bundles. She worked with the older woman, tending the herbal gardens, collecting the medicines, and learning the meanings of the marks on wood and leather. Although she was a good student, whenever Calm Water spoke of the five essential relationships and the need for their adoption, Mala appeared bored.

One afternoon as Calm Water sat in the afternoon sun, the wind blew through the cliff face, giving the impression of rustling wings. *The great beast stirs,* she thought. She leaned forward, stretching, still feeling tired from the journey to the southwest. Moon cycles passed, yet she still felt drained. *Perhaps it was the death of Raven?*

Calm Water shook her head sadly; *I must bring him food soon,* she thought. *He will not come for it.* Wildcat had returned several weeks after the main party, bringing Ravens' body back to the valley and buried it with the other sisters. Even though Calm Water begged him to come live with her, he'd refused, taking a position at the side of the grave. "I failed her once," he said, "never again."

Calm Water's thoughts were interrupted as she felt a small hand on her shoulder. "Mother, would you like me to take him food? Why don't you rest?"

She smiled at Mala. "No, daughter. It is something for me to do."

Calm Water took a bowl of spicy soup to Wildcat and found him sitting beside Ravens's grave, talking to her. His once strong body had shrunk, and his skin seemed stretched across a thin skeleton and cavernous face. Seeming not to notice Calm Water, he continued to talk. "Are you cold? I could bring a warm fur." He pointed to a blossoming tree. "I know how you love plum blossoms; I could gather some for you. Would you like that?"

Looking down at him, Calm Water was overcome with sorrow. She closed her eyes, gathering strength, and put out her hand to touch his shoulder. Wildcat looked startled. "I've brought you food," she said. "You must eat. Raven would want you to eat."

Without speaking he reached for the bowl and brought it to his lips. After struggling to swallow the first few sips, he returned the bowl. Then, as if Calm Water were not there, his eyes returned to Raven's grave. "Do you remember when you gave me the plant that quenches thirst?" He turned his head, listened, and smiled.

Tears came to Calm Water's eyes and she turned to make her way back to the camp. Seeing her sadness, Mala held her close. "It will be all right Mother. It will be all right." Mala helped Calm Water to her seat, wrapped a blanket around her, and put several fresh pieces of wood on the fire. Calm Water sat staring into the flames, her shoulders shaking beneath the blanket.

A movement at the edge of camp caught Mala's attention. Looking up, she saw her brother, He Looks Up. She smiled, pulled the blanket closer about Calm Water's shoulder, and then went to him. Reaching one another, they kissed and moved away so as not to be heard. "My brother, what is the occasion of your visit?"

"The time has come for the Sun Born's rebirth," he said. "I have many followers; they await the sign. Can you get the power bundles for the temple? We must show that they reside with us, that our magic is greater than the Witches in White."

Mala giggled and kissed him. "Of course. The six most powerful sisters will soon be here to celebrate Sun-Stand-Strong and plan the winter conference. They'll bring the most powerful bundles with them."

"Yes, but can you get them?" When the wind rustled through the cliff face, He Looks Up glanced about nervously. He hated and feared this valley of the winged beast. What if the stories were true? "There is power here, Sister. Do not be fooled."

Mala laughed at her brother's fear. "These are but women and a painted bird. They are no match for Sun Born. Our time has come." She kissed him. "You must leave, brother. I have planning to do."

For several weeks, Calm Water and Mala prepared for the

mid-summer meeting. They selected fresh herbs from the garden for drying. Six powerful shamanic women, each drawn from the Sisterhood of the Osage and Trading clans, arrived. There was Peeing Woman from the Osage upper river people-known as She Who Does Not Squat, Buffalo Hump from the High Pass People known as She Who The Buffalo Follow, and Sage Blossom from the Great Mound village whose touch cooled fevers. Last came the companionship of Pretty Feather and Radiant One. Calm Water was the sixth and final sister. Each of the six were leaders of the Sisterhood, women greatly admired for their wisdom and healing skills, even by those who called them witches.

On the morning of Sun-Stand-Strong, the six women sat in darkness, waiting for a beam of light to appear in the east. Standing before them, Calm Water said, "Sisters, today the sun's rays are strongest, and Father Sun will hold darkness away. The Sisterhood has set aside this day to plan. By the time the sun sets tonight, we shall know which acolytes are to be moved forward into the Sisterhood, which companionships will be recalled, and what lessons will be given at the Sun-Stand-Still meeting to bless our families. We have much to consider, but Father Sun has agreed to stay with us for a long time today. While we wait his arrival, I have asked Mala, an acolyte with great understanding, to provide tea to keep the morning chill away." Calm Water took a seat facing the east. After providing hot tea and sweet breads, Mala sat down next to Calm Water.

Smiling, Calm Water placed an arm around Mala. The tea was hot, warming her against the cold. Mala stared at her intently, waiting for something. "Are you alright, daughter?" Calm Water heard a buzzing in her head, and she suddenly felt tired. She looked around the group and saw women slumping in their seats. "What have you done?" she whispered, clutching at Mala, but her fingers were numb and would not hold. "Why did you do this? We saved you from the cage. We love you."

"Saved us?" Mala screeched, spitting in her face. "You didn't save us. You fool, you destroyed us. We were to be the sacrifice to the gods, not her." Like a mask removed, Mala's face distorted into a visage of hate and rage. "Grandfather promised us, and then chose the woman Raven instead. She robbed us."

Mala stood, went about the women, kicking them to be sure that none were alive, and collected their medicine bundles. Dragging forth a travois, she placed the medicine bundles on it. Her hand hesitated over Calm Water's bundle, the symbols seeming to shine in the early light, but she finally took it, along with the buffalo skin. She turned facing the rising sun and raised her arms upward. "Iyee," she screamed in triumph, "Iyee." She felt a presence behind her and turned to see a man.

Wildcat looked at the bodies and then at Mala. He slapped her, splitting her lip and knocking her down. He went to the travois and took Calm Water's medicine bundle and buffalo skin. "Raven's," he said. "Raven's. Belongs to Raven. Belongs Sister of the valley." Then as if he'd forgotten her presence, he stumbled back toward the grave, carrying the buffalo skin and medicine bundle in his arms.

Sucking the blood from her lip, Mala sprang to her feet and yelled after him, "Fool." She first thought to retrieve the medicine bundle and skin from him, but then looked at those already gathered. "Fool," she yelled again. Grabbing the handles of the travois, she made her way toward the village.

Chapter 34 - The Accusation

When Lauren and Daniel arrived at the university Monday morning, Jared Davidson was sitting outside their offices. *He looks like hell*, Daniel thought. "What's the matter, buddy. You look like your dog died."

Lauren frowned, giving Daniel her, *'How very sensitive you are'* look.

Daniel corrected himself, "You okay? Maria and the kids okay?"

Jared shook his head, his face a mirror of pain. "I need to talk to you. Something terrible happened."

"Sure." Daniel reached for his keys. "Come in. We can talk in my office. Okay if Lauren comes too?

Jared shook his head. "No, No. Please, it's too embarrassing."

Daniel looked at Lauren and shrugged. Lauren said, "I'll go get us coffee." She turned to Jared, "It'll be all right; Daniel will help. Just tell me no one's sick or hurt at home.

"No, they're fine. Everyone's fine." He looked ready to cry. Daniel opened the door, allowing Jared to enter his office. Taking the seat next to him, Daniel waited for him to speak.

Jared closed his eyes, as if closing out a painful image. "You know I gave Jenn Rausch a ride to the Winter Solstice presentation?"

Daniel nodded.

"I said I'd bring her when I thought you and I would be carpooling together." Jared took a deep breath. "I generally don't allow myself to be alone in a car with a woman who is not my wife. It's Church policy to *Avoid the Very Appearance of Evil*."

Daniel leaned forward, fearing what was coming next.

"Anyway, on the way home, Jenn was saying how much she admired you and Lauren. Suddenly, I don't know what happened; she was leaning on me, rubbing my leg, telling me how much she admired me as a professor." He was on the verge of tears. "I let her unzip my pants and touch me. I stopped her then, and nothing further happened. I swear. I don't know what to do. I told Maria, and we called Bishop Anderson."

Daniel sat there taken aback, not sure what to say. "Look Jared, I know you're a Mormon, but as you explained it, almost nothing happened." He touched his colleagues arm. "These are strange times for young students, and we seem powerful to them. They depend on us for information and evaluation, and as a result they sometime get confused. This sounds like one of those times. I'm sure Jenn is embarrassed by what happened. I would stay away from her. The matter is probably over." He leaned back. "She's lucky she didn't run into one of those creeps who think sexual relations with students are part of the perks. Hell, there's a recent article in Harper's Magazine where a female graduate student had sex with her professors, and then went on to have sex with her students. The article was titled '*Higher Yearning*,' or some crap like that. The author seems to think a 'sexually charged' atmosphere produces the best work." Daniel laughed. "I think she's one horny broad."

Jared looked somewhat relieved. "But I should have known better. I'm the faculty member; it's my duty to protect students."

Daniel smiled. "You're being too hard on yourself buddy, you didn't intend for any of this to happen."

Lauren knocked on the door. "Mind if I come in?" She handed

Daniel a cup of coffee. "Jared, I know you don't drink coffee. Will non-caffeinated tea work? You guys still need privacy, or can I join?"

Betty looked up as the door opened and Jenn Rausch walked in. The student appeared distressed, her eyes red and puffy. The secretary rose from her desk and took the young woman in her arms. "Are you okay, honey?" She felt Jenn shiver in her arms. "Anything I can do for you? Here, let me help you to a seat."

"I need to speak to Dr. Eldrege. Is he here?"

"Yes, he's here. Can I tell him what this is about?"

Jenn shook her head. "No, I just need to speak to Dr. Eldrege."

"Of course, honey." Betty went to her desk and rang into the department head's office. "Dr. Eldrege, Jenn Rausch is here to see you. I think it's important."

Eldrege looked at his clock. *Christ I'm busy*, he thought. However, Betty's tone told him this was a matter to be handled now. "Show her in Betty. Thanks." Eldrege stood as Jenn entered the room and was seated. He looked at Betty, trying to discern what this was about. "Jenn, do you mind if Betty stays?"

Jenn shook her head no, she didn't mind. Eldrege took his seat behind his desk. "Betty, lock the outer door, will you? I don't want to be disturbed."

Jenn sat crying quietly while Betty locked the door. When the older woman returned, she sat beside Jenn, putting an arm around her. "Honey, you tell Dr. Eldrege what's on your mind. I'm sure he will help." She handed Jenn a tissue.

Jenn smiled gratefully. "I'm sorry. I just don't know what to do." She sniffed and blew her nose. "I was at the Winter Solstice presentation yesterday and rode home with Dr. Davidson. He always seemed so nice, so I wasn't worried. I was telling him how much I admired him, when he suddenly pulled off the road and grabbed me. I was so surprised; I didn't know what to do. He started kissing and fondling me. It was on one of those side streets with no homes, so no one could help." Her voice became a mere whisper. "He exposed himself and pushed my face into his lap." She shuddered.

Eldrege cleared his throat. "Did it go any further than that?"

Jenn paused as if not wanting to tell more. "I did what he wanted, and he took me home. Look, I don't want him to get into trouble. He has a wife and kids. He didn't even talk to me on the way back, just dropped me off." She turned her head into Betty's shoulder.

"Jenn," Eldrege said, "this is a serious matter. I'm glad you brought it to me. I promise to do a thorough investigation. Our university does not take this type of thing lightly. Now, I want you to go with Betty to the Dean of Students Office. We have a counselor there named Marla Jensen; Ms. Jenson is trained in these matters and she is very good." He looked at his secretary. "Betty will stay with you until you have an opportunity to discuss this with the counselor."

As Jenn and Betty walked down the hall outside the office, they were stopped by Josh Green. "Is Dr. Eldrege around? He asked me to make an appointment."

Betty stopped, hardly looking at him. "Thank you for coming in, Josh. Uh…Dr. Eldrege is very busy right now. We'll have to reschedule. How about I call you if he still needs you?" She put her arm around Jenn and they continued down the hall.

Watching them go through the outer door, Josh laughed. "No, No. Thank you!"

The phone rang in Jared Davidson's office and he picked up.

"Dr. Davidson, this is Dr. Eldrege. I wonder if you could come to my office."

Jared's face went pale. "Sure, I'll be right there." He knocked on Daniel's door, and stuck in his head. "Eldrege called. He wants to see me. My God, Daniel, he knows."

Chapter 35 ~ Cahokia

As Mala approached the village of the Trading People, she was met by a group of young men. Each man carried a flint mace and wore only a kilt and sandals. Fresh tattoos showing a winged serpent adorned their arms. One came forward. "I am Wolf Killer, first to follow the Son of the Sun. He paused. "Lord He Looks Up awaits his royal sister on the great mound." Mala looked at him. He was tall and strong, a bit older than the others, perhaps thirty summers in age. His face, scarred and tattooed, was that of a warrior, but his most startling feature was his dark eyes which burned with the intensity of the true believer. He beckoned, and several men came forward to carry the travois. As she walked past a small mound, the smell of rotting flesh assailed her. Smiling Wolf Killer said, "They who opposed us are being prepared. Their blood has refreshed the Great Sun."

Walking through the streets toward the great mound, Mala was struck by the silence. No sounds came from the thatched huts; no children played at the doors. The air was filled with anticipation, and she felt wary eyes watching her from the shadows. When they reached the foot of the mound, groups of young men similarly dressed in kilts and sandals gave way so they could pass. Wolf Killer led the way, those carrying the travois followed. As she climbed the mound, Mala could see her brother He Looks Up, at the top. When she reached him, he said, "It is good to see you, sister. What have you brought me?"

They kissed. "I have brought five bundles of power, enough to show everyone our magic is more powerful than the Sisterhood."

He looked at her accusingly. "Five? You said there were six."

Mala quickly told how Wildcat stole the final medicine bundle from her. Looking at her torn swollen lip, He Looks Up leaned down, licked the cut, and laughed. But then as if a cloud passed across the sky, his countenance changed from light to dark. "He will pay. Doubt it not my sister, no one hits a Sun Born and lives. No one!" Then as quickly, his mood changed. "It is of no matter for now…we have five."

He Looks Up turned to Wolf Killer. "See the emblems inscribed on the power bundles? Paint these on the temple walls, so that all below can see the power resides with me. From now on, the Son of the Sun will predict the movement of animals, the best hour to begin journeys, and the times for planting and harvest." He laughed. "Without the power bundles, the Sisters of White Buffalo Calf Woman are just women. Nothing more. Just women. Place the power bundles on display in the temple."

He Looks Up reached into his clothing and brought out a small bag. He wet a finger with his tongue, dipped it into the bag, coating it with a fine dust, and then licked the substance from his hand. Mala shivered in recognition. *He has found the dream plant*, she thought. *He communes with the world of the spirits. That is why his mind races back and forth so.*

He Looks Up turned to Wolf Killer, his eyes hard and cold. "Have the members of the Senior Council accepted my generous offer?"

Wolf Killer looked uncomfortable. "Lord, all but four have accepted your leadership. The four remaining remind you that it is they who took you in and cared for you. They ask you to remember that wisdom comes from age. They would serve you as advisers."

Before Wolf Killer finished speaking, He Looks Up silenced him with a blow across the face. "They would remind me? Age makes fools." He raised his arms to the sun. "A new age comes, the age of the Sun Born. Only I make decisions here. Have the fools brought before me."

"As you command, Lord." Wolf Killer gave the order to bring the men to the mound.

Mala watched as the four remaining council members were brought and thrown to the ground before them. *How frail they look,* she thought. *Before, they seemed so wise and powerful. Now they are just old men.*

Laughing, He Looks Up walked among the old men kicking them. "Choose now; obey or die. The Son of the Sun needs no counsel."

One of the old men looked at Wolf Killer. "Be ashamed of this day," he said. "You have been taught better. The world of all those who have gone before is watching. You may kill us today, but we shall find you in the next. Be ashamed."

Several of the warriors who carried the travois looked nervously around them, as though expecting the spirit world to intervene. He Looks Up laughed, picked up an axe, and struck the old man in the neck, severing his head. He Looks Up captured the blood gushing from the body in a large vessel. With his next blows, he chopped off the old man's hands. "In the next world you will be eyeless and handless. We will not fear you. How can you harm us?"

The three other men, who'd been brought to the mound, began to beg and promise obedience.

"Too late!" He Looks Up screamed. "The Son of the Sun spews the weak like bitter milk from his mouth. The servants of the Sun

Born will be quicker to follow." His warriors held the old men while He Looks Up quickly decapitated each, carefully collecting their blood. He then chopped their hands off. Turning to Wolf Killer, he commanded, "Take the bodies and bury them together." He stopped, struck by a funny thought. "Be sure to link them arm-to-arm. I do not wish them to lose each other in the next world. Place their heads on poles, and be sure every villager sees what disobedience brings." He giggled.

Mala watched as the bodies were taken from the mound. *He's crazed by the dream plant,* she thought. He Looks Up took the vessel of blood and carried it to the edge of the mound. Facing the sun, he lifted the vessel, and poured the blood over his own body, the young men below began yelling in affirmation. Turning to Mala, laughing, he grabbed her arm and dragged her into the temple to his private quarters.

The next morning at sun rise He Looks Up stood at the temple door, awaiting the bead of light in the east. Looking down, he saw those faithful to him at the foot of the mound also awaiting the sun.

Wolf Killer came and kneeled before his Lord. He Looks Up placed his hand on his shoulder and bade him to rise. "What news do you bring? Is there resistance?"

"No, Lord. There is no resistance, but many families have fled into the woods. Shall we hunt them down?"

He Looks Up laughed. "No, they will come back to me. I am their God. They will come back. We shall harvest all mahiz and place it in the temple. When the cold season comes, and food is scarce, they will come back to beg." He looked out over the village. "See the houses of the old council and leading merchants? They are to be taken by loyal Sun Born. Assign the merchants and craftsmen the houses beyond ours. The remaining will be for commoners. There will be no clan leadership. All food and goods will be brought to me here at the temple. I and I alone decide who eats. I am the Son of the Sun." He looked at his blood-crusted body. "Send women with water to bath and dress me. After I am dressed and fed, bring the merchants."

In the temple Mala lay back on He Looks Up's sleeping furs. She felt dazed, every movement of her body bringing pain. The welts where He Looks Up had bitten her were crusted over with blood rubbed from his body. *He is driven by the power of the dream plant,* she thought. When she tried to ward him off, he hit her, telling her that they were Sun Born, true sons and daughters of the Sun. As his sister, she was the only acceptable vessel of his seed. Tears came to her eyes when she remembered Calm Water's comforting arms, always there whenever she hurt herself. *Mother, I am sorry.*

Chapter 36 ~ A Matter of Principle

Eldrege looked across his desk at Lauren and Daniel. "Look, I know you like Dr. Davidson. Hell, I like him too, but I have to take a complaint like this seriously. I've placed him on paid leave until we can get this sorted out. I will not have a Lothario among my faculty."

Lauren almost choked. "Lothario? Fred, this is 2009, and we're talking about Jared. He's my kid's assistant Cub Master for crying-out-loud!"

Daniel smiled at Lauren. "Fred, we think Jared is telling the truth. According to his story, the girl came on to him. Maybe he should have been more pro-active in stopping her, or not allowed himself to be alone in the car with her, but come on..."

Eldrege shook his head. "Like I said, I like him too. But, this is his word versus hers. I can understand why he might be lying, but not her. I'll keep investigating. For now he's on leave. If I get substantiation in regard to any use of force, it will be permanent." He took a deep breath, wanting them to understand. "Look, even the statistics are against him. A national survey conducted between 1991 and 2000 found that roughly 290,000 students experienced some sort of physical sexual abuse. Even if he's telling the truth and she seduced him, it is still wrong. With such disparity of power between the people involved, mutual consent does not work as a defense. Physical intimacy with students is not now and never will be acceptable, and cannot be defended by evoking fantasies of devoted professors and sophisticated students being denied the right to 'true love.' To make matters worse, in this case if the intimidation and force part is true, this may not only be unethical, he may have crossed the line legally." He shook his head, "I'm sorry. It's just wrong."

Lauren and Daniel looked at each other and remained silent. Eldrege was right. Students needed to be protected. Why would Jenn Rausch lie about such a thing?

Eldrege shook his head. "Actually, I didn't call you over to talk about the Davidson matter. I want to talk to a few of our students about the lost artifacts from our collection. I thought as senior faculty you could sit in. Maybe someone saw or heard something."

Daniel nodded. "Sure Fred. Who's coming in?

Looking at his watch, Eldrege said, "Only three this morning: Josh Green, Samantha Johnson, and if she feels up to it, Jenn Rausch."

Daniel looked at him. "Did you ever talk to Josh about Aaron Smirl?"

"No." Eldrege shook his head. "Betty tells me he tried to make an appointment, but I've been too busy. I'll get to it when I have some time." He hit the intercom button. "Betty, if Josh is out there, please send him in."

Josh appeared at the door, wearing a t-shirt with a picture of a Pilgrim Father in a circle with a line through it. The caption under the picture read, 'Please don't feed the Pilgrims.' Eldrege motioned for him to take a seat. "Josh, thanks for coming in. Of late, we've been concerned about some lost artifacts from our collection. No major pieces, but still important." When Josh tensed, Eldrege laughed, "Don't worry; we're not accusing you of anything. In fact, Dr. French here," he pointed toward Lauren, "has been telling me about what a great job you're doing at the burial sites. She thinks you have a future in archaeology. We just thought that asking a few of our students might help us, perhaps you've seen or heard something."

Josh's face broke into a smile, glad the conversation was not about him. "Well, no. I haven't heard any students talking about artifacts. Are you sure they weren't just misfiled, put in the wrong drawer, or left in someone's classroom? I can't imagine anyone stealing from the collection. If you need any help looking, I'm here."

Eldrege looked at him, "We have many individual pieces in our collection, so I can't be sure, but I think I'm the only one who actually uses the missing items. They shouldn't be in some classroom. I'm certain they were put back properly, but another look around wouldn't hurt. Thanks for offering."

"Well, if I can be of any help..." Josh rose.

As a passing thought, Daniel asked, "Oh, Josh…Dr. Davidson said he saw you at the site the other night? What were you looking for?"

Josh looked at Daniel. "Nothing, really. I forgot a soil sample bag and wanted to get it to the lab. I can't believe what people are saying about Dr. Davidson. I hope it's not true."

Eldrege cleared his throat and gave Daniel a warning glance. He didn't want the conversation to go there. "Yes, ah, well, so do we, Josh. But I'm sure it will sort itself out. Anyway, thanks for coming in. You've been very helpful." When the door closed, he hit the call button. "Betty, send Samantha Johnson in.

Samantha Johnson entered and took a seat. She was wearing an oversized LSU sweatshirt, shorts, and running shoes, giving an overall impression of health and Southern wholesomeness. She smiled at the instructors, and apologized for her casual wear. "I just didn't have time to go back to the dorm this morning after my run."

Eldrege waved his hand dismissing her concerns. "That's fine, Samantha; we appreciate your time. We called you in this morning because we have a problem."

Before he could continue, Samantha broke in. "Yes, I heard. Isn't it just terrible what happened to Jenn. It is so hard for me to believe that about Dr. Davidson. He seems like such a nice man. He's a great instructor."

Lauren frowned and leaned in. "Is Dr. Davidson's problem common knowledge among the students?"

Samantha looked at her. "Uh, yes. All the students know. Josh, especially seems angry. He thinks something should be done about Dr. Davidson. I saw him talking to other students. I think he's trying to get a petition together or something."

Eldrege momentarily closed his eyes and cleared his throat. "Actually, what we called you in for this morning has nothing to do with Dr. Davidson. We wanted to talk to you about some missing artifacts from our collections. Now, don't panic. We don't think you took artifacts, but we are missing a few things and thought that perhaps the students might have seen or heard something."

"Oh, I'm sorry. I just thought it was the other problem since all the students are talking about it." Samantha was crestfallen. "I didn't mean to gossip. Like I said, I really like Dr. Davidson." She breathed deeply, "What part of the collection is missing?"

"We're missing a few pieces from the Piasa Creek collection, Eldrege said. Nothing big: a birdman tablet, a few bone hairpins, some leptoxis shell beads, and a green turtle effigy gorget. We're concerned because departments in Chicago and Springfield have reported missing items, and some think the thefts may be linked to the CAS. We thought we might bring in a few graduate students, and see if they can remember seeing these pieces in a classroom somewhere, or if they've heard anyone talking about them."

"I haven't seen or heard anything, but I've been working on my grades of late and really don't hang out with my classmates." Samantha frowned. "I can't imagine anyone in our group being involved with the CAS. There're criminals. A few of the students are pretty intense in regard to global warming and saving the environment, but they're not anarchists."

Daniel put his hands behind his head and leaned back. "I suppose you're right, Samantha. We thought you might have seen the artifacts in a classroom or misfiled someplace."

"No, I really haven't, but I'll keep my eyes open. I can't imagine pieces from the collection just lying around though. People are really careful," Samantha smiled, "maybe even anal about making notes and getting everything back into place. That seems to be a big part of the archaeology thing."

Eldrege nodded and smiled. "You're right, Samantha. Keeping notes and putting things where you can find them again is a big part of archaeology. Anyway, thanks for coming in, and if you see or hear anything, let us know, will you?" He punched the call button. "Betty, is Jenn Rausch out there?

Jenn and Samantha passed one another in the doorway. Samantha gave her a brief hug, and a sympathetic look, but they didn't speak.

Eldrege waited until she was seated. "Jenn, thanks for coming in. Sorry to bother you, but the department is missing a few pieces from the collection, and we're asking students if they've seen them lying about in some classroom or perhaps put away in a drawer somewhere or heard any conversations about them."

Jenn smiled, "I haven't heard or seen anything, Dr. Eldrege. I've been sorta," she paused and looked down gathering herself, "in a funk of late."

"Thats okay, Jenn, we just thought that maybe one of the students might have heard or seen something. How is the other matter coming along? Was the counselor helpful?"

"She was, and Betty has been so sweet. I'm just sorry this has happened. I hope nothing bad happens to Dr. Davidson. He has a wife, you know."

Lauren nodded her head. "It's a terrible thing. Have the other students been supportive?"

Jenn paused. "I don't know, I've tried to keep this to myself. I don't think anyone else knows."

Lauren said, "I asked because Josh mentioned it to us earlier. I know you two are friends."

"I'm surprised he knows," Jenn said. "Josh and I have worked together on the burial site dig, but we don't hang out together socially."

Lauren stood and walked behind Jenn. She picked up a book from the shelf and appeared to examine it. "Who knows where he heard it," she said, "but I'm glad it's not common student knowledge." Standing behind Jenn, Lauren drug one finger across her thumb.

Eldrege frowned. "Jenn, we're sorry to have brought you in this morning. We know you have other things on your mind, but if you do see or hear anything, please let me know. And in regard to the other matter, if there is anything further I can do for you, please don't hesitate to ask. My door is open."

Jenn rose to leave. "Thank you, Dr. Eldrege. You've been so kind." She smiled at Lauren and Daniel. "If I see or hear anything, I'll be sure to tell you."

As the door closed, Eldrege looked at Lauren. "What was that about?"

"She's lying." Lauren shook her head. "I don't know why, but she is." She turned to Daniel. "Remember when we invited Josh and Jenn to work with us on the dig? I called the number Josh gave me and got an answering machine. It was Jenn's voice. I'm sure of it because she said something cute about not wanting to speak to solicitors. The voice on the machine clearly said Josh and Jenn were not in. They are, or at least were, a couple."

Eldrege leaned over and picked up the phone, checked his student directory, and dialed a number. He listened, as an answering machine picked up. He turned to Lauren, "Well, the message only has Josh now. Are you sure?"

Lauren thought for a moment. "Gosh Fred. I'm pretty sure. I will have erased it from my home phone by now, but I'm pretty sure. That's why it seemed strange to me that she denied telling him about it. Also, did you notice that neither Josh nor Jenn asked us what artifacts were missing?"

Eldrege laced his fingers together, and put them to his lips. "So what? What does it tell us? Suppose she and Josh are roommates?" He shrugged his shoulders.

Lauren laughed. "You're right, I guess. But I'm sure she was lying. Not sure what that tells us, but she was lying. Is there anything else we can check to see whether this lying thing is anything bigger than just trying to keep a personal relationship personal?"

Daniel shook his head. "You remember when I asked Josh what he was doing at the site the other night when Davidson saw him? He said he was picking up a soil sample for the lab. We could check the cameras in the lab to see if he really dropped by that night."

"Forget it," Eldrege said, looking at Lauren and Daniel. "You two have read too many *Encyclopedia Brown* and *Nancy Drew* books as kids. Even if Jenn lied about a relationship with Josh, and Josh didn't immediately take the soil sample to the lab, what would it prove?" He rubbed his forehead, and took in a deep breath. "Besides, we have bigger problems. If Josh is getting the students to sign a petition over the Davidson matter…well, can you just imagine it?"

Chapter 37 ~ He Comes!

Timid Girl hid in a small grove of trees and looked down on the great mound city. It always surprised her. *So many people*, she thought. In her sixteen summers she'd watched the fields of green spread outward as trees were removed and more of the land was planted in mahiz. The small creeks which crossed the valley were now straight ditches bringing water to the city. She remembered her brothers and father fishing and gathering mussels from the creeks, but now the water was dead. It seemed as if the increasing fields of green created a great swirling current, drawing people and goods in, pushing out all other life. At times she wished she could join the families below, but the Sisters in White were banished. Only her mother, Forest Water, Witch of the Medicine Valley guarded by the winged beast, lived in peace. None dared harm the woman who lived with the winged beast and tended the medicine gardens. Conferences of the Sisterhood were still held each Sun Stand Still, but now in secret.

Timid Girl's mind wandered, but then was drawn to activity at the river's edge. A trading canoe landed and a large foreign man jumped out and waded to shore. He was a giant, towering over the others. In the distance his skin and beard appeared to glow in the morning sun. On his back he carried a large pack, and furs covered his body.

It is them, she thought, *the strangers who will come. They for whom we have waited. I must tell Mother.* She was without breath as she raced into the valley. "They've come! Mother, they've come. Strangers come."

Forest Water looked up when her daughter ran into camp. "Who?"

"Strangers, Mother. The strangers have come. I saw one. He is in Mound City. He comes to trade."

Forest Water grabbed her daughter. "Are you sure it is not one of us? Perhaps from a distant tribe?"

"No, Mother. It is a stranger." Timid Girl described the man. "He is not one of us. He is tall and strong, like a giant."

Forest Water laughed, "They have come. We must bring him to the valley. He must see the great winged beast on the cliff. We must give him Snow Pine's record." She danced in joy. "Daughter, go and when he is alone, give him this." She removed the small coin necklace which had been passed from generation to generation of women of the valley and gave it to Timid Girl. "The necklace will bring him here."

Timid Girl ran to the city. She found the stranger sitting in the marketplace, surrounded by merchants and onlookers. A blanket was spread before him and the goods from his pack were laid out in display. The curiously designed items looked to be weapons. Several hours passed before the crowds dispersed and she could approach him. Smiling, she sat by his side. When she held out the necklace, he took it from her, looked at its design, brought it to his mouth, and bit it.

"Gold, Little One. This is gold. Where did you get it?"

Not understanding his language, Timid Girl only smiled. She reached for his hand, urging him to come.

He looked about, there were no more customers. "Gold and

a sweet woman," he laughed, thinking of his good fortune. He repacked his goods and slung the huge pack over his shoulder. "Gold and sweet woman," he laughed heartily, allowing her to lead the way.

Forest Water watched as the man and Timid Girl came into the valley. She had changed into the white dress of the Sisterhood and scented her body. *They come*, she thought, *they upon whom we have waited so long, have come.* She looked around to see that all was prepared. The fire burned brightly and the aroma of spicy food filled the camp.

When Timid Girl and the man came into camp Forest Water came forward and knelt at his feet. "We welcome you," she said.

He laughed, not understanding her words. Reaching down, he lifted her to her feet. "Gold and two sweet woman," He laughed again, brought out the small coin necklace, pointed at it, and looked about. "Where come from?"

Forest Water laughed, not understanding. *He wants to see the winged beast,* she thought. She grabbed his hand urging him to come.

He allowed himself to be led to the cliff side overlooking the river. Forest Water pointed at the Great Winged Beast painted on the cliff and looked at him.

The man drew the large axe he wore at his side, threw it at the Painted Bird and yelled, "I am Thornfeld Skullsplitter. I fear not demons." As the axe fell back to the ground, he picked it up, and daring the beast above to do its worst, he grabbed Forest Water and dragged her back to camp.

Returning to camp, he released her and took a seat by the fire. He pointed to the food, then to his mouth. "I'm hungry." While she prepared the food, he muttered to himself, "I fear no demons. Gold and two sweet woman." He patted the furs next to him, indicating he wanted Timid Girl to join him.

Timid Girl looked at her mother, who nodded that she should sit. "I can't understand him," Forest Water said. "He is not as I supposed."

Thornfeld reached into his pack and brought out a drinking vessel. He took a long swig, laughed, and offered it to Timid Girl. She again looked at her mother, who only shrugged. When she drank the liquid, it burned her throat and made her cough. Forest Water rushed to her side, but Thornfeld pushed her away, laughing and pointed to his mouth.

Forest Water watched in disgust as he ate. *He is a beast,* she thought. He removed his helmet, revealing yellow hair, matted and dirty. He grunted, ran his fingers around the bowl, scooping up the last bits of vegetables and meat, then wiped his fingers clean against his furs. Laughing, he pulled Timid Girl onto his lap. "Gold and two sweet woman." Forest Water rushed to the girl and tried to pull her away, but the man backhanded her across the face, and she fell.

Scrambling to her feet, Forest Water screamed at him, momentarily distracting him from disrobing Timid Girl. She pulled up her white dress and dropped it aside. His smile deepened and he released Timid Girl. Extending his arms to Forest Water. she jumped at him, scratching at his face. He laughed and wrestled with her, pinning her arms to the ground. She looked up and saw a wide eyed Timid Girl watching. "Run, Daughter. Hide. It will be alright."

He pulled away his clothing and fell upon her, his beard scratching her face. She could smell the liquid he drank, mixed with meat, vegetables and unwashed body. He moved above her, his weight was oppressive. Finally, he grunted and fell aside. Within minutes, he was snoring, and she carefully slid from beneath him.

When Thornfeld awoke the next morning the sun was already

up. The woman, with her back to him, was cooking at the fire. He smiled, she was still without clothes. "Gold, and two sweet woman," he muttered. Hearing his voice, Forest Water came and kissed him. In response he stroked her breasts and belly. She moved from his arms, went back to the fire, and brought him food. *Good woman*, he thought, as she spooned the food into his mouth. *Good woman.*

Forest Water watched as the ku poison took him and he lie writhing on the ground. She searched his clothing, found the small coin-shaped necklace, put it around her neck, then pulled on her white dress. *This beast is not who we wait for,* she thought. *We must continue.* She called for Timid Girl to come and help undress him and drag the body away from camp. Rather than give him the honor of burial, they would allow their wild cousins to consume him.

They returned to camp and sat by the fire. The wind rustled along the cliff side. Forest Water looked at her daughter, and said. "The Winged Beast is restless." She picked up the man's pack and clothing and with her daughter went to the cliff side under the great beast. They flung the pack and clothing into the river below and stood watching as they sank. Looking up at the great winged beast, Forest Water raised her arms. "Mother Snow Pine," she called, "I'm sorry. He was not the one!"

A summer later, Forest Water sat by the fire with the buffalo skin across her lap. On the other side of the fire, Timid Girl held a baby. *Such a beautiful child, yellow hair like his father. Strong, like his father, too.* Forest Water smiled, and winced, her breasts sore from his suckling. *Tall, strong sons are good.*

She unfolded the great buffalo skin and traced her fingers across the row of women. First, Buffalo Woman, she who brought peace to the Osage. Then, Mother Snow Pine, the foreign woman, wife of Sun Kai, who lives in the mountain and rides the winged beast. Then Ming, daughter of Snow Pine, gentle lover of ku. Then Cassie, the mindless one, healer of the people. Then Raven, bringer of the golden kernels. Then Calm Water, she who was betrayed by the evil one. Forrest Water's mind paused in her telling of the figures. The character of Raven on the great skin was a woman with a green stalk flowing from her forehead. Off to her side was Wildcat. It was Wildcat who brought Raven home to the valley and placed her in the grave of the sisters. Faithful Wildcat, who failed to protect her in life, who then sat by her grave refusing to leave her. It was Wildcat who saved the valley's great skin of memory and medicine bundle of power. Tears came to Forest Water's eyes, thinking of the love between Raven and Wildcat. A love made greater by loss.

Her finger slid to the next figure, Moon Blossom. It was Moon Blossom who received the power bundle and great skin of memory. As Raven's sister-companion, Wildcat brought them to her. Her fingers moved across the other keepers of the valley: Snake Maiden, Strong Deer, Sacred Dancer, and Secret Butterfly. Healers all, and when necessary, users of ku.

With her marking stick Forest Water drew the figure of a tall bearded man armed with an axe. She smiled, *I will be the next figure, then Timid Girl. Our wait continues.*

Chapter 38 - The Protest

Daniel pushed his hair back from his eyes and quickly sorted through a folder of overheads labeled '*Secrets of the Ancient Dead.*' Earlier Eldrege had called and asked him to cover his seminar that morning. He selected ten overheads from his deciphering the past from tombs, graves, and mummies collection. *Better bring something*, he thought, *in case one of the students is not prepared to present.* He looked at his watch, 7:45. *Better get a move on, it's Show Time!*

At 8:00 am, he walked into the seminar room, and nodded to several graduate students he had in other classes. *A good group*, he thought, *should be fun.* He took a seat at the head of the table, and cleared his throat. "Good morning. Dr. Eldrege called and asked me to sub for him. This morning is scheduled for student presentations. Let's see…" he looked at the note in front of him. "Josh Green? Anyone know where he is?"

The students stared back blankly, no one seeming to know Josh's whereabouts or why he was not present. Daniel looked at his watch. "Well, let's give him a few minutes. I think Josh was doing a presentation on the burials at Cahokia. Maybe we can kick around some ideas until he shows up. What do we know?"

Samantha Johnson raising her hand said, "Well, at this point, and given all the construction that's gone on around the site, we probably will never know if they had a burial site in the sense of a community cemetery. But just south of the Twin Mounds, which we think functioned as a funereal preparation point, they've found extensive and interesting burial activity."

Daniel smiled; it was good to have Samantha in a class. *Smart students make class interesting*, he thought. "You mean Mound 72, if so, what makes it interesting?"

"Well, one of the skeletons is apparently a very important early leader. He died in his early 40s…" She glanced down at her notes, "Around1050 CE."

"Why do we think he was important?"

"The grave goods." She again looked at her notes. "He was laid to rest on a bird shaped platform made of 20,000 shell ornaments, along with eight-hundred apparently unused arrows with finely made heads. They also recovered a staff and 15 Chunkey stones."

Daniel snorted, "Maybe not a great leader at all, perhaps a sports hero?"

Now Samantha smiled. "Well if he was, they were real fans. Interred near him were four men with their heads and hands cut off and arms interlinked and nearby, fifty three young women apparently strangled. The women's ages were between fifteen and twenty five years, which suggests human sacrifice."

Another student cut in. "I know some Cardinal fans who would off their own kids to get another World Series Championship."

Daniel shook his head. "You're probably right, but not everyone is as rabid as a Cardinal fan."

"Besides," another student broke in, "there's the matter of the two hundred forty skeletons haphazardly thrown into a nearby pit, some beheaded and others with arrowheads in their backs. Seems to me that not everyone was loyal to the regime."

Daniel nodded in agreement. "That's interesting. The way they were buried, tossed into a single pit, indicates dishonor. Maybe a crushed rebellion or a successful one?"

The student who'd given the Cardinal fan comment spoke out. "Maybe it was the fans of the losing side." Several students laughed.

Daniel raised his hand, bringing the group back into focus. "In any case, Mound 72 and the Twin Mounds, which seem to have been charnel areas, have sparked considerable debate among anthropologists and archaeologists. Some speculate the four men with arms interlocked, without heads or hands, represent the four cardinal directions on a compass." He shrugged his shoulders. "To others the sacrifices represent a cultural diffusion from the Mayan or Aztec cultures. Whatever the truth is, the huge number of people sacrificed is unparalleled north of Mexico."

Samantha Johnson raised her hand. "I know this is way off topic, but is it true one of the skeletons at the site you're currently working shows signs of knife chips and cuts like it was disarticulated or rendered?"

Daniel frowned. "Well, yes. One of the female skeletons seems to have been taken apart, and then put back together for burial. The cuts and chips on the bones are consistent with dismembering. I really don't want to say much more because at this time, it's just a guess."

"But…" Samantha protested, clearly engaged and interested, "do you have any ideas? Do you think it was ritual sacrifice, cannibalism?"

Daniel laughed to himself. *This is the downside of smart students*, he thought. *They're actually interested.* "Samantha, as I said, our findings are too premature to come to any conclusions."

Before she could ask another question, Samantha was drowned out by a bull horn blaring outside the window: *LYNCH THE LECH! LYNCH THE LECH! LYNCH THE LECH!*

Suddenly, all the students were at the window peering out. Daniel joined them. He saw several hundred students, milling about the quad, chanting. Josh Green stood on a stool in front of chanting students, bull horn in hand. Josh's t-shirt had a picture of several Mescalero Apache warriors on horseback under the slogan, *Department of Immigration…for when they just won't leave.* Daniel closed his eyes. *Little bastard has good taste in t-shirts anyway. Eldrege is going to tear him a new one for this.* He shook his head in disgust. *Might as well close up,* Daniel thought. *With all that going on outside, this class is over. The students will never get focused.* Besides, he wanted to have a chat with Josh. "Class, lets call it a day. Seems like we have too much competition to get much done this morning. Samantha, you'll be the lead presenter for next class. I'm sure Dr. Eldrege will be back by then."

Daniel walked out of the building and watched the demonstration. From the signs being waved, he identified several student fringe groups: Gay and Lesbian Alliance, Earth Liberation, Women Against Exploitation. He recognized several faculty from the Women's Study Center. Off to the side, local and St. Louis press stood, cameras and feed trucks at the ready. Daniel closed his eyes, shaking his head. *Just in time for the 12 o'clock news cycle,* he thought. *This will be all over the country before it finishes. My conversation with young Josh will need to wait. Guess I better contact the Old Man.*

He walked over to the department office to see if he could speak to Eldrege. "Hi, Betty. Fred about?"

Betty looked up. "No, Dr. Eldrege is out of town. I don't expect to see him again until tomorrow morning. He left a number, if you really need him." She laughed. "I guess you really do need to talk to him. I just got off the phone with the secretary from Liberal Arts. Has Josh Green lost his mind?"

"I dunno, Betty, but I do need to talk to Dr. Eldrege. This could become very unfunny, if it goes much further." She handed him a slip of paper with the number. "Mind if I use Fred's office to make the call?"

Daniel dialed the number. "Dr. Manley's office, can we help you?

Carol Manley's office, Daniel thought, *Eldrege is in Chicago.* "Ah, yes. Is Dr. Frederick Eldrege there? This is Dr. French at SIUE. I'm sorry to bother him, but it's important."

"Well, he's in a meeting with Dr. Manley, but if it's really important, I can ring in and see if he can talk."

"Thanks, I do need to speak to him, and it's a bit urgent." Daniel waited while she made the connection."

"Fred Eldrege, can I help you?"

"Fred, this is Daniel French. Sorry to bother you, but we have a situation here. You remember Samantha Johnson saying that Josh Green was trying to get a petition signed? Well, he did that and more. At this moment he's leading a demonstration outside the department, demanding the firing of Jared Davidson."

There was a long silence at the other end of the line, and Daniel wondered whether they'd been cut off. Then he heard Eldrege sigh. "Okay… ah… look, Daniel, I'll take the afternoon plane back to St. Louis and meet you and Lauren at my home at seven. Will that work for you?"

"Sure Fred. We'll be there."

"In the meantime, have Betty make an appointment for me with the Dean as early as possible, and then with our young friend Josh Green. Oh, and ask Betty to ask the Dean if it would be possible to have university legal counsel attend our meeting."

"Sorry to be the bearer of bad news, Fred. Lauren and I will see you at seven." After the call, Daniel sat deep in thought. Finally, he hit the button, connecting to Betty. "Betty, Dr. Eldrege wants to set up several meetings early in the morning. He wants a meeting with the Dean and university counsel if she's available, and then a meeting with Josh Green. If you need me, I will be in Lauren's office. If you get the meetings set, call Marge Eldrege and tell her, so she can relay the message to Fred. He's coming home this evening. Oh, also tell her Dr. Eldrege invited Lauren and me over this evening at seven. Just in case he forgets."

Lauren and Daniel rang the Eldrege doorbell at 6:45. Marge answered, hugged Lauren, and said to Daniel, "Thanks for the warning about your coming this evening. Fred did forget, but you know you're always welcome. Go right on in. He's in the study."

Eldrege looked up when they came in. "Take a seat; thanks for coming. Sounds like you guys had an interesting day. Get you anything to drink? Beer? Wine? Soda? Water? Juice? I'm sure whatever you want, Marge has it cold."

Looking at Lauren, Daniel said, "No thanks, we're fine."

Eldrege leaned forward in his chair. "Well, tell me about it. I was in Chicago this morning, then on the plane coming back, so I haven't seen the news. How big of a deal is the press making of it?"

"Pretty bad Fred," Lauren replied. "It spread like wildfire across the campus gossip line, it made the 12:00, and 5:00 news both locally and in St. Louis. Lots of quotes by crazies who want to make Jared a symbol of all the problems of male/female relationships. The way people speak, you'd think this was a rape case."

Eldrege looked at Daniel, and said "This was being orchestrated by Josh Green?"

"Yeah, he seemed like he was having fun out there. Practically the leader of the band." Daniel shook his head. "What do you suppose has gotten into him?"

"I don't know, but I do know what will get into him soon, my boot. As you know, I met with Dr. Manley. They've found Aaron Smirl, the guy stealing artifacts. When I confronted him with the buffalo skin theft, and threatened to press charges, he sang like a bird. Gave up Josh Green and Jenn Rausch as CAS members. Little bastards are leaders of something called the Berenger Cell." He laughed ruefully, "If you can believe that."

Daniel laughed. "A CAS Cell here? Who would have imagined! Does this help Jared? Maybe I'll have a beer to celebrate."

Eldrege shook his head. "I'll get you the beer, but I can't see how it helps Davidson. The CAS nonsense is one thing, the accusation of sexual abuse with threat of force, is quite another. With all the publicity, charging Jenn with involvement will look like pretty small potatoes. It may even be viewed as an attempt to keep her quiet."

Daniel stood up. "Forget the beer. Do you really think Jared could be charged? That's just not fair!"

"Sit down Daniel. We need to let this play out and see where the pieces fall. I've an appointment with the Dean for 8:00 in the morning. We'll know more after that, but I've got a bad feeling about this."

The next morning, Daniel and Lauren sat in her office anxiously waiting for Eldrege to return from his meeting with the Dean. Around 9:30 he knocked on the door. Lauren looked at him. "Fred, you look like hell. It couldn't have gone that bad. You want coffee or something?"

"No thanks," Eldrege took a deep breath before continuing. "I asked university legal counsel to be at my meeting with the Dean because I wanted to think through the theft of artifacts from our collections and Josh Green's involvement. Unfortunately, university administration isn't interested in the CAS problem. They're focused on the demonstration and the bad press. Their solution is to axe Dr. Davidson. They hope that decisive action by them will take the steam out of the situation. He's to be the sacrifice."

Daniel burst out incredulously. "Jared fired? Fred, couldn't you do something?"

Eldrege looked at him, his shoulders drooping, his face clearly fatigued. "Well, yes, Daniel, I can do something." He held up a folded piece of paper. "My resignation. And as my last official duty as department head, I am appointing you temporary head until a search can be done to find a replacement." He placed the letter in an envelope, licking the seal. "I included a recommendation for your promotion as temporary head in the letter. I hope you will apply for the permanent position. You and Lauren are important to the department. I'm getting too old for this shit."

Eldrege stood to leave, and Daniel rose and shook his hand. "Fred, this isn't right. It isn't fair."

Eldrege closed his eyes, and sighed. "I know you're a believer Daniel. As a kid, you probably believed in Santa and the Easter Bunny, but, and this is perhaps the saddest truth ever, there never was a Fair Fairy." He reached out and hugged Daniel. "The one thing I know for certain is, this too shall pass."

He stopped at the door. "Betty, set up an appointment for me with Josh this morning. I may not be able to do much to him, but perhaps I can scare the little shit. He's through as an archaeology major at SIU, that's for damn certain."

After the office door closed, Lauren looked at Daniel. "This is not right; Josh and Jenn should not be allowed to destroy his career. Jared is too nice a guy. We've got to do something."

Daniel shook his head in resignation. "Maybe Eldrege is right. Life is just not fair. Jared is getting screwed, and Eldrege is resigning. I've wanted to be department head someday, but not this way." He looked at Lauren, "Any ideas?"

"No, but I'll think of one."

Jenn Rausch sat in her apartment waiting for Josh to call. When he left for his meeting with Dr. Eldrege, he'd been in high spirits. The demonstration and the press coverage was everything he'd hoped for. 'Who cares what Eldrege has to say. We're in control.' She laughed, remembering Josh's puppet master imitation as he walked out the door. The phone rang; she looked at her watch. *Its too early for Josh to be calling about the meeting,* she thought, picking up the phone. "Hello, this is Jenn."

"Hi, Jenn. This is Laura French. I was wondering whether you'd be able to watch the kids for a few hours this afternoon. I'm sorry. I know I'm calling late, but something came up, and I need to be away for a couple of hours right after lunch. I'd really appreciate it. I'm in a real bind."

Because she wanted to stay and hear what Josh had to say about his meeting with Eldrege, Jenn started to say no, but then it occurred to her that this might be a way for her to learn what the other side was thinking. Also, it would make her look good. "Sure. Dr. French, I think I can be there. You said it's just for a couple hours?"

When Jenn arrived, she noticed two cars in the French's driveway. When she rang the door bell, Lauren responded quickly, as though she'd been standing there. "Come on in. Thanks so much for doing this."

"That's okay. Where're the kids?"

"Back here." Lauren led her toward the kitchen. When they entered, Jenn stopped. Sitting at the kitchen table was Maria Davidson.

"Take a seat," Lauren said. "I thought we girls might have a little chat while you wait for your boyfriend to finish his meeting with Dr. Eldrege."

"He's not my boyfriend, only a fellow student. I don't like this, it's not fair."

Lauren laughed. "That fairness thing again. Look, Jenn, yesterday Dr. Eldrege was in Chicago talking with Dean Manley and a student you know, Aaron Smirl. In order to save his hide, Mr. Smirl told Fred he gave Josh and you the buffalo skin. Now, I know you're lying about your relationship with Josh. You are, shall we say, a very intimate acquaintance of his. I also know you're lying about Dr. Davidson. I don't know why, but you are. I invited Maria here so that perhaps you could explain it to her."

"I don't have to put up with this crap. I'm leaving."

"Leave if you want, but Eldrege is grilling Josh right now, and he will probably go to jail for stealing the buffalo skin. At least he'll be thrown out of the university. The real question is this—do you want to join him?

"But I didn't do anything."

"Look, Smirl said you were at the CAS meeting. That makes you an accomplice. If you come clean, I'll do everything in my power to help you. Continue to lie, and you'll get the same treatment as Josh. I wanted Maria here so that you could see and understand the pain your deception is causing. Dr. Davidson will be fired from the university because of your story. If he loses his position under these circumstances, it is unlikely he'll ever be hired by an academic institution again. You mentioned fairness. Is that fair?"

"But I didn't mean to get him fired. Josh said..."

Lauren cut her off. "Screw Josh. Tell us what happened that morning with Dr. Davidson. Did you lie?"

Jenn bit her lip and tears flowed. "I'm so sorry; I didn't mean to hurt anyone." She looked at Maria. "Dr. Davidson didn't do anything."

Lauren reached out and took her into her arms. "That's all right. Thanks for telling the truth. What you did was very wrong, but you can fix it. And I promise I'll do everything in my power to help."

She turned, picked up the phone, and dialed Eldrege's office. "Here, you tell him what you've told me. It will be okay. Honest."

Later that afternoon when Jenn returned to the apartment, she found Josh jumping about like a wild man, hitting the walls, screaming. "The bastards kicked me out. Fuck em. They won't get away with this." Finally, he noticed her tear stained face. "What the fuck is your problem. It's me they're kicking out."

Jenn sat down and cried. "I didn't want this to happen. I didn't want Dr. Davidson fired. I told Dr. French."

"You did what?" Josh screamed. "You told them?" He came at her and slapped her across the mouth, cutting her lip. "How fucking stupid." Then, as if he had a new idea, he turned and grabbed the phone. "I'll get even with the bastards." He dialed a number, "Hello, Richard? This is Josh Green. You remember me? We met at the Cahokia pow-wow. Man, I just quit the fucking university archaeology department, couldn't take it anymore. They're doing some strange shit with the bones we dug up at the Alton site. You suppose I could come talk to you?"

Jenn saw a transformation come over Josh as he completed the phone call. Suddenly, he was confident and sure of himself again. He took her into his arms and kissed her, seeming to forget he'd just hit her. "I'm sorry. We'll get em baby. Take my word… they'll pay."

He began to undress her. She stiffened, standing straight in front of him. *Sex? Isn't this the guy who just hit me?*

Afterwards, Jenn lay thinking how mechanical the sex had been. Tears came to her eyes, whatever just happened would have been hard to describe as love making. She licked her lip, tasting blood.

Chapter 39 - They Come

Leaning against the railing, Admiral Zhou Wen watched the sun sink below the horizon. The ship rocked slowly in the calm sea. Around him the lights of countless other vessels blinked on as night watches were set. He bowed his head and prayed to the goddess. "Ah, Mazu, Protectress of Mariners, bring winds to our sails, rescue us from the still." He reached into his jacket, found a piece of fresh fruit, and dropped it into the sea. Completing his prayers, he looked around. *Better check the watch*, he thought. Although the fleet had nothing to fear from barbarians, discipline still must be maintained. Zheng He, The Grand Eunuch, Lord Admiral of All Oceans, was not a man one wished to fail.

Zheng He was not only his lord but also the greatest of all admirals. No less than Zhu Di, rightful occupant of the Dragon Throne, Son of Heaven, Emperor on Horseback, had selected him for the special task of taking Chinese culture to the world, his seven voyages sailing to the ends of the earth.

It was now time for the grand flotilla to divide. The Lord Admiral planned to visit Mecca for the Hajj before turning homeward toward China. *A devout man*, thought Zhou Wen, *one who serves the Emperor well*. Zheng He had dressed in his formal uniform, a long red robe and tall hat, at their last meeting. Zhou Wen smiled at the memory. Zheng He was a mountain of a man, twice the height and weight of two, yet he strode the deck as lightly as a tiger.

Zheng He sailed the grand flotilla to the southern tip of Africa, and invited the fleet's admirals to his treasure ship to give them orders. He planned to divide the armada into three, each under an admiral. As a special gift he handed each a scroll of calligraphy inked by his own hand, stamped with his personal chop at the bottom. On each was inscribed three symbols: clouds, open sky, and the character for ten thousand. After handing each man a scroll, he blessed him. "May your voyages be free of clouds for ten thousand li. May you serve the Emperor. Do my will."

"You are to sail outward to the ends of the earth. Chart your path, so others may follow. Inform all you meet that their true lord is our Lord, the Emperor Zhu Di. Bring them under China's family as younger brothers, so they can be taught and blessed with the great civilizing effects of Confucian harmony." Zheng He frowned. "Also seek out any trace of the fugitive traitor-pretender Zhu Yunwen, who supposedly escaped abroad. We must have him, so all will know that the rightful occupant of the Dragon Throne, the Emperor on Horseback, the Son of Heaven, is Zhu Di."

"Tonight I invite you to stay on board. Concubines will be provided." He laughed in self deprecation. "I, of course, will not join you, but wish you bliss. If you need vitalization, we have ample bald chicken potion. The men laughed, looking at each other. Zheng He continued. "As Confucius taught, *'Of all the 10,000 things created by heaven, man is the most precious. Of all things that make man prosper none can be compared to sexual intercourse. It is modeled after heaven'.*"

He smiled. "I give you the power of life and death over those you command. Ninety captains, ships and crews, are entrusted to each of you. I have led you to the tip of this land. I shall return home now, confident you will handle your fleets as I have taught you. Do my will."

The next morning Zhou Wen watched the ships move outward as their sails caught the winds. The sails were red in the morning light, giving the appearance of flying houses. "Bald chicken potion indeed." He laughed to himself, at the personal joke of the Great Eunuch, Admiral Zheng He.

He smiled thinking of last night's exertions. According to legend, a seventy-year old-prefect from Shu once drank a potion to enhance his sexual vitality. His wife, exhausted by his vigor, could neither sit nor lie down. She insisted her husband throw the elixir away. A yard rooster then ate it, jumped on a hen, and continued to copulate without interruption, pecking the hen's head until it was completely bald.

As part of last night's gift, Admiral Zheng He allowed each admiral to select five concubines from the treasure ship to accompany them on their voyages. Zhu Wen selected three Tanka women, a minority people known for their sexual skills. "Bald Chicken, indeed."

For the next several weeks, the ships ran with the wind. Suddenly from a clear sky a great storm erupted, threatening to swamp the smaller vessels and drive the fleet apart. Fearing the storm's ferocity, Zhu Wen and his officers gathered in the temple room of the flagship to pray to Mazu. He prostrated himself before the stature of the goddess, portrayed as a young woman dressed in white. On the wall above her was a painted rainbow. As he completed his ninth kowtow before the goddess, a miraculous, luminous light gleamed at the tips of the masts. And the winds ceased. Zhu Wen rose, laughing. "Our fleet is under the divine protection of the goddess. Admiral Zheng He was right. Our sky is clear for 10,000 li."

As the fleet moved out into the unknown, good fortune followed them. The ships were well provisioned with soybeans, wheat, millet and rice. The physicians had required that enough citrus fruit–limes, oranges, and lemons-be taken aboard to protect every man from disease. Fresh vegetables-cabbages, turnips, and bamboo shoots-were stored. When these ran out, the cooks sprouted soy beans. The ship's meat rations included tubs of frogs, specially bred dogs, and pigs. Fresh, salted, dried, and fermented fish were stored in great abundance. Though chickens were on board, they were only used for divination. A huge quantity of fresh water for both crew and animals was stored, and at each stop along the way, the water was replenished. Zhu Wen was confident that if necessary he could cross the broadest of oceans without re-provision.

Completing his daily log, Zhu Wen noted it had been a year since they set sail from Nanjing. How far they had come, the ocean seemed endless. After making port in Malacca, where logs of teak were taken aboard for repairs, they landed in Calicut to purchase cotton, then to Africa for ivory.

Since the division of the flotilla, his fleet enjoyed the protection of the goddess; no ship had been lost, even though the winds and currents pulled them outward into the unknown. "Mazu be praised," he uttered. His pen moved across the paper, concluding the note. *It has been a strange day. Several exotic birds of beautiful color flew over the ship, but no land is in sight. Although it might have been my imagination, today the air seemed sweetly fragranced.*

He covered the ink, placed his pens in their holders, folded his log, and prepared to retire. His mind went to Sula, his favorite concubine, who even now would be warming his bed. *Such a skillful woman*, he thought. At first he was repulsed by her large ugly feet since Tanka mothers did not bind their daughter's feet into the form of the golden lotus. *But tiny feet were not everything.* She'd proven to be an imaginative lover with great dexterity and endless energy. He laughed. "Perhaps I should have taken the bald chicken elixir."

Like he did every morning, Zhu Wen rose in the darkness, put on his robe and slippers, and went to the ships rail to await the sun. "Let's see what Mazu has brought." He took a deep breath, filling his lungs and nostrils with the pungent smell of flowers.

As the light of day pushed back the darkness, a large mountainous land mass slowly came into view. *Fusang,* he thought, *Fusang, the mystical paradise spoken of by the Buddhist monk Hoei-Shin.* The priest claimed to have visited a land twenty thousand li east of China. He named the land Fusang, after a fragrant red pear tree that grew there.

The full dawn revealed a string of tropical islands. The largest had a volcanic peak rising to an immense height. From its sides huge waterfalls cascaded downward, like mists from heaven. Flocks of the brightly colored birds he saw yesterday winged their way between islands. The air was laden with the sweet smell of wet foliage and flowers. *We will go ashore,* he thought, *and replenish our water supplies.* While he stood looking at this primitive paradise, a cry came from the watch tower: "To the west, a ship. One of our ships has beached."

Turning his attention Zhu Wen saw one of the smaller vessels lying on its side after drifting into a rocky reef during the night. As the light intensified, he saw native canoes tied to the vessel and naked people crawling over it. "Captain, prepare a party and rescue our crew. Take a military contingent until we know their intentions. Do my will!"

Zhu Wen watched as several longboats rowed toward the wreck site. Seeing the approaching boats, the natives took to their canoes and fled for the island. Behind them, the foundering ship burst into flame. The rescuers pursued the canoes to land. Ahead of them the natives pulled several of the wrecked ship's crew out of the canoes, across the beach, and into the jungle. He closed his eyes, praying to Mazu to protect them. *Like roses, even paradise has thorns,* he thought.

Why did I allow myself to be lulled? The longboats landed in good order, and a small contingent was left to guard the boats while a larger armed force went into the jungle to rescue the crew. *These are but naked barbarians,* he thought. *They are no match for us.*

After several hours Zhu Wen saw a plume of smoke from an inland fire. More hours passed before he saw the troops return to the beach and the longboats cast off for their return.

Impatient for information, Zhu Wen went to where the crew would board. First to cross the rail was Captain Yang Qing, who quickly prostrated himself. He allowed the captain to remained face to deck until all rescuers came aboard, then ordered him to, "Stand and report."

"Lord Admiral, we pursued the barbarians into the jungle until we reached their village. There, we found only women and children because all the men fled in terror at our approach." Yang Qing paused, unwilling to continue. "The stench was terrible, they are cannibals. We found our men dismembered and hung for curing. Parts of others were roasting before a fire."

"Did any of our men survive?"

Yang Qing avoided his gaze, fearing to answer. "No. We searched the jungle for the savages who did this, but were unsuccessful. We returned to the village, and killed everyone." He pointed to the smoke on the horizon. "We placed our dead comrades in a thatched hut and burned the whole village to the ground. Returning to our boats, we could hear the barbarians wailing their loss, but they did not attack. We brought back one prisoner for you to question. We think these people call themselves Caribs." He gestured, and a woman was brought forward and thrown at Zhu Wen's feet.

He looked down at her, a thing of little value. Today had begun with his fantasies of finding Fusan, the mystical paradise, yet all he gained was a lost vessel, dead crew, and a worthless woman. "Bind her and throw her overboard; I have nothing to learn from this trash. Do my will!"

"Captain Yang Qing, order all crew to prepare. Let us leave this cursed place. There will be no further landings here. I hoped to replenish water, but that can wait." Zhu Wen turned and strode back to his apartment. He shook his head, thinking of the day's losses. *Perhaps Sula can ease my mind*, he thought.

Two weeks later the fleet came to a large land mass that seemed to extend endlessly in both directions. This time Zhu Wen was careful not to allow his mind to wander with Fusan fantasies. Once water was replenished, the fleet made its way westward along the coast until reaching a mighty river. Naked primitives were seen on the beaches, but when approached, they fled.

He called his captains to the treasure ship. "I will take ten longboats and crews upriver to see this place." He shook his head in annoyance. "Perhaps we will find advanced people. In my absence, Captain Yang Qing will serve in my place. You are to remain in anchorage here. Do not go ashore except for provisions, and then only with overwhelming security." He turned to Yang Qing, "You will lose no further ships or crew in my absence. Do my will."

"Lord Admiral, how long will you be away?"

Zhu Wen looked at the man, and said. "I do not know, but we are now in early summer. I will return before autumn colors."

For the next several weeks the crews pulled the longboats up river. Although the mid-river current was great, the men attached ropes to themselves and pulled the boats along the river's shallow edge. People came to stare at them, but when approached, they vanished from site. *A land of primitives*, Zhu Wen thought. *Too backward to benefit from contact with us. Is this land empty of all civilization?*

On the sixtieth day they came to a city surrounded by a great wall of wood. *Finally*, he thought, *civilization*. The boats were beached, and Zhu Wen posted guards. He left Captain Hong in charge of securing the longboats and selected Captain Gao to accompany him, along with a military contingent.

Surprisingly, no one came to greet them from the city above. He laughed to himself, and said. "Perhaps we are too frightening. Fear is good in situations like these."

Arraying the contingent of soldiers around them, Zhu Wen and Gao moved toward the city. As they approached the great wooden wall, Gao stopped and pointed. "Admiral, the wall is strong and secure, but the gate hangs open." Looking out across the valley, Zhu Wen saw the land stripped of trees and barren of crops. Only bushes and weeds grew from the cracked and dusty soil.

They passed through an area of thatched huts, many in need of repair. Entering through the gate, they saw great mounds with buildings on their crests. The air hung heavy and still with no sound nor movement. Zhu Wen felt his neck hair prickle. He wondered if the Goddess Mazu, Protectress of Mariners followed them inland. This is a city of the dead. Perhaps, disease has emptied this place? Perhaps starvation? He remembered how caring the farmers of China were for their land. Obviously, these barbarians had taken and not given back to the land, abusing it, until the God's had punished them. He turned, not willing to go further into this dead place. "What we seek is not here. Return to the boats."

The next morning as they prepared to move up river, Zhu Wen called his crew together. "Maybe the people of the dead city have moved up river for new land. We will seek them for one more day. If we find nothing, it is time to return to our ships and explore west."

That day the current grew stronger and the river became muddier. When they came around a bend, they saw a second but smaller great river adding its waters to the first. They chose to keep to the river they'd been following. In late afternoon, they came to an area where great cliffs rose above the river. Staring down at them was something so unbelievable that Zhu Wen quickly beached the boats. Above them painted on the cliff in bright colors was the immediately recognizable Qin Dragon Banner. While he stood staring at the painting, Captain Goa and the crew around him threw themselves prostrate on the ground. "Mazu," came from their throats.

Zhu Wen raised his eyes to the top of the cliff and saw a young woman dressed in white staring down at them. His mind screamed the question, *Could it be the Goddess?*

The apparition disappeared from view. Minutes later the woman came running down the path to the beach. Standing before Zhu Wen, she said, "I am granddaughter of Radient Jewel. I am She Who Remembers, Daughter of White Buffalo Calf Woman, Servant to the Winged Beast, and keeper of the medicine valley. I, Wind Sage, welcome you. Please accept these humble gifts." She smiled, placing the journal of Sun Kai, the great buffalo skin of memory, and a small bag of golden kernels at his feet.

Zhu Wen stood staring at the woman, not understanding her words. To his surprise, she showed no fear of them. He received her gifts, and with sign language invited her to come with them.

Tears came to the woman's eyes. 'You've come," she said.

Chapter 40 ~ The Memory Skin

It was after 5:00 pm, and the department was empty when Lauren and Daniel used their key to Eldrege's office. He looked up and smiled. Around him were boxes of books and papers. His awards and pictures had been taken from the wall. "Good. Glad you're here. I could use a strong, young back to get this stuff out to the car."

Lauren reached out and touched his arm. "Fred, you don't have to do this. The administration has dropped all charges against Jared. Jenn Rausch has cooperated fully and been allowed to continue in the program. Hopefully, she'll avoid Dr. Davidson's classes. Josh Green's been forced to drop everything and resign from the university." She paused. "Little bastard's getting off way too easy, but it saves us the hassle of prosecuting him." She looked at Daniel to show she was speaking for the both of them. "Fred, we don't want you to give up the department head position. The administration wants you to take back the resignation."

He placed his hand on hers, shaking his head. "Thanks, but no thanks. It's time for me to go do something else. This last bit of circus convinced me that administration is not what I want to do with this last portion of my life. The university is allowing me to take a sabbatical for a year, retire, and then return as an emeritus professor. Seems like a plan to me."

Eldrege turned to Daniel. "Funny, you're always going on about China, and I just received an invitation to visit Beijing University. Remember, when I told you I did some articles on Native American art and stories painted on buffalo skins? Someone in Beijing read my articles and decided I'm the man they need to look at an artifact in their collection. Apparently it's very old, not in Chinese culture terms, but old. How they managed to get a Native American skin in their collection is beyond me, probably some curio bought in the late 1800's. Anyway, they want me to come and look at it, and give some lectures on Native American archaeology. Marge has been after me to take some time off and travel. She's excited to go. By the way, I recommend keeping Betty as your secretary; she knows all the comings and goings of the university. You couldn't make a better choice."

"Fred," Daniel said in exasperation, "We don't want you to leave."

"Daniel, I know you don't, and I appreciate it." He scratched his beard. "What's that great line from Lewis Carroll?"

The time has come, the Walrus said,

To talk of many things:

Of shoes--and ships--and sealing-wax--

Of cabbages--and kings—

"Truth is Daniel," Eldrege laughed, "it's time for this old walrus to do something else. The China gig has real appeal to Marge and me. In fact, she's at home closing up right now. We're leaving as soon as we get the visas complete. Let's not talk about this anymore. Don't want to get maudlin. Give me a hand with these boxes."

Two weeks later they saw Fred and Marge off at Lambert International Airport. As the plane gained altitude and banked toward the west, it was lit up by the rising sun. Putting his arm around Lauren, Daniel said, "You know I envy them. Beijing

University is the Harvard of China. They'll have a great time."

She smiled. "It'll be our turn someday; we still have to prove China discovered America. Where better to find the evidence?"

Daniel laughed. "I love you cuz you a crazy person. You never give up."

Lauren looked at her watch. "You know, we have time to do lunch before we go back. Why don't we go to the Hill? Best Italian restaurants this side of Rome. You can feed this crazy person."

Monday morning, at 7:30am, Betty looked up and saw Daniel coming through the door. She smiled. *A chip off the old block,* she thought. "Good morning Dr. French. Here's your coffee."

"Morning, Betty. After our meeting this morning, Lauren and Jared are joining me for a review of the burial site findings. We'll probably do some preliminary planning in regard to where we go next spring. You don't need to join us for this confab, but please clear my calendar until at least noon."

"Sure, Dr. French. By the way, I received an e-mail from Dr. Eldrege this morning. She laughed. "Nothing particularly important. Mostly grousing about his swollen feet from the 18 hour flight. Couldn't get his shoes back on when he got there. He gave me a number where we can reach him; they have an on-campus guest house for foreign experts. He's about to start work on their buffalo skin."

Daniel was placing some of his pictures and awards on the office wall when Lauren and Jared came in. "Seems strange, doesn't it? I almost feel like I'm desecrating the place with my stuff. I guess I'll get used to it. Can I get you guys' coffee?"

When they were settled, Lauren handed them printouts containing all the information gained from the dig site. "Now, all this is very preliminary, but it will give us a foundation, telling us where to begin next season. So far we have uncovered thirty-six skeletons. The fact that they are all female removes coincidence from the equation. This is a female grave site, and it appears the burials went on for hundreds of years. Mostly, they are in a straight line across a small valley. I say mostly because the first two are about a meter higher than the others. Looking at the soil samples, the difference was caused by an earth shift, probably from a New Madrid event. About every three hundred years, the area gets a major earthquake."

Jared nodded. "I did a paper on the fault once. About a billion years ago, the continent of North America was part of a much larger body of land that geologists call Rodinia. Sometime between 700 and 550 million years ago Rodinia separated into smaller pieces. In the breakup, smaller rifts occurred, including one that ran north from the Gulf coast up into what is now the bootheel region of Missouri. For unknown reasons, the rifting and process of separation stopped. The rift valley in the bedrock extends over an area more than three hundred fifty miles long and more than fifty miles wide, throughout what would later become the lower Mississippi Valley." Jared smiled, "Sorry, it's a teacher thing; always tell em more than they want to know."

Recognizing the academic syndrome, Lauren and Daniel laughed.

Daniel asked, "You ever read the book, *When the Mississippi Ran Backward*, by Jay Feldman? Fun read. About the quake that occurred in December 1811. Apparently the earthquake really moved things around. They reported exploding earth fissures anywhere from ten feet wide to four and five miles long. Huge geysers spewed out a variety of substances. Some were circular sand geysers; they say one of them threw up a fossilized skull of an extinct buffalo species."

Lauren laughed. "Guys, try to focus will you?" She looked back at the notes in the folder. "There doesn't seem to be much of interest at the site beyond the skeletons. Some of the flotation samples show a heavy concentration of an interesting variety of seeds and pods. It appears as if some of the area might have served as a pharmaceutical garden for an extended period of time."

Daniel interjected, "But the real interesting part is the skeletons. There are only a few grave goods. We found an obsidian knife, which we think was associated with skeleton number one." He pointed to the grid map. "We found what appears to be a small jade mouth amulet with grave number two. Then there are no more artifacts until we get to grave number sixteen. This is the skeleton which shows signs of knife cuts, as though the body were dismembered. At this sight we found a small necklace with a flat stone, Birdman etched into it. The Birdman is significant because it relates to other findings at the Cahokia site. None of the other skeletons are associated with any grave goods."

Daniel looked at Lauren who nodded in approval. He reached into his briefcase, brought out a book, and handed it to Jared. "Ever read, *Flight of the Piasa,* by Raymond Scott Edge?"

Jared turned the book over, quickly scanning the back cover. "Can't say I have, but then again, I don't read much fiction."

Daniel took a deep breath. "Well, actually, I wrote that book based on some artifacts Lauren and I found as graduate students. Eldrege made us promise we wouldn't tie our ideas to the department, so I wrote it under a pen name and called it fiction." Daniel laughed. "Eldrege didn't want a crazy China discovered America story coming from his department."

Now it was Jared's turn to laugh. "I know how that feels. Remember, I believe that some Native Americans are ancient Israelites. Try selling an article proposing that to a department head, outside of Utah."

They all laughed. "Sorry, about that Jared," Daniel said. "Tell you what... we won't make fun of your Mormon mania, and you keep an open mind to our China discovers America theory. But that brings us to a matter we want to discuss with you, skeleton number two, the one with the jade mouth amulet. The skeleton didn't seem quite right to us, so I invited Father Bill Archer, a Paleontologist from St. Louis University, to take a look. He came over, measured the length of the skull, the shapes of the seams where joints of the skull come together, structure of the jawbone, and features of the smaller facial bones. Although he's not one hundred percent certain and wouldn't bet his Jesuit robes on it, it seemed Caucasian to him."

Jared blinked. "Caucasian? Like Kennewick Man, the nine-thousand-year-old skeleton found in Washington State?"

Lauren nodded. "Yep, like Kennewick Man. In this case more like Kennewick Woman, but to make things even weirder, once we put it with a jade mouth amulet like those used in ancient China, it leads us to believe the skeleton might be Snow Pine, the heroine in the book you're holding."

"Yes... but..." Jared stammered his mind trying to fill in the blanks of the story. "Wouldn't this Snow Pine be Chinese if you guys have it right?"

"Well, no." Daniel said. "If we have it right, she would be from a minority people who arrived in northern China from Europe several thousand years ago, like the Loulan Beauty mummy of the Uyghur area in northwest China, making her caucasian."

Jared looked at the book. "Looks like I need to read it. This will sure make next year's work interesting. Wow, now I understand why Eldrege made you two promise. This story truly is crazy."

Betty opened the door, and said. "I'm sorry, Dr. French. I know you asked not be disturbed, but we have a delegation in the waiting room, and they are demanding to see you." She handed him a business card.

He turned the card in his hand, noting the name. "Hmm, Mr. Richard Longbow, Chairman, Illini Confederation." Daniel looked puzzled. "Wonder what they want?"

Betty shrugged. "He didn't say, but it's a delegation. I think you should see them."

Daniel turned to Lauren and Jared. "Could you guys excuse me for a minute? Just wait outside. This shouldn't take long. Probably something Eldrege had going with the tribe or Cahokia Visitor's Center."

Betty showed the three men into the room. They were all dressed in dark business suits, but their cowboy boots and braids left no doubt that this was not your usual business delegation. The leader of the group, putting out his hand, said, "Dr. French? I'm Richard Longbow. My two colleagues, Dr. Myron Mankiller and Dr. Joseph Robinson, are both tribal lawyers."

Daniel smiled, "It is nice to meet you." He nodded to Myron Mankiller. "You related to Wilma Mankiller? I'm a great admirer of hers."

Mankiller nodded. "She's my great auntie, the family is very proud of her accomplishments."

Richard Longbow interrupted. "Excuse me, Dr. French... this is not a social visit." He reached into his briefcase, brought out a sheet of legal paper, and handed it to Daniel. "You're familiar with the Native American Graves Protection and Repatriation Act of 1990?

Daniel nodded apprehensively.

"The tribal council has met on this matter and feels the gravesites you are investigating fall under this statute. We have begun the repatriation process to return these skeletons to the proper tribal authorities for reburial; we would appreciate your cooperation and immediate compliance."

Daniel's face flushed red. "Ah, gentlemen. I'm familiar with the APGRA statute, but don't think it applies in this case. We're an academic institution, empowered by the State to carry out archaeological studies and to collect and house associated human remains and artifacts. Naturally we consult with any affected Native American group, but the Illini Confederation would not seem to be an affected party."

Myron Mankiller cut him off. "Look, we're here today to request that you immediately cease all further work at the site and any further study. These are not specimens. They are ancestors. The council has received information in regard to the nature of your studies, and, frankly, they're outraged and offended. It's sacrilegious."

Daniel could feel himself losing control of the situation. "Received information? What source?"

"We are not at liberty to reveal our sources."

"Well then, I guess that concludes what we can do at the moment." Daniel took in a deep breath calming himself. "I will study your paperwork, consult with University Counsel, and get back to you within the week. However, let me assure you, no faculty member of this institution has done anything sacrilegious to human remains. Perhaps, you should check your sources of information." He stood and motioned toward the door. "Gentlemen."

When Lauren and Jared entered the office, they found Daniel sitting in his chair, head in hands. Looking up, he said, "You will not believe this. This could mean the end of our work at the dig site."

"But why?" Jared asked.

He held up Longbow's paper. "The Illini Confederation has a bug up their butt about our work at the burial site. Remember our discussion of Kennewick Man? He was discovered in 1996 along the Columbia River in Washington. The legal fight over that skeleton is still going on. If these guys press the case, we might be in court for years."

He looked at Lauren, and said, "I'm sorry babe; I thought we just might make it this time—Snow Pine, Sun Kai, the whole ball of wax." He sat back and scratched his forehead, pushing his hair from his eyes. Reaching over, he punched the button for his secretary. "Betty, can you get Dr. Eldrege on the line for me?"

"Sure Dr. French, if you don't mind waking him up at 1:00 o'clock in the morning. Remember? He's in China.

The three of them sat looking at each other. The road forward was blocked, the energy sucked from the room. Jared leaned back closed his eyes and stretched. "Guess I'll go back to the office. See you later."

Nothing further was said. Lauren and Daniel just waved weakly as Jared left the room. When the phone rang, Daniel didn't reach for it. "Betty'll get it."

When he didn't pick up, Betty pushed the intercom button. "Dr. French, I have Dr. Eldrege on the line."

Daniel shook his head in disbelief. "I thought you said it was past midnight there and we shouldn't wake him.

"Well, yes, it's about one o'clock in the morning there, but he's calling you."

Daniel grabbed for the phone. "Fred, everything all right? You and Marge okay?"

Fred chuckled on the other end. "Daniel, I'm sitting here looking at the damndest thing I ever saw. Remember, I told you they invited me here to look at a painted buffalo skin? The one I have in front of me has pictures of Cahokia mounds, the Birdman Tablet, Woodhenge, crops of corn, and across the top are what appear to be thirty six figures of women in white. Plus, if that's not crazy enough, there's Chinese calligraphy, but the guys here can't read it. They say it is very old script. And, oh yes, there's a little figure that looks like a Viking."

There was a long pause. "Tell you what… let me fax you a picture." Daniel heard a yawn. "Never mind. My mind must be getting cloudy, the fax is off for the night. I'll send it in the morning." Another yawn. "Talk to you tomorrow, okay?"

The line went dead, and Daniel sat there holding the phone. Lauren came to his side, "Daniel, are Fred and Marge okay?"

He put down the phone, took her into his arms, and swirled her around. "They are just perfect, better than fine. And do you know what? I think we're about to receive a letter from Snow Pine."

ALSO BY Raymond Scott Edge

Flight Of the Piasa

Daniel looked up at the wall clock. "Well that brings us to the end of our time, but I should tell you that the last sighting of the Piasa Bird was April 1948. Guy named Coleman, while riding on horseback about four miles from Alton, claimed to have sighted a bird "bigger than an airplane." The students were now standing, packing their bags, adjusting their coats, readying themselves to leave."Oh, by the way, be careful out there," Daniel laughed. "And remember to look up now and then, you never know. When Daniel French, a graduate student of archaeology, sets out for a romantic picnic under a mysterious local cliff painting known as the Piasa Bird, he unwittingly finds himself involved in an ancient tale filled with passion, sacrifice, love, and loss. The Piasa is a famous petroglyph overlooking the Mississippi River near Alton, Illinois. First described by French explorers Marquette and Joliet in 1673 and later called "America's most fascinating free roadside attraction," the origin of the Piasa is shrouded in legend and obscured by time, with no known date of creation, name of creator, or purpose. As Daniel French seeks to unravel the mystery surrounding the ancient work of art, he learns that there is more to the Piasa than meets the eye.

Learn more at:
http://www.outskirtspress.com/FLIGHTOFTHEPIASA
http://www.redoubtbooks.com

LaVergne, TN USA
17 February 2011
216835LV00002B/27/P